YULETIDE IN NEW ENGLAND

I have been summoned to this festival—older than Bethlehem and Babylon, older than Memphis and mankind—by the writings of my forefathers who had founded the Yule worship in Kingsport.

Out of the unimaginable blackness beyond the gangrenous glare of the cold flame, out of the tartarean leagues through which the oily river rolled uncanny, unheard, and unsuspected, there flopped rhythmically a horde of tame, trained, hybrid winged things that no sound eye could every wholly grasp, or sound brain ever wholly remember. They were not altogether crows, nor moles, nor buzzards, nor ants, nor vampire bats, nor decomposed human beings, but something I cannot and must not recall.

P8-AUM-360

By H. P. Lovecraft
Published by Ballantine Books:

AT THE MOUNTAINS OF MADNESS
and Other Tales of Terror

BLOODCURDLING TALES OF HORROR AND
THE MACABRE: The Best of H. P. Lovecraft

THE CASE OF CHARLES DEXTER WARD

THE DOOM THAT CAME TO SARNATH
and Other Stories

THE DREAM-QUEST OF UNKNOWN KADATH

THE LURKING FEAR
and Other Stories

THE TOMB
and Other Tales

THE TOMB

and Other Tales

by H. P. Lovecraft

A Del Rey Book

BALLANTINE BOOKS • NEW YORK

A Del Rey Book
Published by Ballantine Books

These stories were originally published as part of the collection *Dagon and Other Macabre Tales* by Arkham House.

ISBN 0-345-33661-5

This edition published by arrangement with Arkham House

Printed in Canada

First Ballantine Books Edition: December 1970
Twenty-first Printing: September 1993

Cover Art by Michael Whelan

SC
LOVECRAFT

Contents

The Tomb

In relating the circumstances which have led to my confinement within this refuge for the demented, I am aware that my present position will create a natural doubt of the authenticity of my narrative. It is an unfortunate fact that the bulk of humanity is too limited in its mental vision to weigh with patience and intelligence those isolated phenomena, seen and felt only by a psychologically sensitive few, which lie outside its common experience. Men of broader intellect know that there is no sharp distinction betwixt the real and the unreal; that all things appear as they do only by virtue of the delicate individual physical and mental media through which we are made conscious of them; but the prosaic materialism of the majority condemns as madness the flashes of supersight which penetrate the common veil of obvious empricism.

My name is Jervas Dudley, and from earliest childhood I have been a dreamer and a visionary. Wealthy beyond the necessity of a commercial life, and temperamentally unfitted for the formal studies and social recreation of my acquaintances, I have dwelt ever in realms apart from the visible world; spending my youth and adolescence in ancient and little known books, and in roaming the fields and groves of the region near my ancestral home. I do not think that what I read in these books or saw in these fields and groves was exactly what other boys read and saw there; but of this I must say little, since detailed speech would but confirm those cruel slanders upon my intellect which I sometimes overhear from the whispers of the stealthy attendants around me. It is sufficient for me to relate events without analyzing causes.

I have said that I dwelt apart from the visible world, but I have not said that I dwelt alone. This no human creature may do; for lacking the fellowship of the living, he inevitably draws upon the companionship of things that are not, or are no longer, living. Close by my home there lies a singular wooded hollow, in whose twilight deeps I spent

most of my time; reading, thinking, and dreaming. Down
its moss-covered slopes my first steps of infancy were taken,
and around its grotesquely gnarled oak trees my first fancies of boyhood were woven. Well did I come to know the
presiding dryads of those trees, and often have I watched
their wild dances in the struggling beams of a waning moon
– but of these things I must not now speak. I will tell only
of the lone tomb in the darkest of the hillside thickets; the
deserted tomb of the Hydes, an old and exalted family
whose last direct descendant had been laid within its black
recesses many decades before my birth.

The vault to which I refer is of ancient granite, weathered
and discolored by the mists and dampness of generations.
Excavated back into the hillside, the structure is visible only
at the entrance. The door, a ponderous and forbidding slab
of stone, hangs upon rusted iron hinges, and is fastened
ajar in a queerly sinister way by means of heavy iron chains
and padlocks, according to a gruesome fashion of half a
century ago. The abode of the race whose scions are here
inurned had once crowned the declivity which holds the
tomb, but had long since fallen victim to the flames which
sprang up from a stroke of lightning. Of the midnight storm
which destroyed this gloomy mansion, the older inhabitants of the region sometimes speak in hushed and uneasy
voices; alluding to what they call 'divine wrath' in a manner that in later years vaguely increased the always strong
fascination which I had felt for the forest-darkened sepulcher. One man only had perished in the fire. When the last
of the Hydes was buried in this place of shade and stillness,
the sad urnful of ashes had come from a distant land, to
which the family had repaired when the mansion burned
down. No one remains to lay flowers before the granite
portal, and few care to brave the depressing shadows which
seem to linger strangely about the water-worn stones.

I shall never forget the afternoon when first I stumbled
upon the half-hidden house of death. It was in mid-
summer, when the alchemy of nature transmutes the sylvan
landscape to one vivid and almost homogeneous mass of
green; when the senses are well-nigh intoxicated with the
surging seas of moist verdure and the subtly indefinable

odors of the soil and the vegetation. In such surroundings the mind loses its perspective; time and space become trivial and unreal, and echoes of a forgotten prehistoric past beat insistently upon the enthralled consciousness.

All day I had been wandering through the mystic groves of the hollow; thinking thoughts I need not discuss, and conversing with things I need not name. In years a child of ten, I had seen and heard many wonders unknown to the throng; and was oddly aged in certain respects. When, upon forcing my way between two savage clumps of briars, I suddenly encountered the entrance of the vault, I had no knowledge of what I had discovered. The dark blocks of granite, the door so curiously ajar, and the funeral carvings above the arch, aroused in me no associations of mournful or terrible character. Of graves and tombs I knew and imagined much, but had on account of my peculiar temperament been kept from all personal contact with churchyards and cemeteries. The strange stone house on the woodland slope was to me only a source of interest and speculation; and its cold, damp interior, into which I vainly peered through the aperture so tantalizingly left, contained for me no hint of death or decay. But in that instant of curiosity was born the madly unreasoning desire which has brought me to this hell of confinement. Spurred on by a voice which must have come from the hideous soul of the forest, I resolved to enter the beckoning gloom in spite of the ponderous chains which barred my passage. In the waning light of day I alternately rattled the rusty impediments with a view to throwing wide the stone door, and essayed to squeeze my slight form through the space already provided; but neither plan met with success. At first curious, I was now frantic; and when in the thickening twilight I returned to my home, I had sworn to the hundred gods of the grove that *at any cost* I would some day force an entrance to the black, chilly depths that seemed calling out to me. The physician with the iron-grey beard who comes each day to my room, once told a visitor that this decision marked the beginning of a pitiful monomania; but I will leave final judgment to my readers when they shall have learnt all.

The months following my discovery were spent in futile attempts to force the complicated padlock of the slightly open vault, and in carefully guarded inquiries regarding the nature and history of the structure. With the traditionally receptive ears of the small boy, I learned much ; though an habitual secretiveness caused me to tell no one of my information or my resolve. It is perhaps worth mentioning that I was not at all surprised or terrified on learning of the nature of the vault. My rather original ideas regarding life and death had caused me to associate the cold clay with the breathing body in a vague fashion ; and I felt that the great and sinister family of the burned-down mansion was in some way represented within the stone space I sought to explore. Mumbled tales of the weird rites and godless revels of bygone years in the ancient hall gave to me a new and potent interest in the tomb, before whose door I would sit for hours at a time each day. Once I thrust a candle within the nearly closed entrance, but could see nothing save a flight of damp stone steps leading downward. The odor of the place repelled yet bewitched me. I felt I had known it before, in a past remote beyond all recollection; beyond even my tenancy of the body I now possess.

The year after I first beheld the tomb, I stumbled upon a worm-eaten translation of Plutarch's *Lives* in the book-filled attic of my home. Reading the life of Theseus, I was much impressed by that passage telling of the great stone beneath which the boyish hero was to find his tokens of destiny whenever he should become old enough to lift its enormous weight. The legend had the effect of dispelling my keenest impatience to enter the vault, for it made me feel that the time was not yet ripe. Later, I told myself, I should grow to a strength and ingenuity which might enable me to unfasten the heavily chained door with ease; but until then I would do better by conforming to what seemed the will of Fate.

Accordingly my watches by the dank portal became less persistent, and much of my time was spent in other though equally strange pursuits. I would sometimes rise very quietly in the night, stealing out to walk in those church-

yards and places of burial from which I had been kept by
my parents. What I did there I may not say, for I am not
now sure of the reality of certain things; but I know that
on the day after such a nocturnal ramble I would often
astonish those about me with my knowledge of topics almost forgotten for many generations. It was after a night
like this that I shocked the community with a queer con-
ceit about the burial of the rich and celebrated Squire
Brewster, a maker of local history who was interred in
1711, and whose slate headstone, bearing a graven skull
and crossbones, was slowly crumbling to powder. In a moment of childish imagination I vowed not only that the
undertaker, Goodman Simpson, had stolen the silver-
buckled shoes, silken hose, and satin small-clothes of the
deceased before burial; but that the Squire himself, not
fully inanimate, had turned twice in his mound-covered
coffin on the day after interment.

But the idea of entering the tomb never left my thoughts;
being indeed stimulated by the unexpected genealogical
discovery that my own maternal ancestry possessed at least
a slight link with the supposedly extinct family of the
Hydes. Last of my paternal race, I was likewise the last of
this older and more mysterious line. I began to feel that
the tomb was *mine*, and to look forward with hot eagerness
to the time when I might pass within that stone door and
down those slimy stone steps in the dark. I now formed the
habit of listening very intently at the slightly open portal,
choosing my favorite hours of midnight stillness for the
odd vigil. By the time I came of age, I had made a small
clearing in the thicket before the mold-stained façade of
the hillside, allowing the surrounding vegetation to encircle
and overhang the space like the walls and roof of a sylvan
bower. This bower was my temple, the fastened door my
shrine, and here I would lie outstretched on the mossy
ground, thinking strange thoughts and dreaming strange
dreams.

The night of the first revelation was a sultry one. I must
have fallen asleep from fatigue, for it was with a distinct
sense of awakening that I heard the voices. Of these tones
and accents I hesitate to speak; of their quality I will not

speak; but I may say that they presented certain uncanny differences in vocabulary, pronunciation, and mode of utterance. Every shade of New England dialect, from the uncouth syllables of the Puritan colonists to the precise rhetoric of fifty years ago, seemed represented in that shadowy colloquy, though it was only later that I noticed the fact. At the time, indeed, my attention was distracted from this matter by another phenomenon; a phenomenon so fleeting that I could not take oath upon its reality. I barely fancied that as I awoke, a *light* had been hurriedly extinguished within the sunken sepulcher. I do not think I was either astounded or panic-stricken, but I know that I was greatly and permanently *changed* that night. Upon returning home I went with much directness to a rotting chest in the attic, wherein I found the key which next day unlocked with ease the barrier I had so long stormed in vain.

It was in the soft glow of late afternoon that I first entered the vault on the abandoned slope. A spell was upon me, and my heart leaped with an exultation I can but ill describe. As I closed the door behind me and descended the dripping steps by the light of my lone candle, I seemed to know the way; and though the candle sputtered with the stifling reek of the place, I felt singularly at home in the musty, charnel-house air. Looking about me, I beheld many marble slabs bearing coffins, or the remains of coffins. Some of these were sealed and intact, but others had nearly vanished, leaving the silver handles and plates isolated amidst certain curious heaps of whitish dust. Upon one plate I read the name of Sir Geoffrey Hyde, who had come from Sussex in 1640 and died here a few years later. In a conspicuous alcove was one fairly well preserved and untenanted casket, adorned with a single name which brought me both a smile and a shudder. An odd impulse caused me to climb upon the broad slab, extinguish my candle, and lie down within the vacant box.

In the gray light of dawn I staggered from the vault and locked the chain of the door behind me. I was no longer a young man, though but twenty-one winters had chilled my bodily frame. Early-rising villagers who observed my homeward progress looked at me strangely, and marveled at the signs of ribald revelry which they saw in one whose life was known to be sober and solitary. I did not appear before my parents till after a long and refreshing sleep.

Henceforward I haunted the tomb each night; seeing, hearing, and doing things I must never recall. My speech, always susceptible to environmental influences, was the first thing to succumb to the change; and my suddenly acquired archaism of diction was soon remarked upon. Later a queer boldness and recklessness came into my demeanor, till I unconsciously grew to possess the bearing of a man of the world despite my lifelong seclusion. My formerly silent tongue waxed voluble with the easy grace of a Chesterfield or the godless cynicism of a Rochester. I displayed a peculiar erudition utterly unlike the fantastic, monkish lore over which I had pored in youth; and covered the fly-leaves of my books with facile impromptu epigrams which brought up suggestions of Gay, Prior, and the sprightliest of the Augustan wits and rimesters. One morning at breakfast I came close to disaster by declaiming in palpably liquorish accents an effusion of Eighteenth Century bacchanalian mirth, a bit of Georgian playfulness never recorded in a book, which ran something like this:

Come hither, my lads, with your tankards of ale,
And drink to the present before it shall fail;
Pile each on your platter a mountain of beef,
For 'tis eating and drinking that bring us relief:
  So fill up your glass,
  For life will soon pass;
When you're dead ye'll ne'er drink to your king or your
    lass!

Anacreon had a red nose, so they say;
But what's a red nose if ye're happy and gay?
Gad split me! I'd rather be red whilst I'm here,
Than white as a lily — and dead half a year!
  So Betty, my miss,
  Come give me kiss;
In hell there's no innkeeper's daughter like this!

Young Harry, propp'd up just as straight as he's able,
Will soon lose his wig and slip under the table,
But fill up your goblets and pass 'em around —
Better under the table than under the ground!
    So revel and chaff
    As ye thirstily quaff:
Under six feet of dirt 'tis less easy to laugh!

The fiend strike me blue! I'm scarce able to walk,
And damn me if I can stand upright or talk!
Here, landlord, bid Betty to summon a chair;
I'll try home for a while, for my wife is not there!
    So lend me a hand;
    I'm not able to stand,
But I'm gay whilst I linger on top of the land!

About this time I conceived my present fear of fire and thunderstorms. Previously indifferent to such things, I had now an unspeakable horror of them; and would retire to the innermost recesses of the house whenever the heavens threatened an electrical display. A favorite haunt of mine during the day was the ruined cellar of the mansion that had burned down, and in fancy I would picture the structure as it had been in its prime. On one occasion I startled a villager by leading him confidently to a shallow sub-cellar, of whose existence I seemed to know in spite of the fact that it had been unseen and forgotten for many generations.

At last came that which I had long feared. My parents, alarmed at the altered manner and appearance of their only son, commenced to exert over my movements a kindly espionage which threatened to result in disaster. I had told no one of my visits to the tomb, having guarded my secret purpose with religious zeal since childhood; but now I was forced to exercise care in threading the mazes of the wooded hollow, that I might throw off a possible pursuer. My key to the vault I kept suspended from a cord about my neck, its presence known only to me. I never carried out of the sepulcher any of the things I came upon whilst within its walls.

One morning as I emerged from the damp tomb and

fastened the chain of the portal with none too steady hand,
I beheld in an adjacent thicket the dreaded face of a watcher. Surely the end was near; for my bower was discovered, and the objective of my nocturnal journeys revealed. The man did not accost me, so I hastened home in
an effort to overhear what he might report to my careworn
father. Were my sojourns beyond the chained door about
to be proclaimed to the world? Imagine my delighted as-
tonishment on hearing the spy inform my parent in a cautious whisper *that I had spent the night in the bower outside
the tomb*; my sleep-filmed eyes fixed upon the crevice where
the padlocked portal stood ajar! By what miracle had the
watcher been thus deluded? I was now convinced that a
supernatural agency protected me. Made bold by this
heaven-sent circumstance, I begin to resume perfect open-
ness in going to the vault; confident that no one could wit-
ness my entrance. For a week I tasted to the full joys of
that charnel conviviality which I must not describe, when
the *thing* happened, and I was borne away to this accursed
abode of sorrow and monotony.

I should not have ventured out that night; for the taint
of thunder was in the clouds, and a hellish phosphoresence
rose from the rank swamp at the bottom of the hollow. The
call of the dead, too, was different. Instead of the hillside
tomb, it was the charred cellar on the crest of the slope
whose presiding demon beckoned to me with unseen fingers. As I emerged from an intervening grove upon the
plain before the ruin. I beheld in the misty moonlight a
thing I had always vaguely expected. The mansion, gone
for a century, once more reared its stately height to the
raptured vision; every window ablaze with the splendor of
many candles. Up the long drive rolled the coaches of the
Boston gentry, whilst on foot came a numerous assemb-
lage of powdered exquisites from the neighboring man-
sions. With this throng I mingled, though I knew I belonged
with the hosts rather than with the guests. Inside the hall
were music, laughter, and wine on every hand. Several faces
I recognized; though I should have known them better had
they been shriveled or eaten away by death and decomposi-
tion. Amidst a wild and reckless throng I was the wildest

and most abandoned. Gay blasphemy poured in torrents from my lips, and in shocking sallies I heeded no law of God, or nature.

Suddenly a peal of thunder, resonant even above the din of the swinish revelry, clave the very roof and laid a hush of fear upon the boisterous company. Red tongues of flame and searing gusts of heat engulfed the house; and the roysterers, struck with terror at the descent of a calamity which seemed to transcend the bounds of unguided nature, fled shrieking into the night. I alone remained, riveted to my seat by a groveling fear which I had never felt before. And then a second horror took possession of my soul. Burnt alive to ashes, my body dispersed by the four winds, *I might never lie in the tomb of the Hydes!* Was not my coffin prepared for me? Had I not a right to rest till eternity amongst the descendants of Sir Geoffrey Hyde? Aye! I would claim my heritage of death, even though my soul go seeking through the ages for another corporeal tenement to represent it on that vacant slab in the alcove of the vault. *Jervas Hyde* should never share the sad fate of Palinurus!

As the phantom of the burning house faded, I found myself screaming and struggling madly in the arms of two men, one of whom was the spy who had followed me to the tomb. Rain was pouring down in torrents, and upon the southern horizon were flashes of lightning that had so lately passed over our heads. My father, his face lined with sorrow, stood by as I shouted my demands to be laid within the tomb, frequently admonishing my captors to treat me as gently as they could. A blackened circle on the floor of the ruined cellar told of a violent stroke from the heavens; and from this spot a group of curious villagers with lanterns were prying a small box of antique workmanship, which the thunderbolt had brought to light.

Ceasing my futile and now objectless writhing, I watched the spectators as they viewed the treasure-trove, and was permitted to share in their discoveries. The box, whose fastenings were broken by the stroke which had unearthed it, contained many papers and objects of value, but I had eyes for one thing alone. It was the porcelain miniature of a young man in a smartly curled bag-wig, and bore the initials 'J. H.' The face was such that as I gazed, I might well have been studying my mirror.

On the following day I was brought to this room with the barred windows, but I have been kept informed of certain things through an aged and simple-minded servitor, for whom I bore a fondness in infancy, and who, like me, loves the churchyard. What I have dared relate of my experiences within the vault has brought me only pitying smiles. My father, who visits me frequently, declares that at no time did I pass the chained portal, and swears that the rusted padlock had not been touched for fifty years when he examined it. He even says that all the village knew of my journeys to the tomb, and that I was often watched as I slept in the bower outside the grim façade, my half-open eyes fixed on the crevice that leads to the interior. Against these assertions I have no tangible proof to offer, since my key to the padlock was lost in the struggle on that night of horrors. The strange things of the past which I have learned during those nocturnal meetings with the dead he dismisses as the fruits of my lifelong and omnivorous browsing amongst the ancient volumes of the family library. Had it not been for my old servant Hiram, I should have by this time become quite convinced of my madness.

But Hiram, loyal to the last, has held faith in me, and has done that which impels me to make public at least part of my story. A week ago he burst open the lock which chains the door of the tomb perpetually ajar, and descended with a lantern into the murky depths. On a slab in an alcove he found an old but empty coffin whose tarnished plate bears the single word: *Jervas*. In that coffin and in that vault they have promised me I shall be buried.

The Festival

*Efficiut Daemones, ut quae non sunt, sic tamen quasi sint,
conspicienda bominibus exhibeant.*

— LACTANTIUS

I was far from home, and the spell of the eastern sea was
upon me. In the twilight I heard it pounding on the rocks,
and I knew it lay just over the hill where the twisting willows writhed against the clearing sky and the first stars of
evening. And because my fathers had called me to the old
town beyond, I pushed on through the shallow, new-fallen
snow along the road that soared lonely up to where Aldebaran twinkled among the trees; on toward the very ancient town I had never seen but often dreamed of.

It was the Yuletide, that men call Christmas though they
know in their hearts it is older than Bethlehem and Babylon, older than Memphis and mankind. It was the Yuletide, and I had come at last to the ancient sea town where
my people had dwelt and kept festival in the elder time
when festival was forbidden; where also they had com-
manded their sons to keep festival once every century, that
the memory of primal secrets might not be forgotten. Mine
were an old people, and were old even when this land was
settled three hundred years before. And they were strange,
because they had come as dark furtive folk from opiate
southern gardens of orchids, and spoken another tongue
before they learnt the tongue of the blue-eyed fishers. And
now they were scattered, and shared only the rituals of
mysteries that none living could understand. I was the only
one who came back that night to the old fishing town as
legend bade, for only the poor and the lonely remember.

Then beyond the hill's crest I saw Kingsport outspread
frostily in the gloaming; snowy Kingsport with its ancient
vanes and steeples, ridgepoles and chimney-pots, wharves
and small bridges, willow-trees and graveyards; endless
labyrinths of steep, narrow, crooked streets, and dizzy
church-crowned central peak that time durst not touch;

ceaseless mazes of colonial houses piled and scattered at
all angles and levels like a child's disordered blocks; antiquity hovering on grey wings over winter-whitened gables
and gambrel roofs; fanlights and small-paned windows one
by one gleaming out in the cold dusk to join Orion and the
archaic stars. And against the rotting wharves the sea poun-
ded; the secretive, immemorial sea out of which the people
had come in the elder time.

Beside the road at its crest a still higher summit rose,
bleak and windswept, and I saw that it was a burying-ground
where black gravestones stuck ghoulishly through the snow
like the decayed fingernails of a gigantic corpse. The print-
less road was very lonely, and sometimes I thought I heard
a distant horrible creaking as of a gibbet in the wind. They
had hanged four kinsmen of mine for witchcraft in 1692,
but I did not know just where.

As the road wound down the seaward slope I listened
for the merry sounds of a village at evening, but did not
hear them. Then I thought of the season, and felt that these
old Puritan folk might well have Christmas customs strange
to me, and full of silent hearthside prayer. So after that I
did not listen for merriment or look for wayfarers, kept on
down past the hushed lighted farmhouses and shadowy
stone walls to where the signs of ancient shops and sea
taverns creaked in the salt breeze, and the grotesque knock-
ers of pillared doorways glistened along deserted unpaved
lanes in the light of little, curtained windows.

I had seen maps of the town, and knew where to find the
home of my people. It was told that I should be known
and welcomed, for village legend lives long; so I hastened
through Back Street to Circle Court, and across the fresh
snow on the one full flagstone pavement in the town, to
where Green Lane leads off behind the Market House. The
old maps still held good, and I had no trouble; though at
Arkham they must have lied when they said the trolleys
ran to this place, since I saw not a wire overhead. Snow
would have hid the rails in any case. I was glad I had chosen
to walk, for the white village had seemed very beautiful
from the hill; and now I was eager to knock at the door of
my people, the seventh house on the left in Green Lane,

with an ancient peaked roof and jutting second story, all
built before 1650.

There were lights inside the house when I came upon it,
and I saw from the diamond window-panes that it must
have been kept very close to its antique state. The upper
part overhung the narrow grass-grown street and nearly
met the over-hanging part of the house opposite, so that I
was almost in a tunnel, with the low stone doorstep wholly
free from snow. There was no sidewalk, but many houses
had high doors reached by double flights of steps with iron
railings. It was an odd scene, and because I was strange to
New England I had never known its like before. Though it
pleased me, I would have relished it better if there had been
footprints in the snow, and people in the streets, and a few
windows without drawn curtains.

When I sounded the archaic iron knocker I was half
afraid. Some fear had been gathering in me, perhaps because of the strangeness of my heritage, and the bleakness
of the evening, and the queerness of the silence in that aged
town of curious customs. And when my knock was answered I was fully afraid, because I had not heard any footsteps before the door creaked open. But I was not afraid
long, for the gowned, slippered old man in the doorway had
a bland face that reassured me ; and though he made signs
that he was dumb, he wrote a quaint and ancient welcome
with the stylus and wax tablet he carried.

He beckoned me into a low, candle-lit room with massive
exposed rafters and dark, stiff, sparse furniture of the
seventeenth century. The past was vivid there, for not an
attribute was missing. There was a cavernous fireplace and
a spinning-wheel at which a bent old woman in loose wrap-
per and deep poke-bonnet sat back toward me, silently
spinning despite the festive season. An indefinite dampness
seemed upon the place, and I marvelled that no fire should
be blazing. The high-backed settle faced the row of curtained windows at the left, and seemed to be occupied,
though I was not sure. I did not like everything about what
I saw, and felt again the fear I had had. This fear grew
stronger from what had before lessened it, for the more I
looked at the old man's bland face the more its very bland-

ness terrified me. The eyes never moved, and the skin was
too much like wax. Finally I was sure it was not a face at
all, but a fiendishly cunning mask. But the flabby hands,
curiously gloved, wrote genially on the tablet and told me I
must wait a while before I could be led to the place of the
festival.

Pointing to a chair, table, and pile of books, the old man
now left the room ; and when I sat down to read I saw that
the books were hoary and mouldy, and that they included
old Morryster's wild *Marvells of Science*, the terrible
Saducismus Triumphatus of Joseph Glanvil, published in
1681, the shocking *Daemonolatreia* of Remigius, printed in
1595 at Lyons, and worst of all, the unmentionable *Necronomicon* of the mad Arab Abdul Alhazred, in Olaus
Wormius' forbidden Latin translation ; a book which I had
never seen, but of which I had heard monstrous things
whispered. No one spoke to me, but I could hear the creaking of signs in the wind outside, and the whir of the wheel
as the bonneted old woman continued her silent spinning,
spinning. I thought the room and the books and the
people very morbid and disquieting, but because an old
tradition of my fathers had summoned me to strange feast-
ings, I resolved to expect queer things. So I tried to read,
and soon became tremblingly absorbed by something I
found in that accursed *Necronomicon* ; a thought and a
legend too hideous for sanity or consciousness, but I disliked it when I fancied I heard the closing of one of the
windows that the settle faced, as if it had been stealthily
opened. It had seemed to follow a whirring that was not of
the old woman's spinning-wheel. This was not much,
though, for the old woman was spinning very hard, and
the aged clock had been striking. After that I lost the feeling that there were persons on the settle, and was reading
intently and shudderingly when the old man came back
booted and dressed in a loose antique costume, and sat
down on that very bench, so that I could not see him. It
was certainly nervous waiting, and the blasphemous book
in my hands made it doubly so. When eleven struck, however, the old man stood up, glided to a massive carved
chest in a corner, and got two hooded cloaks ; one of which

he donned, and the other of which he draped round the old woman, who was ceasing her monotonous spinning. Then they both started for the outer door; the woman lamely creeping, and the old man, after picking up the very book I had been reading, beckoning me as he drew his hood over that unmoving face or mask.

We went out into the moonless and tortuous network of that incredibly ancient town; went out as the lights in the curtained windows disappeared one by one, and the Dog Star leered at the throng of cowled, cloaked figures that poured silently from every doorway and formed monstrous processions up this street and that, past the creaking signs and antediluvian gables, the thatched roofs and diamond-paned windows; threading precipitous lanes were de-caying houses overlapped and crumbled together, gliding across open courts and churchyards where the bobbing lanthorn made eldritch drunken constellations.

Amid these hushed throngs I followed my voiceless guides; jostled by elbows that seemed preternaturally soft, and pressed by chests and stomachs that seemed abnorm-ally pulpy; but seeing never a face and hearing never a word. Up, up, up, the eery columns slithered, and I saw that all the travellers were converging as they flowed near a sort of focus of crazy alleys at the top of a high hill in the centre of the town, where perched a great white church. I had seen it from the road's crest when I looked at Kingsport in the new dusk, and it had made me shiver because Aldebaran had seemed to balance itself a moment on the ghostly spire.

There was an open space around the church; partly a churchyard with spectral shafts, and partly a half-paved square swept nearly bare of snow by the wind, and lined with unwholesomely archaic houses having peaked roofs and overhanging gables. Death-fires danced over the tombs, revealing gruesome vistas, though queerly failing to cast any shadows. Past the churchyard, where there were no houses, I could see over the hill's summit and watch the glimmer of stars on the harbour, though the town was invisible in the dark. Only once in a while a lanthorn bob-bed horribly through serpentine alleys on its way to overtake the throng that was now slipping speechlessly into the church. I waited till the crowd had oozed into the black doorway, and till all the stranglers had followed. The old man was pulling at my sleeve, but I was determined to be the last. Crossing the threshold into the swarming temple of unknown darkness, I turned once to look at the outside world as the churchyard phosphorescence cast a sickly glow on the hilltop pavement. And as I did so I shuddered. For though the wind had not left much snow, a few patches did remain on the path near the door; and in that fleeting backward look it seemed to my troubled eyes that they bore no mark of passing feet, not even mine.

The church was scarce lighted by all the lanthorns that had entered it, for most of the throng had already vanished. They had streamed up the aisle between the high pews to the trap-door of the vaults which yawned loathsomely open just before the pulpit, and were now squirming noiselessly in. I followed dumbly down the footworn steps and into the dark, suffocating crypt. The tail of that sinuous line of night-marchers seemed very horrible, and as I saw them wriggling into a venerable tomb they seemed more horrible still. Then I noticed that the tomb's floor had an aperture down which the throng was sliding, and in a moment we were all descending an ominous staircase of rough-hewn stone; a narrow spiral staircase damp and peculiarly odorous, that wound endlessly down into the bowels of the hill past monotonous walls of dripping stone blocks and crumbling mortar. It was a silent, shocking descent, and I observed after a horrible interval that the walls and steps were changing in nature, as if chiselled out of the solid rock. What mainly troubled me was that the myriad footfalls made no sound and set up no echoes. After more aeons of descent I saw some side passages or burrows leading from unknown recesses of blackness to this shaft of nighted mystery. Soon they became excessively numerous, like impious catacombs of nameless menace; and their pungent odour of decay grew quite unbearable. I knew we must have passed down through the mountain and beneath the earth of Kingsport itself, and I shivered

that a town should be so aged and maggoty with subterraneous evil.

Then I saw the lurid shimmering of pale light, and heard
the insidious lapping of sunless waters. Again I shivered,
for I did not like the things that the night had brought, and
wished bitterly that no forefather had summoned me to
this primal rite. As the steps and the passage grew broader,
I heard another sound, the thin, whining mockery of a
feeble flute ; and suddenly there spread out before me the
boundless vista of an inner world – a vast fungous shore
litten by a belching column of sick greenish flame and
washed by a wide oily river that flowed from abysses frightful and unsuspected to join the blackest gulfs of immemorial ocean.

Fainting and gasping, I looked at that unhallowed Ere-
bus of titan toadstools, leprous fire and slimy water, and
saw the cloaked throngs forming a semicircle around the
blazing pillar. It was the Yule-rite, older than man and
fated to survive him ; the primal rite of the solstice and of
spring's promise beyond the snows ; the rite of fire and
evergreen, light and music. And in the stygian grotto I
saw them do the rite, and adore the sick pillar of flame,
and throw into the water handfuls gouged out of the vis-
cous vegetation which glittered green in the chlorotic glare.
I saw this, and I saw something amorphously squatted far
away from the light, piping noisomely on a flute ; and as
the thing piped I thought I heard noxious muffled flutter-
ings in the foetid darkness where I could not see. But what
frightened me most was that flaming column ; spouting
volcanically from depths profound and inconceivable, casting no shadows as healthy flame should, and coating the
nitrous stone with a nasty, venomous verdigris. For in all
that seething combustion no warmth lay, but only the
clamminess of death and corruption.

The man who had brought me now squirmed to a point
directly beside the hideous flame, and made stiff ceremonial motions to the semi-circle he faced. At certain
stages of the ritual they did grovelling obeisance, especially when he held above his head that abhorrent *Necronomicon* he had taken with him ; and I shared all the

obeisances because I had been summoned to this festival by
the writings of my forefathers. Then the old man made a
signal to the half-seen flute-player in the darkness, which
player thereupon changed its feeble drone to a scarce
louder drone in another key; precipitating as it did so a
horror unthinkable and unexpected. At this horror I sank
nearly to the lichened earth, transfixed with a dread not of
this or any world, but only of the mad spaces between the
stars.

Out of the unimaginable blackness beyond the gangrenous glare of that cold flame, out of the tartarean leagues
through which that oily river rolled uncanny, unheard, and
unsuspected, there flopped rhythmically a horde of tame,
trained, hybrid winged things that no sound eye could ever
wholly grasp, or sound brain ever wholly remember. They
were not altogether crows, nor moles, nor buzzards, nor
ants, nor vampire bats, nor decomposed human beings;
but something I cannot and must not recall. They flopped
limply along, half with their webbed feet and half with
their membranous wings; and as they reached the throng
of celebrants the cowled figures seized and mounted them,
and rode off one by one along the reaches of that unlighted
river, into pits and galleries of panic where poison springs
feed frightful and undiscoverable cataracts.

The old spinning woman had gone with the throng, and
the old man remained only because I had refused when he
motioned me to seize an animal and ride like the rest. I saw
when I staggered to my feet that the amorphous flute-
player had rolled out of sight, but that two of the beasts
were patiently standing by. As I hung back, the old man
produced his stylus and tablet and wrote that he was the
true deputy of my fathers who had founded the Yule worship in this ancient place; that it had been decreed I should
come back, and that the most secret mysteries were yet to
be performed. He wrote this in a very ancient hand, and
when I still hesitated he pulled from his loose robe a seal
ring and a watch, both with my family arms, to prove that
he was what he said. But it was a hideous proof, because I
knew from old papers that that watch had been buried with
my great-great-great-great-grandfather in 1698.

Presently the old man drew back his hood and pointed to the family resemblance in his face, but I only shuddered, because I was sure that the face was merely a devilish mask. The flopping animals were now scratching restlessly at the lichens, and I saw that the old man was nearly as restless himself. When one of the things began to waddle and edge away, he turned quickly to stop it; so that the suddenness of his motion dislodged the waxen mask from what should have been his head. And then, because that nightmare's position barred me from the stone staircase down which we had come, I flung myself into the oily underground river that bubbled somewhere to the caves of the sea; flung myself into that putrescent juice of earth's inner horrors before the madness of my screams could bring down upon me all the charnel legions these pestgulfs might conceal.

At the hospital they told me I had been found half-frozen in Kingsport Harbour at dawn, clinging to the drifting spar that accident sent to save me. They told me I had taken the wrong fork of the hill road the night before, and fallen over the cliffs at Orange Point; a thing they deduced from prints found in the snow. There was nothing I could say, because everything was wrong. Everything was wrong, with the broad windows showing a sea of roofs in which only about one in five was ancient, and the sound of trolleys and motors in the streets below. They insisted that this was Kingsport, and I could not deny it. When I went delirious at hearing that the hospital stood near the old churchyard on Central Hill, they sent me to St. Mary's Hospital in Arkham, where I could have better care. I liked it there, for the doctors were broad-minded, and even lent me their influence in obtaining the carefully sheltered copy of Alhazred's objectionable *Necronomicon* from the library of Miskatonic University. They said something about a 'psychosis', and agreed I had better get any harassing obsessions off my mind.

So I read that hideous chapter, and shuddered doubly because it was indeed not new to me. I had seen it before, let footprints tell what they might; and where it was I had seen it were best forgotten. There was no one – in waking hours – who could remind me of it; but my dreams are

filled with terror, because of phrases I dare not quote. I
dare quote only one paragraph, put into such English as I
can make from the awkward Low Latin.

'The nethermost caverns,' wrote the mad Arab, 'are not
for the fathoming of eyes that see; for their marvels are
strange and terrific. Cursed the ground where dead thoughts
live new and oddly bodied, and evil the mind that is held
by no head. Wisely did Ibn Schacabao say, that happy is
the tomb where no wizard hath lain, and happy the town at
night whose wizards are all ashes. For it is of old rumour
that the soul of the devil-bought hastes not from his char-
nal clay, but fats and instructs *the very worm that gnaws;*
till out of corruption horrid life springs, and the dull scavengers of earth wax crafty to vex it and swell monstrous to
plague it. Great holes secretly are digged where earth's
pores ought to suffice, and things have learnt to walk that
ought to crawl.'

Imprisoned with the Pharaohs*

Mystery attracts mystery. Ever since the wide appearance of my name as a performer of unexplained feats, I have encountered strange narratives and events which my calling has led people to link with my interests and activities. Some of these have been trivial and irrelevant, some deeply dramatic and absorbing, some productive of weird and perilous experiences and some involving me in extensive scientific and historical research. Many of these matters I have told and shall continue to tell very freely; but there is one of which I speak with great reluctance, and which I am now relating only after a session of grilling persuasion from the publishers of this magazine, who had heard vague rumors of it from other members of my family.

The hitherto guarded subject pertains to my non-professional visit to Egypt fourteen years ago, and has been avoided by me for several reasons. For one thing, I am averse to exploiting certain unmistakably actual facts and conditions obviously unknown to the myriad tourists who throng about the pyramids and apparently secreted with much diligence by the authorities at Cairo, who cannot be wholly ignorant of them. For another thing, I dislike to recount an incident in which my own fantastic imagination must have played so great a part. What I saw – or thought I saw – certainly did not take place; but is rather to be viewed as a result of my then recent readings in Egyptology, and of the speculations anent this theme which my environment naturally prompted. These imaginative stimuli, magnified by the excitement of an actual event terrible enough in itself, undoubtedly gave rise to the culminating horror of that grotesque night so long past.

In January, 1910, I had finished a professional engagement in England and signed a contract for a tour of Australian theatres. A liberal time being allowed for the trip, I determined to make the most of it in the sort of travel which chiefly interests me; so accompanied by my wife I

* With Harry Houdini

drifted pleasantly down the Continent and embarked at
Marseilles on the P. & O. Steamer *Malwa,* bound for Port
Said. From that point I proposed to visit the principal his-
torical localities of lower Egypt before leaving finally for
Australia.

The voyage was an agreeable one, and enlivened by many
of the amusing incidents which befall a magical performer
apart from his work. I had intended, for the sake of quiet
travel, to keep my name a secret; but was goaded into betraying myself by a fellow-magician whose anxiety to as-
tound the passengers with ordinary tricks tempted me to
duplicate and exceed his feats in a manner quite destructive
of my incognito. I mention this because of its ultimate
effect – an effect I should have foreseen before unmasking
to a shipload of tourists about to scatter throughout the
Nile valley. What it did was to herald my identity wherever
I subsequently went, and deprive my wife and me of all the
placid inconspicuousness we had sought. Traveling to seek
curiosities, I was often forced to stand inspection as a sort
of curiosity myself!

We had come to Egypt in search of the picturesque and
the mystically impressive, but found little enough when the
ship edged up to Port Said and discharged its passengers in
small boats. Low dunes of sand, bobbing buoys in shallow
water, and a drearily European small town with nothing of
interest save the great De Lesseps statue, made us anxious
to get on to something more worth our while. After some
discussion we decided to proceed at once to Cairo and the
Pyramids, later going to Alexandria for the Australian boat
and for whatever Greco-Roman sights that ancient metro-
polis might present.

The railway journey was tolerable enough, and consumed only four hours and a half. We saw much of the
Suez Canal, whose route we followed as far as Ismailiya
and later had a taste of Old Egypt in our glimpse of the re-
stored fresh-water canal of the Middle Empire. Then at last
we saw Cairo glimmering through the growing dusk; a
winkling constellation which became a blaze as we halted
at the great Gare Centrale.

But once more disappointment awaited us, for all that we

beheld was European save the costumes and the crowds.
A prosaic subway led to a square teeming with carriages,
taxicabs, and trolley-cars and gorgeous with electric lights
shining on tall buildings ; whilst the very theatre where I was
vainly requested to play and which I later attended as a
spectator, had recently been renamed the 'American Cos-
mograph.' We stopped at Shepheard's Hotel, reached in a
taxi that sped along broad, smartly built-up streets ; and
amidst the perfect service of its restaurant, elevators and
generally Anglo-American luxuries the mysterious East
and immemorial past seemed very far away.

The next day, however, precipitated us delightfully into
the heart of the *Arabian Nights atmosphere*; and in the
winding ways and exotic skyline of Cairo, the Bagdad of
Harun-al-Rashid seemed to live again. Guided by our Bae-
deker, we had struck east past the Ezbekiyeh Gardens along
the Mouski in quest of the native quarter, and were soon in
the hands of a clamorous cicerone who – notwithstanding later developments – was assuredly a master at his
trade.

Not until afterward did I see that I should have applied at
the hotel for a licensed guide. This man, a shaven, peculiarly
hollow-voiced and relatively cleanly fellow who looked like
a Pharaoh and called himself 'Abdul Reis el Drogman,' appeared to have much power over others of his kind ; though
subsequently the police professed not to know him, and to
suggest that *reis* is merely a name for any person in authority, whilst 'Drogman' is obviously no more than a clumsy
modification of the word for a leader of tourist parties –
dragoman.

Abdul led us among such wonders as we had before only
read and dreamed of. Old Cairo is itself a story-book and a
dream – labyrinths of narrow alleys redolent of aromatic
secrets ; Arabesque balconies and oriels nearly meeting
above the cobbled streets ; maelstroms of Oriental traffic
with strange cries, cracking whips, rattling carts, jingling
money, and braying donkeys ; kaleidoscopes of polychrome
robes, veils, turbans, and tarbushes ; water-carriers and
dervishes, dogs and cats, soothsayers and barbers ; and over
all the whining of blind beggars crouched in alcoves, and the

sonorous chanting of muezzins from minarets limned delicately against a sky of deep, unchanging blue.

The roofed, quieter bazaars were hardly less alluring. Spice, perfume, incense beads, rugs, silks, and brass –old Mahomoud Suleiman squats cross-legged amidst his gummy bottles while chattering youths pulverize mustard in the hollowed-out capital of an ancient classic column – a Roman Corinthian, perhaps from neighboring Heliopolis, where Augustus stationed one of his three Egyptian legions. Antiquity begins to mingle with exoticism. And then the mosques and the museum – we saw them all, and tried not to let our Arabian revel succumb to the darker charm of Pharaonic Egypt which the museum's priceless treasures offered. That was to be our climax, and for the present we concentrated on the mediaeval Saracenic glories of the Califs whose magnificent tomb-mosques form a glittering faery necropolis on the edge of the Arabian Desert.

At length Abdul took us along the Sharia Mohammed Ali to the ancient mosque of Sultan Hassan, and the tower-flanked Babel-Azab, beyond which climbs the steep-walled pass to the mighty citadel that Saladin himself built with the stones of forgotten pyramids. It was sunset when we scaled that cliff, circled the modern mosque of Mohammed Ali, and looked down from the dizzy parapet over mystic Cairo – mystic Cairo all golden with its carven domes, its ethereal minarets and its flaming gardens.

Far over the city towered the great Roman dome of the new museum ; and beyond it – across the cryptic yellow Nile that is the mother of eons and dynasties – lurked the menacing sands of the Libyan Desert, undulant and iridescent and evil with older arcana.

The red sun sank low, bringing the relentless chill of Egyptian dusk ; and as it stood poised on the world's rim like that ancient god of Heliopolis – Re-Harakhte, the Horizon-Sun – we saw silhouetted against its vermeil holocaust the black outlines of the Pyramids of Gizeh – the palaeogean tombs there were hoary with a thousand years when Tut-Ankh-Amen mounted his golden throne in distant Thebes. Then we knew that we were done with Saracen Cairo, and that we must taste the deeper mysteries of primal

Egypt – the black Kem of Re and Amen, Isis and Osiris.

The next morning we visited the Pyramids, riding out in a Victoria across the island of Chizereh with its massive leb-bakh trees, and the smaller English bridge to the western shore. Down the shore road we drove, between great rows of lebbakhs and past the vast Zooligical Gardens to the suburb of Gizeh, where a new bridge to Cairo proper has since been built. Then, turning inland along the Sharia-el-Haram, we crossed a region of glassy canals and shabby native villages till before us loomed the objects of our quest, cleaving the mists of dawn and forming inverted replicas in the roadside pools. Forty centuries, as Napoleon had told his campaigners there, indeed looked down upon us.

The road now rose abruptly, till we finally reached our place of transfer between the trolley station and the Mena House Hotel. Abdul Reis, who capably purchased our Pyramid tickets, seemed to have an understanding with the crowding, yelling and offensive Bedouins who inhabited a squalid mud village some distance away and pestiferously assailed every traveler ; for he kept them very decently at bay and secured an excellent pair of camels for us, himself mounting a donkey and assigning the leadership of our animals to a group of men and boys more expensive than useful. The area to be traversed was so small that camels were hardly needed, but we did not regret adding to our experience this troublesome form of desert navigation.

The pyramids stand on a high rock plateau, this group forming next to the northernmost of the series of regal and aristocratic cemeteries built in the neighbourhood of the extinct capital Memphis, which lay on the same side of the Nile, somewhat south of Gizeh, and which flourished between 3400 and 2000 B.C. The greatest pyramid, which lies nearest the modern road, was built by King Cheops or Khufu about 2800 B.C., and stands more than 450 feet in perpendicular height. In a line southwest from this are successively the Second Pyramid, built a generation later by King Khephren, and though slightly smaller, looking even larger because set on higher ground, and the radically smaller Third Pyramid of King Mycerinus, built about 2700 B.C. Near the edge of the plateau and due east of the Second

Pyramid, with a face probably altered to form a colossal portrait of Khephren, its royal restorer, stands the monstrous Sphinx – mute, sardonic, and wise beyond mankind and memory.

Minor pyramids and the traces of ruined minor pyramids are found in several places, and the whole plateau is pitted with the tombs of dignitaries of less than royal rank. These latter were originally marked by *mastabas*, or stone bench-like structures about the deep burial shafts, as found in other Memphian cemeteries and exemplified by Perneb's Tomb in the Metropolitan Museum of New York. At Gizeh, however, all such visible things have been swept away by time and pillage ; and only the rock-hewn shafts, either sand-filled or cleared out by archaeologists, remain to attest their former existence. Connected with each tomb was a chapel in which priests and relatives offered food and prayer to the hovering *ka* or vital principle of the deceased. The small tombs have their chapels contained in their stone *mastabas* or superstructures, but the mortuary chapels of the pyramids, where regal Pharaohs lay, were separate temples, each to the east of its corresponding pyramid, and connected by a causeway to a massive gate-chapel or propylon at the edge of the rock plateau.

The gate-chapel leading to the Second Pyramid, nearly buried in the drifting sands, yawns subterraneously south-east of the Sphinx. Persistent tradition dubs it the 'Temple of the Sphinx' ; and it may perhaps be rightly called such if the Sphinx indeed represents the Second Pyramid's builder Khephren. There are unpleasant tales of the Sphinx before Khephren – but whatever its elder features were, the monarch replaced them with his own that men might look at the colossus without fear.

It was in the great gateway-temple that the life-size diorite statue of Khephren now in the Cairo museum was found ; a statue before which I stood in awe when I beheld it. Whether the whole edifice is now excavated I am not certain, but in 1910 most of it was below ground, with the entrance heavily barred at night. Germans were in charge of the work, and the war or other things may have stopped them. I would give much, in view of my experience and of certain Bedouin whisperings discredited or unknown in Cairo, to know what has developed in connection with a certain well in a transverse gallery where statues of the Pharaoh were found in curious juxtaposition to the statues of baboons.

The road, as we traversed it on our camels that morning, curved sharply past the wooden police quarters, post office, drug store and shops on the left, and plunged south and east in a complete bend that scaled the rock plateau and brought us face to face with the desert under the lee of the Great Pyramid. Past Cyclopean masonry we rode, rounding the eastern face and looking down ahead into a valley of minor pyramids beyond which the eternal Nile glistened to the east, and the eternal desert shimmered to the west. Very close loomed the three major pyramids, the greatest devoid of outer casing and showing its bulk of great stones, but the others retaining here and there the neatly fitted covering which had made them smooth and finished in their day.

Presently we descended toward the Sphinx, and sat silent beneath the spell of those terrible unseeing eyes. On the vast stone breast we faintly discerned the emblem of Re-Harakhte, for whose image the Sphinx was mistaken in a late dynasty; and though sand covered the tablet between the great paws, we recalled what Thutmosis IV inscribed thereon, and the dream he had when a prince. It was then that the smile of the Sphinx vaguely displeased us, and made us wonder about the legends of subterranean passages beneath the monstrous creature, leading down, down, to depths none might dare hint at – depths connected with mysteries older than the dynastic Egypt we excavate, and having a sinister relation to the persistence of abnormal, animal-headed gods in the ancient Nilotic pantheon. Then, too, it was I asked myself an idle question whose hideous significance was not to appear for many an hour.

Other tourists now began to overtake us, and we moved on to the sand-choked Temple of the Sphinx, fifty yards to the southeast, which I have previously mentioned as the great gate of the causeway to the Second Pyramid's mortuary chapel on the plateau. Most of it was still underground, and although we dismounted and descended through a modern passageway to its alabaster corridor and pillared hall, I felt that Adul and the local German attendant had not shown us all there was to see.

After this we made the conventional circuit of the pyramid plateau, examining the Second Pyramid and the peculiar ruins of its mortuary chapel to the east, the Third Pyramid and its miniature southern satellites and ruined eastern chapel, the rock tombs and the honeycombings of the Fourth and Fifth dynasties, and the famous Campbell's Tomb whose shadowy shaft sinks precipitously for fifty-three feet to a sinister sarcophagus which one of our camel drivers divested of the cumbering sand after a vertiginous descent by rope.

Cries now assailed us from the Great Pyramid, where Bedouins were besieging a party of tourists with offers of speed in the performance of solitary trips up and down. Seventy minutes is said to be the record for such an ascent and descent, but many lusty shieks and sons of shieks assured us they could cut it five if given the requisite impetus of liberal *baksheesh*. They did not get this impetus, though we did let Abdul take us up, thus obtaining a view of unprecedented magnificence which included not only remote and glittering Cairo with its crowned citadel background of gold-violet hills, but all the pyramids of the Memphian district as well, from Abu Roash on the north to the Dashur on the south. The Sakkara step-pyramid, which marks the evolution of the low *mastaba* into the true pyramid, showed clearly and alluringly in the sandy distance. It is close to this transition-monument that the famed tomb of Perneb was found – more than four hundred miles north of the Theban rock valley where Tut-Ankh-Amen sleeps. Again I was forced to silence through sheer awe. The prospect of such antiquity, and the secrets each hoary monument seemed to hold and brood over, filled me with a reverence and sense of immensity nothing else ever gave me.

Fatigued by our climb, and disgusted with the importunate Bedouins whose actions seemed to defy every rule of taste, we omitted the arduous detail of entering the cramped interior passages of any of the pyramids, though we saw several of the hardiest tourists preparing for the suffocating crawl through Cheops' mightiest memorial. As we dismissed and overpaid our local bodyguard and drove back to Cairo with Abdul Reis under the afternoon sun, we half regretted the omission we had made. Such fascinating things were whispered about lower pyramid passages not in the guide books; passages whose entrances had been hastily blocked up and concealed by certain uncommunicative archaeologists who had found and begun to explore them.

Of course, this whispering was largely baseless on the face of it; but it was curious to reflect how persistently visitors were forbidden to enter the Pyramids at night, or to visit the lowest burrows and crypt of the Great Pyramid. Perhaps in the latter case it was the psychological effect which was feared – the effort on the visitor of feeling himself huddled down beneath a gigantic world of solid masonry; joined to the life he has known by the merest tube, in which he may only crawl, and which any accident or evil design might block. The whole subject seemed so weird and alluring that we resolved to pay the pyramid plateau another visit at the earliest possible opportunity. For me this opportunity came much earlier than I exected.

That evening, the members of our party feeling somewhat tired after the strenuous program of the day, I went alone with Abdul Reis for a walk through the picturesque Arab quarter. Though I had seen it by day, I wished to study the alleys and bazaars in the dusk, when rich shadows and mellow gleams of light would add to their glamor and fantastic illusion. The native crowds were thinning, but were still very noisy and numerous when we came upon a knot of reveling Bedouins in the Suken-Nahhasin, or bazaar of the coppersmiths. Their apparent leader, an insolent youth with heavy features and saucily cocked tarbush, took some notice of us, and evidently recognized with no great friendliness my competent but admittedly supercilious and sneeringly disposed guide.

Perhaps, I thought, he resented that odd reproduction of the Sphinx's half-smile which I had often remarked with amused irritation; or perhaps he did not like the hollow and

sepulchral resonance of Abdul's voice. At any rate, the
exchange of ancestrally opprobrious language became very
brisk ; and before long Ali Ziz, as I heard the stranger
called when called by no worse name, began to pull violently at Abdul's robe, an action quickly reciprocated and
leading to a spirited scuffle in which both combatants lost
their sacredly cherished headgear and would have reached
an even direr condition had I not intervened and separated
them by main force.

My interference, at first seemingly unwelcome on both
sides, succeeded at last in effecting a truce. Sullenly each
belligerent composed his wrath and his attire, and with an
assumption of dignity as profound as it was sudden, the
two formed a curious pact of honor which I soon learned
is a custom of great antiquity in Cairo – a pact for the settlement of their difference by means of a nocturnal fist fight
atop the Great Pyramid, long after the departure of the last
moonlight sightseer. Each duellist was to assemble a party
of seconds, and the affair was to begin at midnight, proceed-
ing by rounds in the most civilized possible fashion.

In all this planning there was much which excited my
interests. The fight itself promised to be unique and spec-
tacular, while the thought of the scene on that hoary pile
overlooking the antediluvian plateau of Gizeh under the
wan moon of the pallid small hours appealed to every fiber
of imagination in me. A request found Abdul exceedingly
willing to admit me to his party of seconds ; so that all the
rest of the early evening I accompanied him to various dens
in the most lawless regions of the town – mostly northeast
of the Ezbekiyeh – where he gathered one by one a select
and formidable band of congenial cutthroats at his pugilistic
background.

Shortly after nine our party, mounted on donkeys bearing such royal or tourist-reminiscent names as 'Rameses,'
'Mark Twain,' 'J. P. Morgan,' and 'Minnehaha,' edged
through street labyrinths both Oriental and Occidental,
crossed the muddy and mast-forested Nile by the bridge of
the bronze lions, and cantered philosophically between the
lebbakhs on the road to Gizeh. Slightly over two hours were
consumed by the trip, toward the end of which we passed

the last of the returning tourists, saluted the last inbound trolley-car, and were alone with the night and the past and the spectral moon.

Then we saw the vast pyramids at the end of the avenue, ghoulish with a dim atavistical menace which I had not seemed to notice in the daytime. Even the smallest of them held a hint of the ghastly – for was it not in this that they had buried Queen Nitocris alive in the Sixth Dynasty; subtle Queen Nitocris, who once invited all her enemies to a feast in a temple below the Nile, and drowned them by opening the water-gates? I recalled that the Arabs whisper things about Nitocris, and shun the Third Pyramid at certain phases of the moon. It must have been over her that Thomas Moore was brooding when he wrote a thing muttered about by Memphian boatmen:

> 'The subterranean nymph that dwells
> 'Mid sunless gems and glories hid –
> The lady of the Pyramid!'

Early as we were, Ali Ziz and his party were ahead of us; for we saw their donkeys outlined against the desert plateau at Kafr-el-Harem; toward which squalid Arab settlements, close to the Sphinx, we had diverged instead of following the regular road to the Mena House, where some of the sleepy, inefficient police might have observed and halted us. Here, where filthy Bedouins stabled camels and donkeys in the rock tombs of Khephren's courtiers, we were led up the rocks and over the sand to the Great Pyramid, up whose time-worn sides the Arabs swarmed eagerly, Abdul Reis offering me the assistance I did not need.

As most travelers know, the actual apex of this structure has long been worn away, leaving a reasonably flat platform twelve yards square. On this eery pinnacle a squared circle was formed, and in a few moments the sardonic desert moon leered down upon a battle which, but for the quality of the ringside cries, might well have occurred at some minor athletic club in America. As I watched it, I felt that some of our less desirable institutions were not lacking; for every blow, feint, and defense bespoke 'stalling' to my not inexperienced eye. It was quickly over, and despite my misgivings as to methods I felt a sort of proprietary pride when Abdul Reis was adjudged the winner.

Reconciliation was phenomenally rapid, and amidst the singing fraternizing and drinking which followed, I found it difficult to realize that a quarrel had ever occurred. Oddly enough, I myself seemed to be more a center of notice than the antagonists; and from my smattering of Arabic I judged that they were discussing my professional performances and escapes from every sort of manacle and confinement, in a manner which indicated not only a surprising knowledge of me, but a distinct hostility and skepticism concerning my feats of escape. It gradually dawned on me that the elder magic of Egypt did not depart without leaving traces, and that fragments of a strange secret lore and priestly cult-practises have survived surreptitiously amongst the fellaheen to such an extent that the prowess of a strange *hahwi* or magician is resented and disputed. I thought of how much my hollow-voiced guide Abdul Reis looked like an old Egyptian priest or Pharaoh or smiling Sphinx ... and wondered.

Suddenly something happened which in a flash proved the correctness of my reflection and made me curse the denseness whereby I had accepted this night's events as other than the empty and malicious 'frame-up' they now showed themselves to be. Without warning, and doubtless in answer to some subtle sign from Abdul, the entire band of Bedouins precipitated itself upon me; and having produced heavy ropes, soon had me bound as securely as I was ever bound in the course of my life, either on the stage or off.

I struggled at first, but soon saw that one man could make no headway against a band of over twenty sinewy barbarians. My hands were tied behind my back, my knees bent to their fullest extent, and my wrists and ankles stoutly linked together with unyielding cords. A stifling gag was forced into my mouth, and a blindfold fastened tightly over my eyes. Then, as Arabs bore me aloft on their shoulders and began a jouncing descent of the pyramid, I heard the taunts of my late guide Abdul, who mocked and jeered delightedly in his hollow voice, and assured me that I was soon to have my 'magic powers' put to a supreme test which would quickly remove any egotism I might have gained through triumphing over all the tests offered by America and Europe. Egypt, he reminded me, is very old, and full of inner mysteries and antique powers not even conceivable to the experts of today, whose devices had so uniformly failed to entrap me.

How far or in what direction I was carried, I cannot tell; for the circumstances were all against the formation of any accurate judgment. I know, however, that it could not have been a great distance; since my bearers at no point hastened beyond a walk, yet kept me aloft a surprisingly short time. It is this perplexing brevity which makes me feel almost like shuddering whenever I think of Gizeh and its plateau – for one is oppressed by hints of the closeness to everyday tourist routes of what existed then and must exist still.

The evil abnormality I speak of did not become manifest at first. Setting me down on a surface which I recognized as sand rather than rock, my captors passed a rope around my chest and dragged me a few feet to a ragged opening in the ground, into which they presently lowered me with much rough handling. For apparent eons I bumped against the stony irregular sides of a narrow hewn well which I took to be one of the numerous burial-shafts of the plateau until the prodigious, almost incredible depth of it robbed me of all bases of conjecture.

The horror of the experience deepened with every dragging second. That any descent through the sheer solid rock could be so vast without reaching the core of the planet itself, or that any rope made by man could be so long as to dangle me in these unholy and seemingly fathomless profundities of nether earth. were beliefs of such grotesqueness that it was easier to doubt my agitated senses than to accept them. Even now I am uncertain, for I know how deceitful the sense of time becomes when one is removed or distorted. But I am quite sure that I preserved a logical consciousness that far; that at least I did not add any full-grown phantoms of imagination to a picture hideous enough in its reality, and explicable by a type of cerebral illusion vastly short of actual hallucination.

All this was not the cause of my first bit of fainting. The shocking ordeal was cumulative, and the beginning of the latter terrors was a very perceptible increase in my rate of descent. They were paying out that infinitely long rope very swiftly now, and I scraped cruelly against the rough and constricted sides of the shaft as I shot madly downward. My clothing was in tatters, and I felt the trickle of blood all over, even above the mounting and excruciating pain. My nostrils, too, were assailed by a scarcely definable menace: a creeping odor of damp and staleness curiously unlike anything I had ever smelled before, and having faint overtones of spice and incense that lent an element of mockery.

Then the mental cataclysm came. It was horrible – hideous beyond all articulate description because it was all of the soul, with nothing of detail to describe. It was the ecstasy of nightmare and the summation of the fiendish. The suddenness of it was apocalyptic and demoniac – one moment I was plunging agonizingly down that narrow well of milliontoothed torture, yet the next moment I was soaring on batwings in the gulfs of hell; swinging free and swoopingly through illimitable miles of boundless, musty space; rising dizzily to measureless pinnacles of chilling ether, then diving gaspingly to sucking nadirs of ravenous, nauseous lower vacua. . . . Thank God for the mercy that shut out in oblivion those clawing Furies of consciousness which half unhinged my faculties, and tore harpy-like at my spirit! That one respite, short as it was, gave me the strength and sanity to endure those still greater sublimations of cosmic panic that lurked and gibbered on the road ahead.

II

It was very gradually that I regained my senses after that eldritch flight through stygian space. The process was infinitely painful, and colored by fantastic dreams in which my bound and gagged condition found singular embodiment. The precise nature of these dreams was very clear while I was experiencing them, but became blurred in my recollection almost immediately afterward, and was soon reduced to the merest outline by the terrible events – real or imaginary – which followed. I dreamed that I was in the grasp of a great and horrible paw; a yellow, hairy, five-clawed paw which had reached out of the earth to crush and engulf me. And when I stopped to reflect what the paw was, it seemed to me that it was Egypt. In the dream I looked back at the events of the preceding weeks, and saw myself lured and enmeshed little by little, subtly and insidiously, by some hellish ghoul-spirit of the elder Nile sorcery; some spirit that was in Egypt before ever man was, and that will be when man is no more.

I saw the horror and unwholesome antiquity of Egypt, and the grisly alliance it has always had with the tombs and temples of the dead. I saw phantom processions of priests with the heads of bulls, falcons, cats, and ibises; phantom processions marching interminably through subterraneous labyrinths and avenues of titanic propylaea beside which a man is as a fly, and offering unnamable sacrifice to inde-scribable gods. Stone colossi marched in endless night and drove herds of grinning andro-sphinxes down to the shores of illimitable stagnant rivers of pitch. And behind it all I saw the ineffable malignity of primordial necromancy, black and amorphous, and fumbling greedily after me in the dark-ness to choke out the spirit that had dared to mock it by emulation.

In my sleeping brain there took shape a melodrama of sinister hatred and pursuit, and I saw the black soul of Egypt singling me out and calling me in inaudible whispers; calling and luring me, leading me on with the glitter and glamor of a Saracenic surface, but ever pulling me down to the age-mad catacombs and horrors of its *dead* and abys-mal pharaonic heart.

Then the dream faces took on human resemblances, and I saw my guide Abdul Reis in the robes of a king, with the sneer of the Sphinx on his features. And I knew that those features were the features of Khephren the Great, who raised the Second Pyramid, carved over the Sphinx's face in the likeness of his own and built that titanic gateway temple whose myriad corridors the archaeologists think they have dug out of the cryptical sand and the uninforma-

tive rock. And I looked at the long, lean, rigid hand of
Khephren; the long, lean, rigid hand as I had seen it on the
diorite statue in the Cairo Museum – the statue they had
found in the terrible gateway temple – and wondered that
I had not shrieked when I saw it on Abdul Reis. ... That
hand? It was hideously cold, and it was crushing me ; it was
the cold and cramping of the sarcophagus ... the chill and
constriction of unrememberable Egypt. ... It was nighted,
necropolitan Egypt itself ... that yellow paw ... and they
whisper such things of Khephren ...

But at this juncture I began to awake – or at least, to
assume a condition less completely that of sleep than the
one just preceding. I recalled the fight atop the pyramid,
the treacherous Bedouins and their attack, my frightful
descent by rope through endless rock depths, and my mad
swinging and plunging in a chill void redolent of aromatic
putrescence. I perceived that I now lay on a damp rock
floor, and that my bonds were still biting into me with un-
loosened force. It was very cold, and I seemed to detect a
faint current of noisesome air sweeping across me. The cuts
and bruises I had received from the jagged sides of the rock
shaft were paining me woefully, their soreness enhanced
to a stinging or burning acuteness by some pungent quality
in the faint draft, and the mere act of rolling over was
enough to set my whole frame throbbing with untold
agony.

As I turned I felt a tug from above, and concluded that
the rope whereby I was lowered still reached to the surface.
Whether or not the Arabs still held it, I had no idea; nor
had I any idea how far within the earth I was. I knew that
the darkness around me was wholly or nearly total, since
no ray of moonlight penetrated my blindfold; but I did not
trust my senses enough to accept as evidence of extreme
depth the sensation of vast duration which had character-
ized my descent.

Knowing at least that I was in a space of considerable
extent reached from the surface directly above by an opening in the rock, I doubtfully conjectured that my prison
was perhaps the buried gateway chapel of old Khephren –
the Temple of the Sphinx – perhaps some inner corridor

which the guides had not shown me during my morning
visit, and from which I might easily escape if I could find
my way to the barred entrance. It would be a labyrinthine
wandering, but no worse than others out of which I had in
the past found my way.

The first step was to get free of my bonds, gag, and blindfold ; and this I knew would be no great task, since subtler
experts than these Arabs had tried every known species of
fetter upon me during my long and varied career as an
exponent of escape, yet had never succeeded in defeating
my methods.

Then it occurred to me that the Arabs might be ready to
meet and attack me at the entrance upon any evidence of
my probable escape from the binding cords, as would be
furnished by any decided agitation of the rope which they
probably held. This, of course, was taking for granted that
my place of confinement was indeed Khephren's Temple
of the Sphinx. The direct opening in the roof, wherever it
might lurk, could not be beyond easy reach of the ordinary
modern entrance near the Sphinx ; if in truth it were any
great distance at all on the surface, since the total area
known to visitors is not at all enormous. I had not noticed
any such opening during my daytime pilgrimage, but knew
that these things are easily overlooked amidst the drifting
sands.

Thinking these matters over as I lay bent and bound on
the rock floor, I nearly forgot the horrors of abysmal descent and cavernous swinging which had so lately reduced
me to a coma. My present thought was only to outwit the
Arabs, and I accordingly determined to work myself free
as quickly as possible, avoiding any tug on the descending
line which might betray an effective or even problematical
attempt at freedom.

This, however, was more easily determined than effected.
A few preliminary trials made it clear that little could be
accomplished without considerable motion ; and it did not
surprise me when, after one especially energetic struggle, I
began to feel the coils of falling rope as they piled up about
me and upon me. Obviously, I thought, the Bedouins had
felt my movements and released their end of the rope ;

hastening no doubt to the temple's true entrance to lie murderously in wait for me.

The prospect was not pleasing – but I had faced worse in my time without flinching, and would not flinch now. At present I must first of all free myself of bonds, then trust to ingenuity to escape from the temple unharmed. It is curious how implicitly I had come to believe myself in the old temple of Khephren beside the Sphinx, only a short distance below the ground.

That belief was shattered, and every pristine apprehension of preternatural depth and demoniac mystery revived, by a circumstance which grew in horror and significance even as I formulated my philosophical plan. I have said that the falling rope was piling up about and upon me. Now I saw that it was continuing to pile, as no rope of normal length could possibly do. It gained in momentum and became an avalanche of hemp, accumulating mountainously on the floor and half burying me beneath its swiftly multiplying coils. Soon I was completely engulfed and gasping for breath as the increasing convolutions submerged and stifled me.

My senses tottered again, and I vainly tried to fight off a menace desperate and ineluctable. It was not merely that I was tortured beyond human endurance – not merely that life and breath seemed to be crushed slowly out of me – it was the knowledge of what those unnatural lengths of rope implied, and the consciousness of what unknown and incalculable gulfs of inner earth must at this moment be surrounding me. My endless descent and swinging flight through goblin space, then, must have been real, and even now I must be lying helpless in some nameless cavern world toward the core of the planet. Such a sudden confirmation of ultimate horror was insupportable, and a second time I lapsed into merciful oblivion.

When I say oblivion, I do not imply that I was free from dreams. On the contrary, my absence from the conscious world was marked by visions of the most unutterable hideousness. God! ... If only I had not read so much Egyptology before coming to this land which is the fountain of all darkness and terror! This second spell of fainting filled my sleeping mind anew with shivering realization of the country and its archaic secrets, and through some damnable chance my dreams turned to the ancient notions of the dead and their sojournings in soul and body beyond those mysterious tombs which were more houses than graves. I recalled, in dream-shapes which it is well that I do not remember, the peculiar and elaborate construction of Egyptian sepulchers ; and the exceedingly singular and terrific doctrines which determined this construction.

All these people thought of was death and the dead. They conceived of a literal resurrection of the body which made them mummify it with desperate care, and preserve all the vital organs in canopic jars near the corpse ; whilst besides the body they believed in two other elements, the soul, which after its weighing and approval by Osiris dwelt in the land of the blest, and the obscure and portentous *ka* or life-principle which wandered about the upper and lower worlds in a horrible way, demanding occasional access to the preserved body, consuming the food offerings brought by priests and pious relatives to the mortuary chapel, and sometimes – as men whispered – taking its body or the wooden double always buried beside it and stalking noxiously abroad on errands peculiarly repellent.

For thousands of years those bodies rested gorgeously encased and staring glassily upward when not visited by the *ka,* awaiting the day when Osiris should restore both *ka* and soul, and lead forth the stiff legions of the dead from the sunken houses of sleep. It was to have been a glorious rebirth – but not all souls were approved, nor were all tombs inviolate, so that certain grotesque *mistakes* and fiendish *abnormalities* were to be looked for. Even today the Arabs murmur of unsanctified convocations and unwholesome worship in forgotten nether abysses, which only winged invisible *kas* and soulless mummies may visit and return unscathed.

Perhaps the most leeringly blood-congealing legends are those which relate to certain perverse products of decadent priestcraft – *composite mummies* made by the artificial union of human trunks and limbs with the heads of animals in imitation of the elder gods. At all stages of history the sacred animals were mummified, so that consecrated bulls, cats, ibises, crocodiles and the like might return some day to greater glory. But only in the decadence did they mix the human and animal in the same mummy – only in the decadence, when they did not understand the rights and prerogatives of the *ka* and the soul.

What happened to those composite mummies is not told of – at least publicly – and it is certain that no Egyptologist ever found one. The whispers of Arabs are very wild, and cannot be relied upon. They even hint that old Khephren – he of the Sphinx, the Second Pyramid and the yawning gateway temple – lives far underground wedded to the ghoul-queen Nitocris and ruling over the mummies that are neither of man nor of beast.

It was of these – of Khephren and his consort and his strange armies of the hybrid dead – that I dreamed, and that is why I am glad the exact dream-shapes have faded from my memory. My most horrible vision was connected with an idle question I had asked myself the day before when looking at the great carven riddle of the desert and wondering with what unknown depth the temple close to it might be secretly connected. That question, so innocent and whimsical then, assumed in my dream a meaning of frenetic and hysterical madness ... *what huge and loathsome abnormality was the Sphinx originally carven to represent?*

My second awakening – if awakening it was – is a memory of stark hideousness which nothing else in my life – save one thing which came after – can parallel ; and that life has been full and adventurous beyond most men's. Remember that I had lost consciousness whilst buried beneath a cascade of falling rope whose immensity revealed the cataclysmic depth of my present position. Now, as perception returned, I felt the entire weight gone ; and realized upon rolling over that although I was still tied, gagged and blindfolded, *some agency had removed completely the suffocating hempen landslide which had overwhelmed me.* The significance of this condition, of course, came to me only gradually ; but even so I think it would have brought unconsciousness again had I not by this time reached such a state of emotional exhaustion that no new horror could make much difference. I was alone . . . *with what?*

Before I could torture myself with any new reflection, or make any fresh effort to escape from my bonds, an additional circumstance became manifest. Pains not formerly felt were racking my arms and legs, and I seemed coated with a profusion of dried blood beyond anything my former cuts and abrasions could furnish. My chest, too, seemed pierced by a hundred wounds, as though some malign, titanic ibis had been pecking at it. Assuredly the agency which had removed the rope was a hostile one, and had begun to wreak terrible injuries upon me when somehow impelled to desist. Yet at the time my sensations were distinctly the reverse of what one might expect. Instead of sinking into a bottomless pit of despair, I was stirred to a new courage and action ; for now I felt that the evil forces were physical things which a fearless man might encounter on an even basis.

On the strength of this thought I tugged again at my bonds, and used all the art of a lifetime to free myself as I had so often done amidst the glare of lights and the applause of vast crowds. The familiar details of my escaping process commenced to engross me, and now that the long rope was gone I half regained my belief that the supreme horrors were hallucinations after all, and that there had never been any terrible shaft, measureless abyss of interminable rope. Was I after all in the gateway temple of Khephren beside the Sphinx, and had the sneaking Arabs stolen in to torture me as I lay helpless there? At any rate, I must be free. Let me stand up unbound, ungagged, and with eyes open to catch any glimmer of light which might come trickling from any source, and I could actually delight in the combat against evil and treacherous foes!

How long I took in shaking off my encumbrances I cannot tell. It must have been longer than in my exhibition performances, because I was wounded, exhausted, and enervated by the experiences I had passed through. When I was finally free, and taking deep breaths of a chill, damp, evilly spiced air all the more horrible when encountered without the screen of gag and blindfolded edges, I found that I was too cramped and fatigued to move at once. There I lay, trying to stretch a frame bent and mangled, for an indefinite period, and straining my eyes to catch a glimpse of some ray of light which would give a hint as to my position.

By degrees my strengtn and flexibility returned, but my eyes beheld nothing. As I staggered to my feet I peered diligently in every direction, yet met only an ebony blackness as great as that I had known when blindfolded. I tried my legs, blood-encrusted beneath my shredded trousers, and found that I could walk ; yet could not decide in what direction to go. Obviously I ought not to walk at random, and perhaps retreat directly from the entrance I sought ; so I paused to note the direction of the cold, fetid, natron-scented air-current which I had never ceased to feel. Accepting the point of its source as the possible entrance to the abyss, I strove to keep track of this landmark and to walk consistently toward it.

I had a match-box with me, and even a small electric flashlight ; but of course the pockets of my tossed and tattered clothing were long since emptied of all heavy articles. As I walked cautiously in the blackness, the draft grew stronger and more offensive, till at length I could regard it as nothing less than a tangible stream of detestable vapor pouring out of some aperture like the smoke of the genie from the fisherman's jar in the Eastern tale. The East ... Egypt ... truly, this dark cradle of civilization was ever the wellspring of horrors and marvels unspeakable!

The more I reflected on the nature of this cavern wind, the greater my sense of disquiet became ; for although despite its odor I had sought its source as at least an indirect clue to the outer world, I now saw plainly that this foul emanation could have no admixture or connection whatsoever with the clean air of the Libyan Desert, but must be essentially a thing vomited from sinister gulfs still lower down. I had, then, been walking in the wrong direction!

After a moment's reflection I decided not to retrace my steps. Away from the draft I would have no landmarks, for the roughly level rock floor was devoid of distinctive configurations. If, however, I followed up the strange current,

I would undoubtedly arrive at an aperture of some sort, from whose gate I could perhaps work round the walls to the opposite side of this Cyclopean and otherwise unnavigable hall. That I might fail, I well realized. I saw that this was no part of Khephren's gateway temple which tourists know, and it struck me that this particular hall might be unknown even to archaeologists, and merely stumbled upon by the inquisitive and malignant Arabs who had imprisoned me. If so, was there any present gate of escape to the known parts or to the outer air?

What evidence, indeed, did I now possess that this was the gateway temple at all? For a moment all my wildest speculations rushed back upon me, and I thought of that vivid melange of impressions – the descent, suspension in space, the rope, my wounds, and the dreams that were frankly dreams. Was this the end of life for me? Or indeed, would it be merciful if this moment *were* the end? I could answer none of my own questions, but merely kept on, till Fate for a third time reduced me to oblivion.

This time there were no dreams, for the suddenness of the incident shocked me out of all thought either conscious or subconscious. Tripping on an unexpected descending step at a point where the offensive draft became strong enough to offer an actual physical resistance, I was precipitated headlong down a black flight of huge stone stairs into a gulf of hideousness unrelieved.

That I ever breathed again is a tribute to the inherent vitality of the healthy human organism. Often I look back to that night and feel a touch of actual humor in those repeated lapses of consciousness; lapses whose succession reminded me at the time of nothing more than the crude cinema melodramas of that period. Of course, it is possible that the repeated lapses never occurred; and that all the features of that underground nightmare were merely the dreams of one long coma which began with the shock of my descent into that abyss and ended with the healing balm of the outer air and of the rising sun which found me stretched on the sands of Gizeh before the sardonic and dawn-flushed face of the Great Sphinx.

I prefer to believe this latter explanation as much as I

can, hence was glad when the police told me that the barrier
to Krephren's gateway temple had been found unfastened.
and that a sizeable rift to the surface did actually exist in
one corner of the still buried part. I was glad, too, when the
doctors pronounced my wounds only those to be expected
from my seizure, blindfolding, lowering, struggling with
bonds, falling some distance – perhaps into a depression in
the temple's inner gallery – dragging myself to the outer
barrier and escaping from it, and experiences like that . . . a
very soothing diagnosis. And yet I know that there must be
more than appears on the surface. That extreme descent is
too vivid a memory to be dismissed – and it is odd that no
one has ever been able to find a man answering the description of my guide. Abdul Reis el Drogman – the tomb-
throated guide who looked and smiled like King Khephren.

I have digressed from my connected narrative – perhaps
in the vain hope of evading the telling of that final incident;
that incident which of all is most certainly an hallucination.
But I promised to relate it, and I do not break promises.
When I recovered – or seemed to recover – my senses after
that fall down the black stone stairs, I was quite as alone
and in darkness as before. The windy stench, bad enough
before, was now fiendish; yet I had acquired enough fami-
liarity by this time to bear it stoically. Dazedly I began to
crawl away from the place whence the putrid wind came,
and with my bleeding hands felt the colossal blocks of a
mighty pavement. Once my head struck against a hard
object, and when I felt of it I learned that it was the base
of a column – a column of unbelievable immensity – whose
surface was covered with gigantic chiseled hieroglyphics
very perceptible to my touch.

Crawling on, I encountered other titan columns at in-
comprehensible distances apart; when suddenly my attention was captured by the realization of something which
must have been impinging on my subconscious hearing
long before the conscious sense was aware of it.

From some still lower chasm in earth's bowels were pro-
ceeding certain *sounds*, measured and definite, and like
nothing I had ever heard before. That they were very ancient and distinctly ceremonial I felt almost intuitively;

and much reading in Egyptology led me to associate them
with the flute, the sambuke, the sistrum, and the tympanum.
In their rhythmic piping, droning, rattling and beating I felt
an element of terror beyond all the known terrors of earth
— a terror peculiarly dissociated from personal fear, and
taking the form of a sort of objective pity for our planet,
that it should hold within its depths such horrors as must
lie beyond these aegipanic cacophonies. The sounds increased in volume, and I felt that they were approaching.
Then — and may all the gods of all pantheons unite to keep
the like from my ears again — I began to hear, faintly and
afar off, the morbid and millennial tramping of the marching things.

It was hideous that footfalls so dissimilar should move
in such perfect rhythm. The training of unhallowed thousands of years must lie behind that march of earth's inmost
monstrosities ... padding, clicking, walking, stalking,
rumbling, lumbering, crawling ... and all to the abhorrent
discords of those mocking instruments. And then — God
keep the memory of those Arab legends out of my head! —
the mummies without souls ... the meeting-place of the
wandering *kas* ... the hordes of the devil-cursed pharaonic
dead of forty centuries ... the *composite mummies* led
through the uttermost onyx voids by King Khephren and
his ghoul-queen Nitocris. ...

The tramping drew nearer — Heaven save me from the
sound of those feet and paws and hooves and pads and
talons as it commenced to acquire detail! Down limitless
reaches of sunless pavement a spark of light flickered in
the malodorous wind and I drew behind the enormous cir-
cumference of a Cyclopic column that I might escape for a
while the horror that was stalking million-footed toward
me through gigantic hypostyles of inhuman dread and
phobic antiquity. The flickers increased, and the tramping
and dissonant rhythm grew sickeningly loud. In the quivering orange light there stood faintly forth a scene of such
stony awe that I gasped from sheer wonder that conquered
even fear and repulsion. Bases of columns whose middles
were higher than human sight ... mere bases of things that
must each dwarf the Eiffel Tower to insignificance ... hiero-

glyphics carved by unthinkable hands in caverns where daylight can be only a remote legend. . . .

I *would not* look at the marching things. That I desperately resolved as I heard their creaking joints and nitrous wheezing above the dead music and the dead tramping. It was merciful that they did not speak . . . but God! *their crazy torches began to cast shadows on the surface of those stupendous columns. Hippopotami should not have human hands and carry torches . . . men should not have the heads of crocodiles. . . .*

I tried to turn away, but the shadows and the sounds and the stench were everywhere. Then I remembered something I used to do in half-conscious nightmares as a boy, and began to repeat to myself, 'This is a dream! This is a dream!' But it was of no use, and I could only shut my eyes and pray . . . at least, that is what I think I did, for one is never sure in visions – and I know this can have been nothing more. I wondered whether I should ever reach the world again, and at times would furtively open my eyes to see if I could discern any feature of the place other than the wind of spiced putrefaction, the topless columns, and the thaumatrophically grotesque shadows of abnormal horror. The sputtering glare of multiplying torches now shone, and unless this hellish place were wholly without walls, I could not fail to see some boundary or fixed landmark soon. But I had to shut my eyes again when I realized how many of the things were assembling – and when I glimpsed a certain object walking solemnly and steadily *without any body above the waist.*

A fiendish and ululant corpse-gurgle or death-rattle now split the very atmosphere – the charnel atmosphere poisonous with naftha and bitumen blasts – in one concerted chorus from the ghoulish legion of hybrid blasphemies. My eyes, perversely shaken open, gazed for an instant upon a sight which no human creature could even imagine without panic, fear and physical exhaustion. The things had filed ceremonially in one direction, the direction of the noisome wind, where the light of their torches showed their bended heads – or the bended heads of such as had heads. They were worshipping before a great black fetor-

belching aperture which reached up almost out of sight,
and which I could see was flanked at right angles by two
giant staircases whose ends were far away in shadow. One
of these was indubitably the staircase I had fallen down.

The dimensions of the hole were fully in proportion with
those of the columns – an ordinary house would have been
lost in it, and any average public building could easily have
been moved in and out. It was so vast a surface that only
by moving the eye could one trace its boundaries ... so
vast, so hideously black, and so aromatically stinking. ...
Directly in front of this yawning Polyphemus-door the
things were throwing objects – evidently sacrifices or religious offerings, to judge by their gestures. Khephren was
their leader; sneering King Khephren *or the guide Abdul
Reis,* crowned with a golden pshent and intoning endless
formulae with the hollow voice of the dead. By his side
knelt beautiful Queen Nitocris whom I saw in profile for a
moment, noting that the right half of her face was eaten
away by rats or other ghouls. And I shut my eyes again
when I saw what objects were being thrown as offerings to
the fetid aperture or its possible local deity.

It occurred to me that, judging from the elaborateness of
this worship, the concealed deity must be one of considerable importance. Was it Osiris or Isis, Horus or Anubis, or
some vast unknown God of the Dead still more central and
supreme? There is a legend that terrible altars and colossi
were reared to an Unknown One before ever the known
gods were worshipped. ...

And now, as I steeled myself to watch the rapt and sepulchral adorations of those nameless things, a thought of escape flashed upon me. The hall was dim, and the columns
heavy with shadow. With every creature of that nightmare
throng absorbed in shocking raptures, it might be barely
possible for me to creep past to the far-away end of one
of the staircases and ascend unseen; trusting to Fate and
skill to deliver me from the upper reaches. Where I was, I
neither knew nor seriously reflected upon – and for a moment it struck me as amusing to plan a serious escape from
that which I knew to be a dream. Was I in some hidden
and unsuspected lower realm of Khephren's gateway

temple – that temple which generations have persistently
called the Temple of the Sphinx? I could not conjecture,
but I resolved to ascend to life and consciousness if wit
and muscle could carry me.

Wriggling flat on my stomach, I began the anxious journey toward the foot of the left-hand staircase, which
seemed the more accessible of the two. I cannot describe
the incidents and sensations of that crawl, but they may be
guessed when one reflects on what I had to watch steadily
in that malign, wind-blown torchlight in order to avoid de-
tection. The bottom of the staircase was, as I have said, far
away in shadow, as it had to be to rise without a bend to
the dizzy parapeted landing above the titanic aperture.
This placed the last stages of my crawl at some distance
from the noisome herd, though the spectacle chilled me
even when quite remote at my right.

At length I succeeded in reaching the steps and began to
climb; keeping close to the wall, on which I observed
decorations of the most hideous sort, and relying for safety
on the absorbed, ecstatic interest with which the monstrosities watched the foul-breezed aperture and the impious
objects of nourishment they had flung on the pavement before it. Though the staircase was huge and steep, fashioned
of vast porphyry blocks as if for the feet of a giant, the
ascent seemed virtually interminable. Dread of discovery
and the pain which renewed exercise had brought to my
wounds combined to make that upward crawl a thing of
agonizing memory. I had intended, on reaching the landing, to climb immediately onward along whatever upper
staircase might mount from there; stopping for no last
look at the carrion abominations that pawed and genu-
flected some seventy or eighty feet below – yet a sudden
repetition of that thunderous corpse-gurgle and death-
rattle chorus, coming as I had nearly gained the top of the
flight and showing by its ceremonial rhythm that it was not
an alarm of my discovery, caused me to pause and peer
cautiously over the parapet.

The monstrosities were hailing something which had
poked itself out of the nauseous aperture to seize the hellish fare proffered it. It was something quite ponderous,

even as seen from my height; something yellowish and hairy, and endowed with a sort of nervous motion. It was as large, perhaps, as a good-sized hippopotamus, but very curiously shaped. It seemed to have no neck, but five separate shaggy heads springing in a row from a roughly cylindrical trunk; the first very small, the second good-sized, the third and fourth equal and largest of all, and the fifth rather small, though not so small as the first.

Out of these heads darted curious rigid tentacles which seized ravenously on the excessively great quantities of unmentionable food placed before the aperture. Once in a while the thing would leap up, and occasionally it would retreat into its den in a very odd manner. Its locomotion was so inexplicable that I stared in fascination, wishing it would emerge farther from the cavernous lair beneath me.

Then it *did emerge* ... it *did* emerge, and at the sight I turned and fled into the darkness up the higher staircase that rose behind me; fled unknowingly up incredible steps and ladders and inclined planes to which no human sight or logic guided me, and which I must ever relegate to the world of dreams for want of any confirmation. It must have been a dream, or the dawn would never have found me breathing on the sands of Gizeh before the sardonic dawn-flushed face of the Great Sphinx.

The Great Sphinx! God! — that idle question I asked myself on that sun-blest morning before ... *what huge and loathsome abnormality was the Sphinx originally carven to represent?* Accursed is the sight, be it in dream or not, that revealed to me the supreme horror – the unknown God of the Dead, which licks its colossal chops in the un-suspected abyss, fed hideous morsels by soulless absurdities that should not exist. The five-headed monster that emer-ged ... that five-headed monsters as large as a hippopta-mus ... the five-headed monster – *and that of which it is the merest forepaw* ...

But I survived, and I know it was only a dream.

This account was ghost-written by H. P. Lovecraft for Harry Houdini (1874–1926) born Erich Weiss in Appleton, Wisconsin, who took his stage name after the great French magician, Jean Eugene, Robert-Houdin (1805–1871). He was for many years an escape artist who had no peer, and was prominent in the exposure of spiritualistic frauds. This account as written by H. H. Lovecraft first appeared in *Weird Tales* for May 1924, and was subsequently reprinted in the issue for July 1939.

He

I saw him on a sleepless night when I was walking desperately to save my soul and my vision. My coming to New York had been a mistake; for whereas I had looked for poignant wonder and inspiration in the teeming labyrinths of ancient streets that twist endlessly from forgotten courts and squares and waterfronts to courts and squares and waterfronts equally forgotten, and in the Cyclopean modern towers and pinnacles that rise blackly Babylonian under waning moons, I had found instead only a sense of horror and oppression which threatened to master, paralyze, and annihilate me.

The disillusion had been gradual. Coming for the first time upon the town, I had seen it in the sunset from a bridge, majestic above its waters, its incredible peaks and pyramids rising flowerlike and delicate from pools of violet mist to play with the flaming clouds and the first stars of evening. Then it had lighted up window by window above the shimmering tides where lanterns nodded and glided and deep horns bayed weird harmonies, and had itself become a starry firmament of dream, redolent of faery music, and one with the marvels of Carcassonne and Samarcand and El Dorado and all glorious and half-fabulous cities. Shortly afterward I was taken through those antique ways so dear to my fancy – narrow, curving alleys and passages where rows of red Georgian brick blinked with small-paned dormers above pillared doorways that had looked on gilded sedans and paneled coaches – and in the first flush of realization of these long-wished things I thought I had indeed achieved such treasures as would make me in time a poet.

But success and happiness were not to be. Garish daylight showed only squalor and alienage and the noxious elephantiasis of climbing, spreading stone where the moon had hinted of loveliness and elder magic; and the throngs of people that seethed through the flumelike streets were squat, swarthy strangers with hardened faces and narrow

eyes, shrewd strangers without dreams and without kinship to the scenes about them, who could never mean aught
to a blue-eyed man of the old folk, with the love of fair
green lanes and white New England village steeples in his
heart.

So instead of the poems I had hoped for, there came only
a shuddering blackness and ineffable loneliness ; and I saw
at last a fearful truth which no one had ever dared to
breathe before – the unwhisperable secret of secrets – the
fact that this city of stone and stridor is not a sentient perpetuation of Old New York as London is of Old London
and Paris of Old Paris, but that it is in fact quite dead, its
sprawling body imperfectly embalmed and infested with
queer animate things which have nothing to do with it as it
was in life. Upon making this discovery I ceased to sleep
comfortably ; though something of resigned tranquillity
came back as I gradually formed the habit of keeping off
the streets by day and venturing abroad only at night,
when darkness calls forth what little of the past still hovers
wraithlike about, and old white doorways remember the
stalwart forms that once passed through them. With this
mode of relief I even wrote a few poems, and still refrained
from going home to my people lest I seem to crawl back
ignobly in defeat.

Then, on a sleepless night's walk, I met the man. It was
in a grotesque hidden courtyard of the Greenwich section,
for there in my ignorance I had settled, having heard of
the place as the natural home of poets and artists. The
archaic lanes and houses and unexpected bits of square
and court had indeed delighted me, and when I found the
poets and artists to be loud-voiced pretenders whose quaintness is tinsel and whose lives are a denial of all that pure
beauty which is poetry and art, I stayed on for love of these
venerable things. I fancied them as they were in their
prime, when Greenwich was a placid village not yet engulfed by the town ; and in the hours before dawn, when
all the revellers had slunk away, I used to wander alone
among their cryptical windings and brood upon the curious arcana which generations must have deposited there.
This kept my soul alive, and gave me a few of those dreams

and visions for which the poet far within me cried out.

The man came upon me at about 2 one cloudy August morning, as I was threading a series of detached court-yards ; now accessible only through the unlighted hallways of intervening buildings, but once forming parts of a con-tinuous network of picturesque alleys. I had heard of them by vague rumor, and realized that they could not be upon any map of today ; but the fact that they were forgotten only endeared them to me, so that I had sought them with twice my usual eagerness. Now that I had found them, my eagerness was again redoubled ; for something in their ar-rangement dimly hinted that they might be only a few of many such, with dark, dumb counterparts wedged ob-scurely betwixt high blank walls and deserted rear tene-ments, or lurking lamplessly behind archways, unbetrayed by hordes of the foreign-speaking or guarded by furtive and uncommunicative artists whose practises do not in-vite publicity or the light of day.

He spoke to me without invitation, noting my mood and glances as I studied certain knockered doorways above iron-railed steps, the pallid glow of traceried transoms feebly lighting my face. His own face was in shadow, and he wore a wide-brimmed hat which somehow blended per-fectly with the out-of-date cloak he affected ; but I was subtly disquieted even before he addressed me. His form was very slight ; thin almost to cadaverousness ; and his voice proved phenomenally soft and hollow, though not particularly deep. He had, he said, noticed me several times at my wanderings ; and inferred that I resembled him in loving the vestiges of former years. Would I not like the guidance of one long practised in these explorations, and possessed of local information profoundly deeper than any which an obvious newcomer could possibly have gained?

As he spoke, I caught a glimpse of his face in the yellow beam from a solitary attic window. It was a noble, even a handsome, elderly countenance ; and bore the marks of a lineage and refinement unusual for the age and place. Yet some quality about it disturbed me almost as much as its features pleased me – perhaps it was too white, or too ex-pressionless, or too much out of keeping with the locality, to make me feel easy or comfortable. Nevertheless I followed him; for in those dreary days my quest for antique beauty and mystery was all that I had to keep my soul alive, and I reckoned it a rare favor of Fate to fall in with one whose kindred seekings seemed to have penetrated so much farther than mine.

Something in the night constrained the cloaked man to silence, and for a long hour he led me forward without needless words; making only the briefest of comments concerning ancient names and dates and changes, and directing my progress very largely by gestures as we squeezed through interstices, tiptoed through corridors, clambered over brick walls, and once crawled on hands and knees through a low, arched passage of stone whose immense length and tortuous twistings effaced at last every hint of geographical location I had managed to preserve. The things we saw were very old and marvelous, or at least they seemed so in the few straggling rays of light by which I viewed them, and I shall never forget the tottering Ionic columns and fluted pilasters and urn-headed iron fenceposts and flaring-linteled windows and decorative fanlights that appeared to grow quainter and stranger the deeper we advanced into this inexhaustible maze of unknown antiquity.

We met no person, and as time passed the lighted windows became fewer and fewer. The streetlights we first encountered had been of oil, and of the ancient lozenge pattern. Later I noticed some with candles; and at last, after traversing a horrible unlighted court where my guide had to lead with his gloved hand through total blackness to a narrow wooded gate in a high wall, we came upon a fragment of alley lit only by lanterns in front of every seventh house – unbelievably Colonial tin lanterns with conical tops and holes punched in the sides. This alley led steeply uphill – more steeply than I thought possible in this part of New York – and the upper end was blocked squarely by the ivy-clad wall of a private estate, beyond which I could see a pale cupola, and the tops of trees waving against a vague lightness in the sky. In this wall was a small, low-arched gate of nail-studded black oak, which the man proceeded to unlock with a ponderous key. Leading me within, he steered a course in utter blackness over what seemed to be a gravel path, and finally up a flight of stone steps to the door of the house, which he unlocked and opened for me.

We entered, and as we did so I grew faint from a reek of infinite mustiness which welled out to meet us, and which must have been the fruit of unwholesome centuries of decay. My host appeared not to notice this, and in courtesy I kept silent as he piloted me up a curving stairway, across a hall, and into a room whose door I heard him lock behind us. Then I saw him pull the curtains of the three small-paned windows that barely showed themselves against the lightening sky ; after which he crossed to the mantel, struck flint and steel, lighted two candles of a candelabrum of twelve sconces, and made a gesture enjoining soft-toned speech.

In this feeble radiance I saw that we were in a spacious, well-furnished and paneled library dating from the first quarter of the Eighteenth Century, with splendid doorway pediments, a delightful Doric cornice, and a magnificently carved overmantel with scroll-and-urn top. Above the crowded bookshelves at intervals along the walls were wel-wrought family portraits ; all tarnished to an enigmatical dimness, and bearing an unmistakable likeness to the man who now motioned me to a chair beside the graceful Chippendale table. Before seating himself across the table from me, my host paused for a moment as if in embarrassment ; then, tardily removing his gloves, wide-brimmed hat, and cloak, stood theatrically revealed in full mid-Georgian costume from queued hair and neck ruffles to knee-breeches, silk hose, and the buckled shoes I had not previously noticed. Now slowly sinking into a lyre-back chair, he commenced to eye me intently.

Without his hat he took on an aspect of extreme age which was scarcely visible before, and I wondered if this unperceived mark of singular longevity were not one of the sources of my disquiet. When he spoke at length, his soft, hollow, and carefully muffled voice not infrequently quavered ; and now and then I had great difficulty in following him as I listened with a thrill of amazement and half-disavowed alarm which grew each instant.

'You behold, Sir,' my host began, 'a man of very eccentrical habits, for whose costume no apology need be offered to one with your wit and inclinations. Reflecting upon better times, I have not scrupled to ascertain their ways, and adopt their dress and manners; an indulgence which offends none if practised without ostentation. It hath been my good fortune to retain the rural seat of my ancestors, swallowed though it was by two towns, first Greenwich, which built up hither after 1800, then New York, which joined on near 1830. There were many reasons for the close keeping of this place in my family, and I have not been remiss in discharging such obligations. The squire who succeeded to it in 1768 studied sartain arts and made sartain discoveries, all connected with influences residing in this particular plot of ground, and eminently desarving of the strongest guarding. Some curious effects of these arts and discoveries I now purpose to show you, under the strictest secrecy; and I believe I may rely on my judgement of men enough to have no distrust of either your interest or your fidelity.'

He paused, but I could only nod my head. I have said that I was alarmed, yet to my soul nothing was more deadly than the material daylight world of New York, and whether this man were a harmless eccentric or a wielder of dangerous arts I had no choice save to follow him and slake my sense of wonder on whatever he might have to offer. So I listened.

'To — my ancestor,' he softly continued, 'there appeared to reside some very remarkable qualities in the will of mankind; qualities having a little-suspected dominance not only over the acts of one's self and of others, but over every variety of force and substance in Nature, and over many elements and dimensions deemed more universal than Nature herself. May I say that he flouted the sanctity of things as great as space and time and that he put to strange uses the rites of sartain half-breed red Indians once encamped upon this hill? These Indians showed choler when the place was built, and were plaguey pestilent in asking to visit the grounds at the full of the moon. For years they stole over the wall each month when they could, and by stealth performed sartain acts. Then, in '68, the new squire catched them at their doings, and stood still at what he saw. Thereafter he bargained with them and exchanged the free access of his grounds for the exact inwardness of what they did; larning that their grandfathers got part of their custom from red ancestors and part from an old Dutchman in the time of the States-General. And pox on him, I'm afeared the squire must have sarved them monstrous bad rum – whether or not by intent – for a week after he larnt the secret he was the only man living that knew it. You, Sir, are the first outsider to be told there is a secret, and split me if I'd have risked tampering that much with – the powers – had ye not been so hot after bygone things.'

I shuddered as the man grew colloquial – and with the familiar speech of another day. He went on.

'But you must know, Sir, that what – the squire – got from those mongrel savages was but a small part of the larning he came to have. He had not been at Oxford for nothing, nor talked to no account with an ancient chymist and astrologer in Paris. He was, in fine, made sensible that all the world is but the smoke of our intellects; past the bidding of the vulgar, but by the wise to be puffed out and drawn in like any cloud of prime Virginia tobacco. What we want, we may make about us; and what we don't want, we may sweep away. I won't say that all this is wholly true in body, but 'tis sufficient true to furnish a very pretty spectacle now and then. You, I conceive, would be tickled by a better sight of sartain other years than your fancy affords you; so be pleased to hold back any fright at what I design to show. Come to the window and be quiet.'

My host now took my hand to draw me to one of the two windows on the long side of the malodorous room, and at the first touch of his ungloved fingers I turned cold. His flesh, though dry and firm, was of the quality of ice; and I almost shrank away from his pulling. But again I thought of the emptiness and horror of reality, and boldly prepared to follow whithersoever I might be led. Once at the window, the man drew apart the yellow silk curtains and directed my stare into the blackness outside. For a moment I saw nothing save a myriad of tiny dancing lights, far, far before me. Then, as if in response to an insidious motion of my host's hand, a flash of heat-lightning played over the scene, and I looked out upon a sea of luxuriant foliage – foliage unpolluted, and not the sea of roofs to be expected by any normal mind. On my right the Hudson glittered wickedly, and in the distance ahead I saw the unhealthy shimmer of a vast salt marsh constellated with nervous fireflies. The flash died, and an evil smile illumined the waxy face of the aged necromancer.

'That was before my time – before the new squire's time. Pray let us try again.'

I was faint, even fainter than the hateful modernity of that accursed city had made me.

'Good God!' I whispered; 'can you do that for *any* time?' And as he nodded, and bared the black stumps of what had once been yellow fangs, I clutched at the curtains to prevent myself from falling. But he steadied me with that terrible, ice-cold claw, and once more made his insidious gesture.

Again the lightning flashed – but this time upon a scene not wholly strange. It was Greenwich, the Greenwich that used to be, with here and there a roof or row of houses as we see it now, yet with lovely green lanes and fields and bits of grassy common. The marsh still glittered beyond, but in the farther distance I saw the steeples of what was then all of New York; Trinity and St. Paul's and the Brick Church dominating their sisters, and a faint haze of wood smoke hovering over the whole. I breathed hard, but not so much from the sight itself as from the possibilities my imagination terrifiedly conjured up.

'Can you – dare you – go far?' I spoke with awe, and I think he shared it for a second, but the evil grin returned.

'Far? What I have seen would blast ye to a mad statue of stone! Back, back – forward, *forward* – look, ye puling lackwit!'

And as he snarled the phrase under his breath he gestured anew; bringing to the sky a flash more blinding than either which had come before. For full three seconds I

could glimpse that pandemoniac sight, and in those seconds
I saw a vista which will ever afterward torment me in
dreams. I saw the heavens verminous with strange flying
things, and beneath them a hellish black city of giant stone
terraces with impious pyramids flung savagely to the moon,
and devil-lights burning from un-numbered windows. And
swarming loathsomely on aerial galleries I saw the yellow,
squint-eyed people of that city, robed horribly in orange
and red, and dancing insanely to the pounding of fevered
kettle-drums, the clatter of obscene crotala, and the mania-
cal moaning of muted horns whose ceaseless dirges rose
and fell undulantly like the waves of an unhallowed ocean
of bitumen.

I saw this vista, I say, and heard as with the mind's ear
the blasphemous domdaniel of cacophony which companioned it. It was the shrieking fulfilment of all the horror
which that corpse-city had ever stirred in my soul, and
forgetting every injunction to silence I screamed and
screamed and screamed as my nerves gave way and the
walls quivered about me.

Then, as the flash subsided, I saw that my host was trem-
bling too; a look of shocking fear half-blotting from his
face the serpent distortion of rage which my screams had
excited. He tottered, clutched at the curtains as I had done
before, and wriggled his head wildly, like a hunted animal.
God knows he had cause, for the echoes of my screaming
died away there came another sound so hellishly suggestive
that only numbed emotion kept me sane and conscious.
It was the steady, stealthy creaking of the stairs beyond
the locked door, as with the ascent of a barefoot or skin-
shod horde; and at last the cautious, purposeful rattling of
the brass latch that glowed in the feeble candlelight. The
old man clawed and spat at me through the moldy air, and
barked things in his throat as he swayed with the yellow
curtain he clutched.

'The full moon – damn ye – ye . . ye yelping dog – ye
called 'em, and they've come for me! Moccasined feet –
dead men – Gad sink ye, ye red devils, but I poisoned no
rum o' yours – han't I kept your pox-rotted magic safe? –

ye swilled yourselves sick, curse ye, and yet must
needs blame the squire – let go, you! Unhand that latch –
I've naught for ye here –'

At this point three slow and very deliberate raps shook
the panels of the door, and a white foam gathered at the
mouth of the frantic magician. His fright, turning to steely
despair, left room for a resurgence of his rage against me;
and he staggered a step toward the table on whose edge I
was steadying myself. The curtains, still clutched in his
right hand as his left clawed out at me, grew taut and finally
crashed down from their lofty fastenings; admitting to the
room a flood of that full moonlight which the brightening
of the sky had presaged. In those greenish beams the
candles paled, and a new semblance of decay spread over
the musk-reeking room with its wormy paneling, sagging
floor, battered mantel, rickety furniture, and ragged
draperies. It spread over the old man, too, whether from
the same source or because of his fear and vehemence, and
I saw him shrivel and blacken as he lurched near and strove
to rend me with vulturine talons. Only his eyes stayed
whole, and they glared with a propulsive, dilated incan-
descence which grew as the face around them charred and
dwindled.

The rapping was now repeated with greater insistence,
and this time bore a hint of metal. The black thing facing
me had become only a head with eyes, impotently trying
to wriggle across the sinking floor in my direction, and
occasionally emitting feeble little spits of immortal malice.
Now swift and splintering blows assailed the sickly panels,
and I saw the gleam of a tomahawk as it cleft the rending
wood. I did not move, for I could not; but watched dazedly
as the door fell in pieces to admit a colossal, shapeless in-
flux of inky substance starred with shining, malevolent eyes.
It poured thickly, like a flood of oil bursting a rotten bulk-
head, overturned a chair as it spread, and finally flowed
under the table and across the room to where the blackened head with the eyes still glared at me. Around that
head it closed, totally swallowing it up, and in another moment it had begun to recede; bearing away its invisible

burden without touching me, and flowing again out that black doorway and down the unseen stairs, which creaked as before, though in reverse order.

Then the floor gave way at last, and I slid gaspingly down into the nighted chamber below, choking with cobwebs and half-swooning with terror. The green moon, shining through broken windows, showed me the hall door half open ; and as I rose from the plaster-strewn floor and twisted myself free from the sagged ceiling, I saw sweep past it an awful torrent of blackness, with scores of baleful eyes glowing in it. It was seeking the door to the cellar, and when it found it, it vanished therein. I now felt the floor of this lower room giving as that of the upper chamber had done, and once a crashing above had been followed by the fall past the west window of something which must have been the cupola. Now liberated for the instant from the wreckage, I rushed through the hall to the front door ; and finding myself unable to open it, seized a chair and broke a window, climbing frenziedly out upon the unkempt lawn where moonlight danced over yard-high grass and weeds. The wall was high, and all the gates were locked ; but moving a pile of boxes in a corner I managed to gain the top and cling to the great stone urn set there.

About me in my exhaustion I could see only strange walls and windows and old gambrel roofs. The steep street of my approach was nowhere visible, and the little I did see succumbed rapidly to a mist that rolled in from the river despite the glaring moonlight. Suddenly the urn to which I clung began to tremble, as if sharing my own lethal dizziness ; and in another instant my body was plunging downward to I knew not what fate.

The man who found me said that I must have crawled a long way despite my broken bones, for a trail of blood stretched off as far as he dared look. The gathering rain soon effaced this link with the scene of my ordeal, and reports could state no more than that I had appeared from a place unknown, at the entrance to a little black court off Perry Street.

I never sought to return to those tenebrous labyrinths, nor would I direct any sane man thither if I could. Of who or what that ancient creature was, I have no idea; but I repeat that the city is dead and full of unsuspected horrors. Whither *he* has gone, I do not know; but I have gone home to the pure New England lanes up which fragrant sea-winds sweep at evening.

The Horror At Red Hook

*There are sacraments of evil as well as of good about us,
and we live and move to my belief in an unknown world, a
place where there are caves and shadows and dwellers in
twilight. It is possible that man may sometimes return on
the track of evolution, and it is my belief that an awful
lore is not yet dead.*

— ARTHUR MACHEN

Not many weeks ago, on a street corner in the village of
Pascoag, Rhode Island, a tall, heavily built, and wholesome-
looking pedestrian furnished much speculation by a singular lapse of behaviour. He had, it appears, been descending
the hill by the road from Chepachet ; and encountering the
compact section, had turned to his left into the main
thoroughfare where several modest business blocks convey
a touch of the urban. At this point, without visible provoca-
tion, he committed his astonishing lapse ; staring queerly
for a second at the tallest of the buildings before him, and
then, with a series of terrified, hysterical shrieks, breaking
into a frantic run which ended in a stumble and fall at
the next crossing. Picked up and dusted off by ready hands,
he was found to be conscious, organically unhurt, and evidently cured of his sudden nervous attack. He muttered
some shamefaced explanations involving a strain he had
undergone, and with downcast glance turned back up the
Chepachet road, trudging out of sight without once looking
behind him. It was a strange incident to befall so large, ro-
bust, normal-featured, and capable-looking a man, and the
strangeness was not lessened by the remarks of a bystander
who had recognised him as the boarder of a well-known
dairyman on the outskirts of Chepachet.

He was, it developed, a New York police detective named
Thomas F. Malone, now on a long leave of absence under
medical treatment after some disproportionately arduous
work on a gruesome local case which accident had made
dramatic. There had been a collapse of several old brick

buildings during a raid in which he had shared, and something about the wholesale loss of life, both of prisoners and of his companions, had peculiarly appalled him. As a result, he had acquired an acute and anomalous horror of any buildings even remotely suggesting the ones which had fallen in, so that in the end mental specialists forbade him the sight of such things for an indefinite period. A police surgeon with relatives in Chepachet had put forward that quaint hamlet of wooden Colonial houses as an ideal spot for the psychological convalescence; and thither the sufferer had gone, promising never to venture among the brick-lined streets of larger villages till duly advised by the Woonsocket specialist with whom he was put in touch. This walk to Pascoag for magazines had been a mistake, and the patient had paid in fright, bruises, and humiliation for his disobedience.

So much the gossips of Chepachet and Pascoag knew; and so much also, the most learned specialists believed. But Malone had at first told the specialists much more, ceasing only when he saw that utter incredulity was his portion. Thereafter he held his peace, protesting not at all when it was generally agreed that the collapse of certain squalid brick houses in the Red Hook section of Brooklyn, and the consequent death of many brave officers, had unseated his nervous equilibrium. He had worked too hard, all said, in trying to clean up those nests of disorder and violence; certain features were shocking enough, in all conscience, and the unexpected tragedy was the last straw. This was a simple explanation which everyone could understand, and because Malone was not a simple person he perceived that he had better let it suffice. To hint to unimaginative people of a horror beyond all human conception – a horror of houses and blocks and cities leprous and cancerous with evil dragged from elder worlds – would be merely to invite a padded cell instead of a restful rustication, and Malone was a man of sense despite his mysticism. He had the Celt's far vision of weird and hidden things, but the logician's quick eye for the outwardly unconvincing; an amalgam which had led him far afield in the forty-two years of his life, and set him in strange places for a Dublin University man born in a Georgian villa near Phoenix Park.

And now, as he reviewed the things he had seen and felt and apprehended, Malone was content to keep unshared the secret of what could reduce a dauntless fighter to a quivering neurotic ; what could make old brick slums and seas of dark, subtle faces a thing of nightmare and eldritch portent. It would not be the first time his sensations had been forced to bide uninterpreted – for was not his very act of plunging into the polyglot abyss of New York's underworld a freak beyond sensible explanation? What could he tell the prosaic of the antique witcheries and grotesque marvels discernible to sensitive eyes amidst the poison cauldron where all the varied dregs of unwholesome ages mix their venom and perpetuate their obscene terrors? He had seen the hellish green flame of secret wonder in this blatant, evasive welter of outward greed and inward blasphemy, and had smiled gently when all the New-Yorkers he knew scoffed at his experiment in police work. They had been very witty and cynical, deriding his fantastic pursuit of unknowable mysteries and assuring him that in these days New York held nothing but cheapness and vulgarity. One of them had wagered him a heavy sum that he could not – despite many poignant things to his credit in the *Dublin Review* – even write a truly interesting story of New York low life ; and now, looking back, he perceived that cosmic irony had justified the prophet's words while secretly confuting their flippant meaning. The horror, as glimpsed at last, could not make a story – for like the book cited by Poe's Germany authority, '*es lasst sich nicht lesen* – it does not permit itself to be read.'

II

To Malone the sense of latent mystery in existence was always present. In youth he had felt the hidden beauty and ecstasy of things, and had been a poet ; but poverty and sorrow and exile had turned his gaze in darker directions, and he had thrilled at the imputations of evil in the world around. Daily life had for him come to be a phantasmagoria of macabre shadow-studies ; now glittering and leering with concealed rottenness as in Beardsley's best manner, now hinting terrors behind the commonest shapes and objects as in the subtler and less obvious work of Gustave Doré. He would often regard it as merciful that most persons of high intelligence jeer at the inmost mysteries; for, he argued, if superior minds were ever placed in fullest contact with the secrets preserved by ancient and lowly cults, the resultant abnormalities would soon not only wreck the world, but threaten the very integrity of the universe. All this reflection was no doubt morbid, but keen logic and a deep sense of humour ably offset it. Malone was satisfied to let his notions remain as half-spied and forbidden visions to be lightly played with ; and hysteria came only when duty flung him into a hell of revelation too sudden and insidious to escape.

He had for some time been detailed to the Butler Street station in Brooklyn when the Red Hook matter came to his notice. Red Hook is a maze of hybrid squalor near the ancient waterfront opposite Governor's Island, with dirty highways climbing the hill from the wharves to that higher ground where the decayed lengths of Clinton and Court Streets lead off toward the Borough Hall. Its houses are mostly of brick, dating from the first quarter to the middle of the nineteenth century, and some of the obscurer alleys and byways have that alluring antique flavour which conventional reading leads us to call 'Dickensian.' The population is a hopeless tangle and enigma ; Syrian, Spanish, Italian, and negro elements impinging upon one another, and fragments of Scandinavian and American belts lying not far distant. It is a babel of sound and filth, and sends out strange cries to answer the lapping of oily waves at its grimy piers and the monstrous organ litanies of the harbour whistles. Here long ago a brighter picture dwelt, with clear-eyed mariners on the lower streets and homes of taste and substance where the larger houses line the hill. One can trace the relics of this former happiness in the trim shapes of the buildings, the occasional graceful churches, and the evidences of original art and background in bits of detail here and there – a worn flight of steps, a battered doorway, a wormy pair of decorative columns of pilasters, or a fragment of once green space with bent and rusted iron railing. The houses are generally in solid blocks, and now and then a many-windowed cupola arises to tell of days when the households of captains and ship-owners watched the sea.

From this tangle of material and spiritual putrescence the blasphemies of an hundred dialects assail the sky. Hordes of prowlers reel shouting and singing along the lanes and thoroughfares, occasional furtive hands suddenly extinguish lights and pull down curtains, and swarthy, sin-pitted faces disappear from windows when visitors pick their way through. Policemen despair of order or reform, and seek rather to erect barriers protecting the outside world from the contagion. The clang of the patrol is answered by a kind of spectral silence, and such prisoners as are taken are never communicative. Visible offences are as varied as the local dialects, and run the gamut from the smuggling of rum and prohibited aliens through diverse stages of lawlessness and obscure vice to murder and mutilation in their most abhorrent guises. That these visible affairs are not more frequent is not to the neighbourhood's credit, unless the power of concealment be an art demanding credit. More people enter Red Hook than leave it – or at least, than leave it by the landwardside – and those who are not loquacious are the likeliest to leave.

Malone found in this state of things a faint stench of secrets more terrible than any of the sins denounced by citizens and bemoaned by priests and philanthropists. He was conscious, as one who united imagination with scientific knowledge, that modern people under lawless conditions tend uncannily to repeat the darkest instinctive patterns of primitive half-ape savagery in their daily life and ritual observances; and he had often viewed with an anthropologist's shudder the chanting, cursing processions of blear-eyed and pockmarked young men which wound their way along in the dark small hours of morning. One saw groups of these youths incessantly; sometimes in leering vigils on street corners, sometimes in doorways playing eerily on cheap instruments of music, sometimes in stupefied dozes or indecent dialogues around cafeteria tables near Borough

Hall, and sometimes in whispering converse around dingy taxicabs drawn up at the high stoops of crumbling and closely shuttered old houses. They chilled and fascinated him more than he dared confess to his associates on the force, for he seemed to see in them some monstrous thread of secret continuity; some fiendish, cryptical and ancient pattern utterly beyond and below the sordid mass of facts and habits and haunts listed with such conscientious technical care by the police. They must be, he felt inwardly, the heirs of some shocking and primordial tradition; the sharers of debased and broken scraps from cults and ceremonies older than mankind. Their coherence and definiteness suggested it, and it showed in the singular suspicion of order which lurked beneath their squalid disorder. He had not read in vain such treatises as Miss Murray's *Witch Cult in Western Europe*; and knew that up to recent years there had certainly survived among peasants and furtive folk a frightful and clandestine system of assemblies and orgies descended from dark religions antedating the Aryan world, and appearing in popular legends as Black Masses and Witches' Sabbaths. That these hellish vestiges of old Turanian–Asiatic magic and fertility-cults were even now wholly dead he could not for a moment suppose, and he frequently wondered how much older and how much blacker than the very worst of the muttered tales some of them might really be.

III

It was the case of Robert Suydam which took Malone to the heart of things in Red Hook. Suydam was a lettered recluse of ancient Dutch family, possessed originally of barely independent means, and inhabiting the spacious but ill-preserved mansion which his grandfather had built in Flatbush when that village was little more than a pleasant group of Colonial cottages surrounding the steepled and ivy-clad Reformed Church with its iron-railed yard of Netherlandish gravestones. In his lonely house, set back from Martense Street amidst a yard of venerable trees, Suydam had read and brooded for some six decades except

for a period a generation before, when he had sailed for
the old world and remained there out of sight for eight
years. He could afford no servants, and would admit but
few visitors to his absolute solitude ; eschewing close friend-
ships and receiving his rare acquaintances in one of the
three ground-floor rooms which he kept in order – a vast,
high-ceiled library, whose walls were solidly packed with
tattered books of ponderous, archaic, and vaguely repellent aspect. The growth of the town and its final absorption
in the Brooklyn district had meant nothing to Suydam, and
he had come to mean less and less to the town. Elderly
people still pointed him out on the streets, but to most of
the recent population he was merely a queer, corpulent
old fellow whose unkempt white hair, stubbly beard, shiny
black clothes and gold headed cane earned him an amused
glance and nothing more. Malone did not know him by
sight till duty called him to the case, but had heard of him
indirectly as a really profound authority on mediaeval
supersitition, and had once idly meant to look up an out-
of-print pamphlet of his on the Kabbalah and the Faustus
legend, which a friend had quoted from memory.

Suydam became a 'case' when his distant and only relatives sought court pronouncements on his sanity. Their
action seemed sudden to the outside world, but was really
undertaken only after prolonged observation and sorrow-
ful debate. It was based on certain odd changes in his
speech and habits ; wild references to impending wonders,
and unaccountable hauntings of disreputable Brooklyn
neighbourhoods. He had been growing shabbier and shabbier with the years, and now prowled about like a veritable
mendicant ; seen occasionally by humiliated friends in subway stations, or loitering on the benches around Borough
Hall in conversation with groups of swarthy, evil-looking
strangers. When he spoke it was to babble of unlimited
powers almost within his grasp, and to repeat with knowing leers such mystical words or names as 'Sephiroth', 'Ash-
modai' and 'Samaël'. The court action revealed that he was
using up his income and wasting his principal in the pur-
chase of curious tomes imported from London and Paris,
and in the maintenance of a squalid basement flat in the

Red Hook district where he spent nearly every night, receiving odd delegations of mixed rowdies and foreigners, and apparently conducting some kind of ceremonial service behind the green blinds of secretive windows. Detectives assigned to follow him reported strange cries and chants and prancing of feet filtering out from these nocturnal rites, and shuddered at their peculiar ecstasy and abandon despite the commonness of weird orgies in that sodden section. When, however, the matter came to a hearing, Suydam managed to preserve his liberty. Before the judge his manner grew urbane and reasonable, and he freely admitted the queerness of demeanour and extravagant cast of language into which he had fallen through excessive devotion to study and research. He was, he said, engaged in the investigation of certain details of European tradition which required the closest contact with foreign groups and their songs and folk dances. The notion that any low secret society was preying upon him, as hinted by his relatives, was obviously absurd; and showed how sadly limited was their understanding of him and his work. Triumphing with his calm explanations, he was suffered to depart unhindered; and the paid detectives of the Suydams, Corlears, and Van Brunts were withdrawn in resigned disgust.

It was here that an alliance of Federal inspectors and police, Malone with them, entered the case. The law had watched the Suydam action with interest, and had in many instances been called upon to aid the private detectives. In this work it developed that Suydam's new associates were among the blackest and most vicious criminals of Red Hook's devious lanes, and that at least a third of them were known and repeated offenders in the matter of thievery, disorder, and the importation of illegal immigrants. Indeed, it would not have been too much to say that the old scholar's particular circle coincided almost perfectly with the worst of the organised cliques which smuggled ashore certain nameless and unclassified Asian dregs wisely turned back by Ellis Island. In the teeming rookeries of Parker Place – since renamed – where Suydam had his basement flat, there had grown up a very unusual colony of unclassified slant-eyed folk who used the Arabic alphabet but were eloquently repudiated by the great mass of Syrians in and around Atlantic Avenue. They could all have been deported for lack of credentials, but legalism is slow-moving, and one does not disturb Red Hook unless publicity forces one to.

These creatures attended a tumble-down stone church, used Wednesdays as a dance-hall, which reared its Gothic buttresses near the vilest part of the waterfront. It was nominally Catholic ; but priests throughout Brooklyn denied the place all standing and authenticity, and policemen agreed with them when they listened to the noises it emitted at night. Malone used to fancy he heard terrible cracked bass notes from a hidden organ far underground when the church stood empty and unlighted, whilst all observers dreaded the shrieking and drumming which accompanied the visible services. Suydam, when questioned, said he thought the ritual was some remnant of Nestorian Christianity tinctured with the Shamanism of Thibet. Most of the people, he conjectured, were of Mongoloid stock, originating somewhere in or near Kurdistan – and Malone could not help recalling that Kurdistan is the land of the Yezidis, last survivors of the Persian devil-worshippers. However this may have been, the stir of the Suydam investigation made it certain that these unauthorised newcomers were flooding Red Hook in increasing numbers; entering through some marine conspiracy unreached by revenue officers and harbour police, overrunning Parker Place and rapidly spreading up the hill, and welcomed with curious fraternalism by the other assorted denizens of the region. Their squat figures and characteristic squinting physiognomies, grotesquely combined with flashy American clothing, appeared more and more numerously among the loafters and nomad gangsters of the Borough Hall section ; till at length it was deemed necessary to compute their numbers, ascertain their sources and occupations, them to the proper immigration authorities. To this task Malone was assigned by agreement of Federal and city and find if possible a way to round them up and deliver forces, and as he commenced his canvass of Red Hook he felt poised upon the brink of nameless terrors, with the shabby, unkempt figure of Robert Suydam as arch-fiend and adversary.

IV

Police methods are varied and ingenious. Malone, through unostentatious rambles, carefully casual conversations, well-timed offers of hip-pocket liquor, and judicious dialogues with frightened prisoners, learned many isolated facts about the movement whose aspect had become so menacing. The newcomers were indeed Kurds, but of a dialect obscure and puzzling to exact philology. Such of them as worked lived mostly as dockhands and unlicensed pedlars, though frequently serving in Greek restaurants and tending corner news stands. Most of them, however, had no visible means of support; and were obviously connected with underworld pursuits, of which smuggling and 'bootlegging' were the least indescribable. They had come in steamships, apparently tramp freighters, and had been unloaded by stealth on moonless nights in rowboats which stole under a certain wharf and followed a hidden canal to a secret subterranean pool beneath a house. This wharf, canal and house Malone could not locate, for the memories of his informants were exceedingly confused, while their speech was to a great extent beyond even the ablest interpreters; nor could be gain any real data on the reasons for their systematic importation. They were reticent about the exact spot from which they had come, and were never sufficiently off guard to reveal the agencies which had sought them out and directed their course. Indeed, they developed something like acute fright when asked the reasons for their presence. Gangsters of other breeds were equally taciturn, and the most that could be gathered was that some god or great priesthood had promised them unheard-of powers and supernatural glories and rulerships in a strange land.

The attendance of both newcomers and old gangsters at Suydam's closely guarded nocturnal meetings was very regular, and the police soon learned that the erstwhile re-

cluse had leased additional flats to accommodate such
guests as knew his password; at last occupying three entire
houses and permanently harbouring many of his queer
companions. He spent but little time now at his Flatbush
home, apparently going and coming only to obtain and
return books; and his face and manner had attained an
appalling pitch of wildness. Malone twice interviewed him,
but was each time brusquely repulsed. He knew nothing, he
said, of any mysterious plots or movements; and had no
idea how the Kurds could have entered or what they wanted. His business was to study undisturbed the folklore of
all the immigrants of the district; a business with which
policemen had no legitimate concern. Malone mentioned
his admiration for Suydam's old brochure on the Kabbalah
and other myths, but the old man's softening was only
momentary. He sensed an intrusion, and rebuffed his visitor in no uncertain way; till Malone withdrew disgusted,
and turned to other channels of information.

What Malone would have unearthed could he have worked continuously on the case, we shall never know. As it
was, a stupid conflict between city and Federal authority
suspended the investigations for several months, during
which the detective was busy with other assignments. But
at no time did he lose interest, or fail to stand amazed at
what began to happen to Robert Suydam. Just at the time
when a wave of kidnappings and disappearances spread its
excitement over New York, the unkempt scholar embarked
upon a metamorphosis as startling as it was absurd. One
day he was seen near Borough Hall with clean-shaven face,
well-trimmed hair, and tastefully immaculate attire, and on
every day thereafter some obscure improvement was noticed in him. He maintained his new fastidiousness without
interruption, added to it an unwonted sparkle of eye and
crispness of speech, and began little by little to shed the
corpulence which had so long deformed him. Now frequently taken for less than his age, he acquired an elasticity
of step and buoyancy of demeanour to match the new
tradition, and showed a curious darkening of the hair
which somehow did not suggest dye. As the months passed,
he commenced to dress less and less conservatively, and

finally astonished his new friends by renovating and re-
decorating his Flatbush mansion, which he threw open in a
series of receptions, summoning all the acquaintances he
could remember, and extending a special welcome to the
fully forgiven relatives who had so lately sought his restraint. Some attended through curiosity, others through
duty ; but all were suddenly charmed by the dawning grace
and urbanity of the former hermit. He had, he asserted,
accomplished most of his allotted work ; and having just
inherited some property from a half-forgotten European
friend, was about to spend his remaining years in a brighter
second youth which ease, care, and diet had made possible
to him. Less and less was he seen at Red Hook, and more
and more did he move in the society to which he was born.
Policemen noted a tendency of the gangsters to congre-
gate at the old stone church and dance-hall instead of
at the basement flat in Parker Place, though the latter
and its recent annexes still overflowed with noxious
life.

Then two incidents occurred – wide enough apart, but
both of intense interest in the case as Malone envisaged it.
One was a quiet announcement in the *Eagle* of Robert Suydam's engagement to Miss Cornelia Gerritsen of Bayside, a
young woman of excellent position, and distantly related
to the elderly bridegroom-elect ; whilst the other was a raid
on the dance-hall church by city police, after a report that
the face of a kidnapped child had been seen for a second
at one of the basement windows. Malone had participated
in this raid, and studied the place with much care when
inside. Nothing was found – in fact, the building was entirely deserted when visited – but the sensitive Celt was
vaguely disturbed by many things about the interior. There
were crudely painted panels he did not like – panels which
depicted sacred faces with pecularly worldly and sardonic
expressions, and which occasionally took liberties that even
a layman's sense of decorum could scarcely countenance.
Then, too, he did not relish the Greek inscription on the
wall above the pulpit ; an ancient incantation which he
had once stumbled upon in Dublin college days, and which
read, literally translated,

'*O friend and companion of night, thou who rejoices in the baying of dogs and spilt blood, who wanderest in the midst of shades among the tombs, who longest for blood and bringest terror to mortals, Gorgo, Mormo, thousand-faced moon, look favourably on our sacrifices!*'

When he read this he shuddered, and thought vaguely of the cracked bass organ notes he fancied he had heard beneath the church on certain nights. He shuddered again at the rust around the rim of a metal basin which stood on the altar, and paused nervously when his nostrils seemed to detect a curious and ghastly stench from somewhere in the neighbourhood. That organ memory haunted him, and he explored the basement with particular assiduity before he left. The place was very hateful to him; yet after all, were the blasphemous panels and inscriptions more than mere crudities perpetrated by the ignorant?

By the time of Suydam's wedding the kidnapping epidemic had become a popular newspaper scandal. Most of the victims were young children of the lowest classes, but the increasing number of disappearances had worked up a sentiment of the strongest fury. Journals clamoured for action from the police, and once more the Butler Street station sent its men over Red Hook for clues, discoveries, and criminals. Malone was glad to be on the trail again, and took pride in a raid on one of Suydam's Parker Place houses. There, indeed, no stolen child was found, despite the tales of screams and the red sash picked up in the area-way; but the paintings and rough inscriptions on the peeling walls of most of the rooms, and the primitive chemical laboratory in the attic, all helped to convince the detective that he was on the track of something tremendous. The paintings were appalling – hideous monsters of every shape and size, and parodies on human outlines which cannot be described. The writing was in red, and varied from Arabic to Greek, Roman, and Hebrew letters. Malone could not read much of it, but what he did decipher was portentous and cabalistic enough. One frequently repeated motto was in a sort of Hebraised Hellenistic Greek, and suggested the most terrible daemon evocations of the Alexandrian decadence:

'HEL . HELOYM . SOTHER . EMMANVEL .
SABAOTH . AGLA . TETRAGRAMMATON . AGY-
ROS . OTHEOS . ISCHYROS . ATHANATOS .
IEHOVA . VA . ADONAI . SADAY . HOMOVSION
MESSIAS . ESCHEREHEYE.'

Circles and pentagrams loomed on every hand, and told
indubitably of the strange beliefs and aspirations of those
who dwelt so squalidly here. In the cellar, however, the
strangest thing was found – a pile of genuine gold ingots
covered carelessly with a piece of burlap, and bearing upon
their shining surfaces the same weird hieroglyphics which
also adorned the walls. During the raid the police encountered only a passive resistance from the squinting Orien-
tals that swarmed from every door. Finding nothing relevant, they had to leave all as it was ; but the precinct captain wrote Suydam a note advising him to look closely to
the character of his tenants and proteges in view of the
growing public clamour.

v

Then came the June wedding and the great sensation.
Flatbush was gay for the hour about high noon, and pen-
nanted motors thronged the streets near the old Dutch
church where an awning stretched from door to highway.
No local event ever surpassed the Suydam-Gerritsen nup-
tials in tone and scale, and the party which escorted the
bride and groom to the Cunard Pier was, if not exactly the
smartest, at least a solid page from the Social Register. At
five o'clock adieux were waved, and the ponderous liner
edged away from the long pier, slowly turned its nose seaward, discarded its tug, and headed for the widening water
spaces that led to old world wonders. By night the outer
harbour was cleared, and late passengers watched the stars
twinkling above an unpolluted ocean.

Whether the tramp steamer or the scream was first to
gain attention, no one can say. Probably they were simultaneous, but it is of no use to calculate. The scream came
from the Suydam stateroom, and the sailor who broke

down the door could perhaps have told frightful things if he had not forthwith gone completely mad – as it is, he shrieked more loudly than the first victims, and thereafter ran simpering about the vessel till caught and put in irons. The ship's doctor who entered the stateroom and turned on the lights a moment later did not go mad, but told nobody what he saw till afterward, when he corresponded with Malone in Chepachet. It was murder – strangulation – but one need not say that the claw-mark on Mrs. Suydam's throat could not have come from her husband's or any other human hand, or that upon the white wall there flickered for an instant in hateful red a legend which, later copied from memory, seems to have been nothing less than the fearsome Chaldee letters of the word 'LILITH.' One need not mention these things because they vanished so quickly – as for Suydam, one could at least bar others from the room until one knew what to think oneself. The doctor has distinctly assured Malone that he did not see IT. The open porthole, just before he turned on the lights, was clouded for a second with a certain phosphorescence, and for a moment there seemed to echo in the night outside the suggestion of a faint and hellish tittering ; but no real outline met the eye. As proof, the doctor points to his continued sanity.

Then the tramp steamer claimed all attention. A boat put off, and a horde of swart, insolent ruffians in officers' dress swarmed· aboard the temporarily halted Cunarder. They wanted Suydam or his body – they had known of his trip, and for certain reasons were sure he would die. The captain's deck was almost a pandemonium ; for at the instant, between the doctor's report from the stateroom and the demands of the men from the tramp, not even the wisest and gravest seaman could think what to do. Suddenly the leader of the visiting mariners, an Arab with a hatefully negroid mouth, pulled forth a dirty, crumpled paper and handed it to the captain. It was signed by Robert Suydam, and bore the following odd message:

In case of sudden or unexplained accident or death on my part, please deliver me or my body unquestioningly in-

to the hands of the bearer and his associates. Everything,
for me, and perhaps for you, depends on absolute com-
pliance. Explanations can come later – do not fail me now.
ROBERT SUYDAM

Captain and doctor looked at each other, and the latter
whispered something to the former. Finally they nodded
rather helplessly and led the way to the Suydam stateroom.
The doctor directed the captain's glance away as he unlocked the door and admitted the strange seamen, nor did
he breathe easily till they filed out with their burden after
an unaccountably long period of preparation. It was wrap-
ped in bedding from the berths, and the doctor was glad
that the outlines were not very revealing. Somehow the
men got the thing over the side and away to their tramp
steamer without uncovering it. The Cunarder started again,
and the doctor and a ship's undertaker sought out the Suydam stateroom to perform what last services they could.
Once more the physician was forced to reticence and even
to mendacity, for a hellish thing had happened. When the
undertaker asked him why he had drained off all of Mrs.
Suydam's blood, he neglected to affirm that he had not
done so ; nor did he point to the vacant bottle-spaces on
the rack, or to the odour in the sink which showed the
hasty disposition of the bottles' original contents. The
pockets of those men – if men they were – had bulged
damnably when they left the ship. Two hours later, and the
world knew by radio all that it ought to know of the horrible affair.

VI

That same June evening, without having heard a word
from the sea, Malone was desperately busy among the
alleys of Red Hook. A sudden stir seemed to permeate
the place, and as if apprised by 'grapevine telegraph' of
something singular, the denizens clustered expectantly
around the dance-hall church and the houses in Parker
Place. Three children had just disappeared – blue eyed
Norwegians from the streets toward Gowanus – and there

were rumours of a mob forming among the sturdy Vikings of that section. Malone had for weeks been urging his colleagues to attempt a general cleanup ; and at last, moved by conditions more obvious to their common sense than the conjectures of a Dublin dreamer, they had agreed upon a final stroke. The unrest and menace of this evening had been the deciding factor, and just about midnight a raiding party recruited from three stations descended upon Parker Place and its environs. Doors were battered in, stragglers arrested, and candle-lighted rooms forced to disgorge unbelievable throngs of mixed foreigners in figured robes, mitres, and other inexplicable devices. Much was lost in the melee, for objects were thrown hastily down unexpected shafts, and betraying odours deadened by the sudden kindling of pungent incense. But spattered blood was everywhere, and Malone shuddered whenever he saw a brazier or altar from which the smoke was still rising.

He wanted to be in several places at once, and decided on Suydam's basement flat only after a messenger had reported the complete emptiness of the dilapidated dance-hall church. The flat, he thought, must hold some clue to a cult of which the occult scholar had so obviously become the centre and leader ; and it was with real expectancy that he ransacked the musty rooms, noted their vaguely charnel odour, and examined the curious books, instruments, gold ingots, and glass-stoppered bottles scattered carelessly here and there. Once a lean, black-and-white cat edged between his feet and tripped him, overturning at the same time a beaker half full of red liquid. The shock was severe, and to this day Malone is not certain of what he saw ; but in dreams he still pictures that cat as it scuttled away with certain monstrous alterations and peculiarities. Then came the locked cellar door, and the search for something to break it down. A heavy stool stood near, and its tough seat was more than enough for the antique panels. A crack formed and enlarged, and the whole door gave way – but from the *other side* ; whence poured a howling tumult of ice-cold wind with all the stenches of the bottomless pit, and whence reached a sucking force not of earth or heaven, which, coiling sentiently about the paralysed detective, dragged him through the aperture and down unmeasured spaces filled with whispers and wails, and gusts of mocking laughter.

Of course it was a dream. All the specialists have told him so, and he has nothing to prove the contrary. Indeed, he would rather have it thus; for then the sight of old brick slums and dark foreign faces would not eat so deeply into his soul. But at the time it was all horribly real, and nothing can ever efface the memory of those nighted crypts, those titan arcades, and those half-formed shapes of hell that strode gigantically in silence holding half-eaten things whose still surviving portions screamed for mercy or laughed with madness. Odours of incense and corruption joined in sickening concert, and the black air was alive with the cloudy, semi-visible bulk of shapeless elemental things with eyes. Somewhere dark sticky water was lapping at onyx piers, and once the shivery tinkle of raucous little bells pealed out to greet the insane titter of a naked phosphorescent thing which swam into sight, scrambled ashore, and climbed up to squat leeringly on a carved golden pedestal in the background.

Avenues of limitless night seemed to radiate in every direction, till one might fancy that here lay the root of a contagion destined to sicken and swallow cities, and engulf nations in the foetor of hybrid pestilence. Here cosmic sin had entered, and festered by unhallowed rites had commenced the grinning march of death that was to rot us all to fungous abnormalities too hideous for the grave's holding. Satan here held his Babylonish court, and in the blood of stainless childhood the leprous limbs of phosphorescent Lilith were laved. Incubi and succubae howled praise to Hecate, and headless moon-calves bleated to the Magna Mater. Goats leaped to the sound of thin accursed flutes, and Ægypans chased endlessly after misshapen fauns over rocks twisted like swollen toads. Moloch and Ashtaroth were not absent; for in this quintessence of all damnation the bounds of consciousness were let down, and man's fancy lay open to vistas of every realm of horror and every forbidden dimension that evil had power to mould. The world and Nature were helpless against such assaults from

unsealed wells of night, nor could any sign or prayer check
the Walpurgis-riot of horror which had come when a sage
with the hateful key had stumbled on a horde with the
locked and brimming coffer of transmitted daemon-lore.

Suddenly a ray of physical light shot through these phan-
tasms, and Malone heard the sound of oars amidst the
blasphemies of things that should be dead. A boat with a
lantern in its prow darted into sight, made fast to an iron
ring in the slimy stone pier, and vomited forth several dark
men bearing a long burden swathed in bedding. They took
it to the naked phosphorescent thing on the carved golden
pedestal, and the thing tittered and pawed at the bedding.
Then they unswathed it, and propped upright before the
pedestal the gangrenous corpse of a corpulent old man
with stubbly beard and unkempt white hair. The phosphoresence thing tittered again, and the men produced
bottles from their pockets and annointed its feet with
red, whilst they afterward gave the bottles to the thing to
drink from.

All a once, from an arcaded avenue leading endlessly
away, there came the daemoniac rattle and wheeze of a
blasphemous organ, choking and rumbling out the mock-
eries of hell in a cracked, sardonic bass. In an instant every
moving entity was electrified; and forming at once into a
ceremonial procession, the nightmare horde slithered away
in quest of the sound – goat, satyr, and Ægypan, incubus,
succubus and lemur, twisted toad and shapeless elemental,
dog-faced howler and silent strutter in darkness – all led
by the abominable naked phosphorescent thing that had
squatted on the carved golden throne, and that now strode
insolently bearing in its arms the glassy-eyed corpse of the
corpulent old man. The strange dark men danced in the
rear, and the whole column skipped and leaped with
Dionysiac fury. Malone staggered after them a few steps,
delirious and hazy, and doubtful of his place in this or in
any world. Then he turned, faltered, and sank down on
the cold damp stone, gasping and shivering as the daemon
organ croaked on, and the howling and drumming and
tinkling of the mad procession grew fainter and fainter.

Vaguely he was conscious of chanted horrors and shock-

ing croakings afar off. Now and then a wail or whine of
ceremonial devotion would float to him through the black
arcade, whilst eventually there rose the dreadful Greek
incantation whose text he had read above the pulpit of
that dance-hall church.

'*O friend and companion of night, thou who rejoicest in
the baying of dogs* (here a hideous howl burst forth) *and
spilt blood* (here nameless sounds vied with morbid shriek-
ings) *who wanderest in the midst of shades among the
tombs,* (here a whistling sigh occurred) *who longest for
blood and bringest terror to mortals,* (short, sharp cries
from myriad throats) *Gorgo,* (repeated as response) *Mormo,* (repeated with ecstasy) *thousand-faced moon,* (sighs
and flute notes) *look favourably on our sacrifices!*

As the chant closed, a general shout went up, and hissing sounds nearly drowned the croaking of the cracked bass
organ. Then a gasp as from many throats, and a babel of
barked and bleated words – 'Lilith, Great Lilith, behold
the Bridegroom!' More cries, a clamour of rioting, and
the sharp, clicking footfalls of a running figure. The footfalls approached, and Malone raised himself to his elbow
to look.

The luminosity of the crypt, lately diminished, had now
slightly increased ; and in that devil-light there appeared the
fleeting form of that which should not flee or feel or breathe
– the glassy-eyed, gangrenous corpse of the corpulent old
man, now needing no support, but animated by some in-
fernal sorcery of the rite just closed. After it raced the
naked, tittering, phosphorescent thing that belonged on
the carven pedestal, and still farther behind panted the
dark men, and all the dread crew of sentient loathsome-
ness. The corpse was gaining on its pursuers, and seemed
bent on a definite object, straining with every rotting muscle toward the carved golden pedestal, whose necromantic
importance was evidently so great. Another moment and
it had reached its goal, whilst the trailing throng laboured
on with more frantic speed. But they were too late, for in
one final spurt of strength which ripped tendon from tendon and sent its noisome bulk floundering to the floor in
a state of jellyish dissolution, the staring corpse which had

been Robert Suydam achieved its object and its triumph. The push had been tremendous, but the force had held out; and as the pusher collapsed to a muddy blotch of corruption the pedestal he had pushed tottered, tipped, and finally careened from its onyx base into the thick waters below, sending up a parting gleam of carven gold as it sank heavily to undreamable gulfs of lower Tartarus. In that instant, too, the whole scene of horror faded to nothingness before Malone's eyes; and he fainted amidst a thunderous crash which seemed to blot out all the evil universe.

VII

Malone's dream, experienced in full before he knew of Suydam's death and transfer at sea, was curiously supplemented by some odd realities of the case; though that is no reason why anyone should believe it. The three old houses in Parker Place, doubtless long rotten with decay in its most insidious form, collapsed without visible cause while half the raiders and most of the prisoners were inside; and of both the greater number were instantly killed. Only in the basements and cellars was there much saving of life, and Malone was lucky to have been deep below the house of Robert Suydam. For he really was there, as no one is disposed to deny. They found him unconscious by the edge of a night-black pool, with a grotesquely horrible jumble of decay and bone, indentifiable through dental work as the body of Suydam, a few feet away. The case was plain, for it was hither that the smugglers' underground canal led; and the men who took Suydam from the ship had brought him home. They themselves were never found, or at least never identified; and the ship's doctor is not yet satisfied with the simple certitudes of the police.

Suydam was evidently a leader in extensive man-smuggling operations, for the canal to his house was but one of several subterranean channels and tunnels in the neighbourhood. There was a tunnel from this house to a crypt beneath the dance-hall church; a crypt accessible from the church only through a narrow secret passage in the north wall, and in whose chambers some singular and terrible things were discovered. The croaking organ was there, as well as a vast arched chapel with wooden benches and a strangely figured altar. The walls were lined with small cells, in seventeen of which – hideous to relate – solitary prisoners in a state of complete idiocy were found chained, including four mothers with infants of disturbingly strange appearance. These infants died soon after exposure to the light; a circumstance which the doctors thought rather merciful. Nobody but Malone, among those who inspected them, remembered the sombre question of old Delrio: *'An sint unquam daemones incubi et succubae, et an ex tali congressu proles enascia quea?*

Before the canals were filled up they were thoroughly dredged, and yielded forth a sensational array of sawed and split bones of all sizes. The kidnapping epidemic, very clearly, had been traced home; though only two of the surviving prisoners could by any legal thread be connected with it. These men are now in prison, since they failed of conviction as accessories in the actual murders. The carved golden pedestal or throne so often mentioned by Malone as of primary occult importance was never brought to light, though at one place under the Suydam house the canal was observed to sink into a well too deep for dredging. It was choked up at the mouth and cemented over when the cellars of the new houses were made, but Malone often speculates on what lies beneath. The police, satisfied that they had shattered a dangerous gang of maniacs and mansmugglers, turned over to the Federal authorities the unconvicted Kurds, who before their deportation were conclusively found to belong to the Yezidi clan of devilworshippers. The tramp ship and its crew remain an elusive mystery, though cynical detectives are once more ready to combat its smuggling and rum-running ventures. Malone thinks these detectives show a sadly limited perspective in their lack of wonder at the myriad unexplainable details, and the suggestive obscurity of the whole case; though he is just as critical of the newspapers, which saw only a morbid sensation and gloated over a minor sadist cult which they might have proclaimed a horror from the universe's very heart. But he is content to rest silent in Chepachet, calming his nervous system and praying that time may gradually transfer his terrible experience from the realm of present reality to that of picturesque and semi-mythical remoteness.

Robert Suydam sleeps beside his bride in Greenwood Cemetery. No funeral was held over the strangely released bones, and relatives are grateful for the swift oblivion which overtook the case as a whole. The scholar's connection with the Red Hook horrors, indeed, was never emblazoned by legal proof; since his death forestalled the inquiry he would otherwise have faced. His own end is not much mentioned, and the Suydams hope that posterity may recall him only as a gentle recluse who dabbled in harmless magic and folklore.

As for Red Hook – it is always the same. Suydam came and went; a terror gathered and faded; but the evil spirit of darkness and squalor broods on amongst the mongrels in the old brick houses, and prowling bands still parade on unknown errands past windows where lights and twisted faces unaccountably appear and disappear. Age-old horror is a hydra with a thousand heads, and the cults of darkness are rooted in blasphemies deeper than the well of Democritus. The soul of the beast is omnipresent and triumphant, and Red Hook's legions of blear-eyed, pockmarked youths still chant and curse and howl as they file from abyss to abyss, none knows whence or whither, pushed on by blind laws of biology which they may never understand. As of old, more people enter Red Hook than leave it on the landward side, and there are already rumours of new canals running underground to certain centres of traffic in liquor and less mentionable things.

The dance-hall church is now mostly a dance hall, and queer faces have appeared at night at the windows. Lately a policeman expressed the belief that the filled-up crypt has been dug out again, and for no simple explainable purpose. Who are we to combat poisons older than history and mankind? Apes danced in Asia to those horrors, and the cancer lurks secure and spreading where furtiveness hides in rows of decaying brick.

Malone does not shudder without cause – for only the other day an officer overheard a swarthy squinting hag teaching a small child some whispered patois in the shadow of an areaway. He listened, and thought it very strange when he heard her repeat over and over again,

'O friend and companion of night, thou who rejoicest in the baying of dogs and spilt blood, who wanderest in the midst of shades among the tombs, who longest for blood and bringest terror to mortals, Gorgo, Mormo, thousand-faced moon, look favourably on our sacrifices!'

The Strange High House in the Mist

In the morning mist comes up from the sea by the cliffs beyond Kingsport. White and feathery it comes from the deep to its brothers the clouds, full of dreams of dank pastures and caves of leviathan. And later, in still summer rains on the steep roofs of poets, the clouds scatter bits of those dreams, that men shall not live without rumor of old strange secrets, and wonders that planets tell planets alone in the night. When tales fly thick in the grottoes of tritons, and conchs in seaweed cities blow wild tunes learned from the Elder Ones, then great eager mists flock to heaven laden with lore, and oceanward eyes on the rocks see only a mystic whiteness, as if the cliff's rim were the rim of all earth, and the solemn bells of buoys tolled free in the aether of faëry.

Now north of archaic Kingsport the crags climb lofty and curious, terrace on terrace, till the northernmost hangs in the sky like a gray frozen wind-cloud. Alone it is, a bleak point jutting in limitless space, for there the coast turns sharp where the great Miskatonic pours out of the plains past Arkham, bringing woodland legends and little quaint memories of New England's hills. The sea-folk of Kingsport look up at that cliff as other sea-folk look up at the pole-star, and time the night's watches by the way it hides or shows the Great Bear, Cassiopeia, and the Dragon. Among them it is one with the firmament, and truly, it is hidden from them when the mist hides the stars or the sun.

Some of the cliffs they love, as that whose grotesque profile they call Father Neptune, or that whose pillared steps they term 'The Causeway'; but this one they fear because it is so near the sky. The Portuguese sailors coming in from a voyage cross themselves when they first see it, and the old Yankees believe it would be much graver matter than death to climb it, if indeed that were possible. Nevertheless there is an ancient house on that cliff, and at evening men see lights in the small-paned windows.

The ancient house has always been there, and people say

One dwells within who talks with the morning mists that come up from the deep, and perhaps sees singular things oceanward at those times when the cliffs rim becomes the rim of all earth, and solemn buoys toll free in the white aether of faëry. This they tell from hearsay, for that forbidding crag is always unvisited, and natives dislike to train telescopes on it. Summer boarders have indeed scanned it with jaunty binoculars, but have never seen more than the gray primeval roof, peaked and shingled, whose eaves come nearly to the gray foundations, and the dim yellow light of the little windows peeping out from under those eaves in the dusk. These summer people do not believe that the same One has lived in the ancient house for hundreds of years, but can not prove their heresy to any real Kingsporter. Even the Terrible Old Man who talks to leaden pendulums in bottles, buys groceries with centuried Spanish gold, and keeps stone idols in the yard of his antediluvian cottage in Water Street can only say these things were the same when his grandfather was a boy, and that must have been inconceivable ages ago, when Belcher or Shirley or Pownall or Bernard was Governor of His Majesty's Province of the Massachusetts-Bay.

Then one summer there came a philosopher into Kingsport. His name was Thomas Olney, and he taught ponderous things in a college by Narragansett Bay. With stout wife and romping children he came, and his eyes were weary with seeing the same things for many years, and thinking the same well-disciplined thoughts. He looked at the mists from the diadem of Father Neptune, and tried to walk into their white world of mystery along the titan steps of The Causeway. Morning after morning he would lie on the cliffs and look over the world's rim at the cryptical aether beyond, listening to spectral bells and the wild cries of what might have been gulls. Then, when the mist would lift and the sea stand out prosy with the smoke of steamers, he would sigh and descend to the town, where he loved to thread the narrow olden lanes up and down hill, and study the crazy tottering gables and odd-pillared doorways which had sheltered so many generations of sturdy sea-folk. And he even talked with the Terrible Old Man, who was not fond of strangers, and was invited into his fearsomely archaic cottage where low ceilings and wormy panelling hear the echoes of disquieting soliloquies in the dark small hours.

Of course it was inevitable that Olney should mark the gray unvisited cottage in the sky, on that sinister northward crag which is one with the mists and the firmament. Always over Kingsport it hung, and always its mystery sounded in whispers through Kingsport's crooked alleys. The Terrible Old Man wheezed a tale that his father had told him, of lightning that shot one night up from that peaked cottage to the clouds of higher heaven ; and Granny Orne, whose tiny gambrel-roofed abode in Ship Street is all covered with moss and ivy, croaked over something her grandmother had heard at second-hand, about shapes that flapped out of the eastern mists straight into the narrow single door of that unreachable place – for the door is set close to the edge of the crag toward the ocean, and glimpsed only from ships at sea.

At length, being avid for new strange things and held back by neither the Kingsporter's fear nor the summer boarder's usual indolence, Olney made a very terrible resolve. Despite a conservative training – or because of it, for humdrum lives breed wistful longings of the unknown – he swore a great oath to scale that avoided northern cliff and visit the abnormally antique gray cottage in the sky. Very plausibly his saner self argued that the place must be tenanted by people who reached it from inland along the easier ridge beside the Miskatonic's estuary. Probably they traded in Arkham, knowing how little Kingsport liked their habitation, or perhaps being unable to climb down the cliff on the Kingsport side. Olney walked out along the lesser cliffs to where the great crag leaped insolently up to consort with celestial things, and became very sure that no human feet could mount it or descend it on that beetling southern slope. East and north it rose thousands of feet perpendicular from the water, so only the western side, inland and toward Arkham remained.

One early morning in August Olney set out to find a path to the inaccessible pinnacle. He worked northwest along pleasant back roads, past Hooper's Pond and the old brick powder-house to where the pastures slope up to the ridge above the Miskatonic and give a lovely vista of Arkham's white Georgian steeples across leagues of river and meadow. Here he found a shady road to Arkham, but no trail at all in the seaward direction he wished. Woods and fields crowded up to the high bank of the river's mouth, and bore not a sign of man's presence; not even a stone wall or a straying cow, but only the tall grass and giant trees and tangles of briars that the first Indian might have seen. As he climbed slowly east, higher and higher above the estuary on his left and nearer and nearer the sea, he found the way growing in difficulty till he wondered how ever the dwellers in that disliked place managed to reach the world outside, and whether they came often to market in Arkham.

Then the trees thinned, and far below him on his right he saw the hills and antique roofs and spires of Kingsport. Even Central Hill was a dwarf from this height, and he could just make out the ancient graveyard by the Congregational Hospital, beneath which rumor said some terrible caves or burrows lurked. Ahead lay sparse grass and scrub blueberry bushes, and beyond them the naked rock of the crag and the thin peak of the dreaded gray cottage. Now the ridge narrowed, and Olney grew dizzy at his loneness in the sky, south of him the frightful precipice above Kingsport, north of him the vertical drop of nearly a mile to the river's mouth. Suddenly a great chasm opened before him, ten feet deep, so that he had to let himself down by his hands and drop to a slanting floor, and then crawl perilously up a natural defile in the opposite wall. So this was the way the folk of the uncanny house journeyed betwixt earth and sky!

When he climbed out of the chasm a morning mist was gathering, but he clearly saw the lofty and unhallowed cottage ahead; walls as gray as the rock, and high peak standing bold against the milky white of the seaward vapors. And he perceived that there was no door on this landward end, but only a couple of small lattice windows with dingy bull's-eye panes leaded in Seventeenth Century fashion. All-

around him was cloud and chaos, and he could see nothing
below the whiteness of illimitable space. He was alone in
the sky with this queer and very disturbing house; and
when he sidled around to the front and saw that the wall
stood flush with the cliff's edge, so that the single narrow
door was not to be reached save from the empty aether, he
felt a distinct terror that altitude could not wholly explain.
And it was very odd that shingles so worm-eaten could
survive, or bricks so crumbled still form a standing chim-
ney.

As the mist thickened, Olney crept around to the windows on the north and west and south sides, trying them
but finding them all locked. He was vaguely glad they were
locked, because the more he saw of that house the less he
wished to get in. Then a sound halted him. He heard a lock
rattle and a bolt shoot, and a long creaking follow as if a
heavy door were slowly and cautiously opened. This was on
the oceanward side that he could not see, where the narrow
portal opened on blank space thousands of feet in the misty
sky above the waves.

Then there was heavy, deliberate tramping in the cottage, and Olney heard the windows opening, first on the
north side opposite him, and then on the west just around
the corner. Next would come the south windows, under the
great low eaves on the side where he stood; and it must be
said that he was more than uncomfortable as he thought of
the detestable house on one side and the vacancy of upper
air on the other. When a fumbling came in the nearer case-
ments he crept around to the west again, flattening himself
against the wall beside the now opened windows. It was
plain that the owner had come home; but he had not come
from the land, nor from any balloon or airship that could
be imagined. Steps sounded again, and Olney edged round
to the north; but before he could find a haven a voice
called softly, and he knew he must confront his host.

Stuck out of the west window was a great black-bearded
face whose eyes were phosphorescent with the imprint of
unheard-of sights. But the voice was gentle, and of a quaint
olden kind, so that Olney did not shudder when a brown
hand reached out to help him over the sill and into that low

room of black oak wainscots and carved Tudor furnishings. The man was clad in very ancient garments, and had about him an unplaceable nimbus of sea-lore and dreams of tall galleons. Olney does not recall many of the wonders he told, or even who he was; but says that he was strange and kindly, and filled with the magic of unfathomed voids of time and space. The small room seemed green with a dim aqueous light, and Olney saw that the far windows to the east were not open, but shut against the misty aether with dull panes like the bottoms of old bottles.

That bearded host seemed young, yet looked out of eyes steeped in the elder mysteries; and from the tales of marvelous ancient things he related, it must be guessed that the village folk were right in saying he had communed with the mists of the sea and the clouds of the sky ever since there was any village to watch his taciturn dwelling from the plain below. And the day wore on, and still Olney listened to rumors of old times and far places, and heard how the kings of Atlantis fought with the slippery blasphemies that wriggled out of rifts in ocean's floor, and how the pillared and weedy temple of Poseidonis is still glimpsed at midnight by lost ships, who knew by its sight that they are lost. Years of the Titans were recalled, but the host grew timid when he spoke of the dim first age of chaos before the gods or even the Elder Ones were born, and when *the other gods* came to dance on the peak of Hatheg-Kla in the stony desert near Ulthar, beyond the River Skai.

It was at this point that there came a knocking on the door; that ancient door of nail-studded oak beyond which lay only the abyss of white cloud. Olney started in fright, but the bearded man motioned him to be still, and tiptoed to the door to look out through a very small peephole. What he saw he did not like, so pressed his fingers to his lips and tiptoed around to shut and lock all the windows before returning to the ancient settle beside his guest. Then Olney saw lingering against the translucent squares of each of the little dim windows in succession a queer black outline as the caller moved inquisitively about before leaving; and he was glad his host had not answered the knocking. For there are strange objects in the great abyss, and the seeker of dreams must take care not to stir up or meet the wrong ones.

Then the shadows began to gather ; first little furtive ones under the table, and then bolder ones in the dark panelled corners. And the bearded man made enigmatical gestures of prayer, and lit tall candles in curiously wrought brass candle-sticks. Frequently he would glance at the door as if he expected some one, and at length his glance seemed answered by a singular rapping which must have followed some very ancient and secret code. This time he did not even glance through the peep-hole, but swung the great oak bar and shot the bolt, unlatching the heavy door and flinging it wide to the stars and the mist.

And then to the sound of obscure harmonies there floated into that room from the deep all the dreams and memories of earth's sunken Mighty Ones. And golden flames played about weedy locks, so that Olney was dazzled as he did them homage. Trident-bearing Neptune was there, and sportive tritons and fantastic nereids, and upon dolphins' backs was balanced a vast crenulate shell wherein rode the gay and awful form of primal Nodens, Lord of the Great Abyss. And the conches of the tritons gave weird blasts, and the nereids made strange sounds by striking on the grotesque resonant shells of unknown lurkers in black sea-caves. Then hoary Nodens reached forth a wizened hand and helped Olney and his host into the vast shell, whereat the conchs and the gongs set up a wild and awesome clamor. And out into the limitless aether reeled that fabulous train, the noise of whose shouting was lost in the echoes of thunder.

All night in Kingsport they watched that lofty cliff when the storm and the mists gave them glimpses of it, and when toward the small hours the little dim windows went dark they whispered of dread and disaster. And Olney's children and stout wife prayed to the bland proper god of Baptists, and hoped that the traveller would borrow an umbrella and rubbers unless the rain stopped by morning. Then dawn swam dripping and mist-wreathed out of the sea, and the buoys tolled solemn in vortices of white aether. And at noon Elfin horns rang over the ocean as Olney, dry and light-footed, climbed down from the cliffs to antique Kingsport with the look of far places in his eyes. He could not recall what he had dreamed in the sky-perched hut of that still nameless hermit, or say how he had crept down that crag untraversed by other feet. Nor could he talk of these matters at all save with the Terrible Old Man, who afterward mumbled queer things in his long white beard ; vowing that the man who came down from that crag was not wholly the man who went up, and that somewhere under that gray peaked roof, or amidst inconceivable reaches of that sinister white mist, there lingered still the lost spirit of him who was Thomas Olney.

And ever since that hour, through dull dragging years of grayness and weariness, the philosopher has labored and eaten and slept and done uncomplaining the svitable deeds of a citizen. Not any more does he long for the magic of farther hills, or sigh for secrets that peer like green reefs from a bottomless sea. The sameness of his days no longer gives him sorrow, and well-disciplined thoughts have grown enough for his imagination. His good wife waxes stouter and his children older and prosier and more useful, and he never fails to smile correctly with pride when the occasion calls for it. In his glance there is not any restless light, and if he ever listens for solemn bells or far elfin horns it is only at night when old dreams are wandering. He has never seen Kingsport again, for his family disliked the funny old houses and complained that the drains were impossibly bad. They have a trim bungalow now at Bristol Highlands, where no tall crags tower, and the neighbors are urban and modern.

But in Kingsport strange tales are abroad, and even the Terrible Old Man admits a thing untold by his grandfather. For now, when the wind sweeps boisterous out of the north past the high ancient house that is one with the firmament, there is broken at last that ominous, brooding silence ever before the bane of Kingsport's maritime cotters. And old folk tell of pleasing voices heard singing there, and of laughter that swells with joys beyond earth's joys ; and say that at evening the little low windows are brighter than formerly. They say, too, that the fierce aurora comes

oftener to that spot, shining blue in the north with visions of
frozen worlds while the crag and the cottage hang black
and fantastic against wild coruscations. And the mists of
the dawn are thicker, and sailors are not quite so sure that
all the muffled seaward ringing is that of the solemn buoys.

Worst of all, though, is the shrivelling of old fears in the
hearts of Kingsport's young men, who grow prone to listen
at night to the north wind's faint distant sounds. They swear
no harm or pain can inhabit that high peaked cottage, for
in the new voices gladness beats, and with them the tinkle of
laughter and music. What tales the sea-mists may bring to
that haunted and northernmost pinnacle they do not know,
but they long to extract some hint of the wonders that knock
at the cliff-yawning door when clouds are thickest. And pat-
riarchs dread lest some day one by one they seek out that
inaccessible peak in the sky, and learn what centuried
secrets hide beneath the steep shingled roof which is part
of the rocks and the stars and the ancient fears of Kingsport. That those venturesome youths will come back they
do not doubt, but they think a light may be gone from
their eyes, and a will from their hearts. And they do not
wish quaint Kingsport with its climbing lanes and archaic
gables to drag listless down the years while voice by voice
the laughing chorus grows stronger and wilder in that unknown and terrible eyrie where mists and the dreams of
mists stop to rest on their way from the sea to the skies.

They do not wish the souls of their young men to leave
the pleasant hearths and gambrel-roofed taverns of old
Kingsport, nor do they wish the laughter and song in that
high rocky place to grow louder. For as the voice which
has come has brought fresh mists from the sea and from the
north fresh lights, so do they say that still other voices will
bring more mists and more lights, till perhaps the olden
gods (whose existence they hint only in whispers for fear
the Congregational parson shall hear) may come out of the
deep and from unknown Kadath in the cold waste and
make their dwelling on that evilly appropriate crag so close
to the gentle hills and valleys of quiet, simple fisher folk.
This they do not wish, for to plain people things not of earth
are unwelcome ; and besides, the Terrible Old Man often

recalls what Olney said about a knock that the lone dweller feared, and a shape seen black and inquisitive against the mist through those queer translucent windows of leaded bull's-eyes.

All these things, however, the Elder Ones only may decide; and meanwhile the morning mist still comes up by that lovely vertiginous peak with the steep ancient house, that gray, low-eaved house where none is seen but where evening brings furtive lights while the north wind tells of strange revels. White and feathery it comes from the deep to its brothers the clouds, full of dreams of dank pastures and caves of leviathan. And when tales fly thick in the grottoes of tritons, and conches in seaweed cities blow wild tunes learned from the Elder Ones, then great eager vapors flock to heaven laden with lore; and Kingsport, nestling uneasy in its lesser cliffs below that awesome hanging sentinel of rock, sees oceanward only a mystic whiteness, as if the cliff's rim were the rim of all earth, and the solemn bells of the buoys tolled free in the aether of faëry.

In the Walls of Eryx

Before I try to rest I will set down these notes in preparation for the report I must make. What I have found is so singular, and so contrary to all past experience and expectations, that it deserves a very careful description.

I reached the main landing on Venus March 18, terrestrial time; VI, 9 of the planet's calendar. Being put in the main group under Miller, I received my equipment – watch tuned to Venus's slightly quicker rotation – and went through the usual mask drill. After two days I was pronounced fit for duty.

Leaving the Crystal Company's post at Terra Nova around dawn, VI, 12, I followed the southerly route which Anderson had mapped out from the air. The going was bad, for these jungles are always half impassable after a rain. It must be the moisture that gives the tangled vines and creepers that leathery toughness; a toughness so great that a knife has to work ten minutes on some of them. By noon it was dryer – the vegetation getting soft and rubbery so that the knife went through it easily – but even then I could not make much speed. These Carter oxygen masks are too heavy – just carrying one half wears an ordinary man out. A Dubois mask with sponge-reservoir instead of tubes would give just as good air at half the weight.

The crystal-detector seemed to function well, pointing steadily in a direction verifying Anderson's report. It is curious how that principle of affinity works – without any of the fakery of the old 'divining rods' back home. There must be a great deposit of crystals within a thousand miles, though I suppose those damnable man-lizards always watch and guard it. Possibly they think we are just as foolish for coming to Venus to hunt the stuff as we think they are for grovelling in the mud whenever they see a piece of it, or for keeping that great mass on a pedestal in their temple. I wish they'd get a new religion, for they have no use for the crystals except to pray to. Barring theology, they would let us take all we want – and even if they learned to

tap them for power there'd be more than enough for their
planet and the earth besides. I for one am tired of passing
up the main deposits and merely seeking separate crystals
out of jungle river-beds. Sometime I'll urge the wiping out
of these scaly beggars by a good stiff army from home.
About twenty ships could bring enough troops across to
turn the trick. One can't call the damned things men for all
their 'cities' and towers. They haven't any skill except building – and using swords and poison darts – and I don't
believe their so-called 'cities' mean much more than ant-
hills or beaver-dams. I doubt if they even have a real language – all the talk about psychological communication
through those tentacles down their chests strikes me as
bunk. What misleads people is their upright posture ; just
an accidental physical resemblance to terrestrial man.

I'd like to go through a Venus jungle for once without
having to watch out for skulking groups of them or dodge
their cursed darts. They may have been all right before we
began to take the crystals, but they're certainly a bad
enough nuisance now – with their dart-shooting and their
cutting of our water pipes. More and more I come to believe that they have a special sense like our crystal-detectors.
No one ever knew them to bother a man – apart from long-
distance sniping – who didn't have crystals on him.

Around 1 P.M. a dart nearly took my helmet off, and I
thought for a second one of my oxygen tubes was punc-
tured. The sly devils hadn't made a sound, but three of
them were closing in on me. I got them all by sweeping in
a circle with my flame pistol, for even though their colour
blended with the jungle, I could spot the moving creepers.
One of them was fully eight feet tall, with a snout like
a tapir's. The other two were average seven-footers. All
that makes them hold their own is sheer numbers – even
a single regiment of flame throwers could raise hell with
them. It is curious, though, how they've come to be domi-
nant on the planet. Not another living thing higher than
the wriggling akmans and skorahs, or the flying tukahs of
the other continent – unless of course those holes in the
Dionaean Plateau hide something.

About two o'clock my detector veered westward, indi-

cating isolated crystals ahead on the right. This checked up
with Anderson, and I turned my course accordingly. It was
harder going – not only because the ground was rising,
but because the animal life and carnivorous plants were
thicker. I was always slashing ugrats and stepping on skorahs, and my leather suit was all speckled from the bursting
darohs which struck it from all sides. The sunlight was all
the worse because of the mist, and did not seem to dry up
the mud in the least. Every time I stepped my feet sank
down five or six inches, and there was a sucking sort of
blup every time I pulled them out. I wish somebody would
invent a safe kind of suiting other than leather for this climate. Cloth of course would rot ; but some thin metallic
tissue that couldn't tear – like the surface of this revolving
decay-proof record scroll – ought to be feasible sometime.

I ate about 3 : 30 – if slipping these wretched food tablets
through my mask can be called eating. Soon after that I
noticed a decided change in the landscape – the bright,
poisonous-looking flowers shifting in colour and getting
wraith-like. The outlines of everything shimmered rhythmically, and bright points of light appeared and danced in the
same slow, steady tempo. After that the temperature seemed
to fluctuate in unison with a peculiar rhythmic drumming.

The whole universe seemed to be throbbing in deep, regular pulsations that filled every corner of space and flowed
through my body and mind alike. I lost all sense of equilibrium and staggered dizzily, nor did it change things in
the least when I shut my eyes and covered my ears with my
hands. However, my mind was still clear, and in a very few
minutes I realised what had happened.

I had encountered at least one of those curious *mirage-
plants* about which so many of our men told stories. Anderson had warned me of them, and described their appearance
very closely – the shaggy stalk, the spiky leaves, and the
mottled blossoms whose gaseous, dream-breeding exhala-
tions penetrate every existing make of mask.

Recalling what happened to Bailey three years ago, I fell
into a momentary panic, and began to dash and stagger
about in the crazy, chaotic world which the plant's exhala-
tions had woven around me. Then good sense came back,

and I realized all I need to do was retreat from the dangerous blossoms – heading away from the source of the pulsations, and cutting a path blindly – regardless of what might seem to swirl around me – until safely out of the plant's effective radius.

Although everything was spinning perilously, I tried to start in the right direction and hack my way ahead. My route must have been far from straight, for it seemed hours before I was free of the mirage-plant's pervasive influence. Gradually the dancing lights began to disappear, and the shimmering spectral scenery began to assume the aspect of solidity. When I did get wholly clear I looked at my watch and was astonished to find that the time was only 4:20. Though eternities had seemed to pass, the whole experience could have consumed little more than a half-hour.

Every delay, however, was irksome, and I had lost ground in my retreat from the plant. I now pushed ahead in the uphill direction indicated by the crystal-detector, bending every energy toward making better time. The jungle was still thick, though there was less animal life. Once a carnivorous blossom engulfed my right foot and held it so tightly that I had to hack it free with my knife ; reducing the flower to strips before it let go.

In less than an hour I saw that the jungle growths were thinning out, and by five o'clock – after passing through a belt of tree-ferns with very little underbrush – I emerged on a broad mossy plateau. My progress now became rapid, and I saw by the wavering of my detector-needle that I was getting relatively close to the crystal I sought. This was odd, for most of the scattered, egg-like spheroids occurred in jungle streams of a sort not likely to be found on this treeless upland.

The terrain sloped upward, ending in a definite crest. I reached the top about 5:30, and saw ahead of me a very extensive plain with forests in the distance. This, without question, was the plateau mapped by Matsugawa from the air fifty years ago, and called on our maps 'Eryx' or the 'Erycinian Highland.' But what made my heart leap was a smaller detail, whose position could not have been far from the plain's exact centre. It was a single point of light, blazing through the mist and seeming to draw a piercing, concentrated luminescence from the yellowish, vapour-dulled sunbeams. This, without doubt, was the crystal I sought – a thing possibly no larger than a hen's egg, yet containing enough power to keep a city warm for a year. I could hardly wonder, as I glimpsed the distant glow, that those miserable man-lizards worship such crystals. And yet they have not the least notion of the powers they contain.

Breaking into a rapid run, I tried to reach the unexpected prize as soon as possible; and was annoyed when the firm moss gave place to a thin, singularly detestable mud studded with occasional patches of weeds and creepers. But I splashed on heedlessly – scarcely thinking to look around for any of the skulking man-lizards. In this open space I was not very likely to be waylaid. As I advanced, the light ahead seemed to grow in size and brilliancy, and I began to notice some peculiarity in its situation. Clearly, this was a crystal of the very finest quality, and my elation grew with every spattering step.

It is now that I must begin to be careful in making my report, since what I shall henceforward have to say involves unprecedented – though fortunately verifiable – matters. I was racing ahead with mounting eagerness, and had come within a hundred yards or so of the crystal – whose position on a sort of raised place in the omnipresent slime seemed very odd – when a sudden, overpowering force struck my chest and the knuckles of my clenched fists and knocked me over backward into the mud. The splash of my fall was terrific, nor did the softness of the ground and the presence of some slimy weeds and creepers save my head from a bewildering jarring. For a moment I lay supine, too utterly startled to think. Then I half mechanically stumbled to my feet and began to scrape the worst of the mud and scum from my leather suit.

Of what I had encountered I could not form the faintest idea. I had seen nothing which could have caused the shock, and I saw nothing now. Had I, after all, merely slipped in the mud? My sore knuckles and aching chest forbade me to think so. Or was this whole incident an illusion brought on by some hidden mirage-plant? It hardly seemed probable, since I had none of the usual symptoms, and since there was no place near by where so vivid and typical a growth could lurk unseen. Had I been on the earth, I would have suspected a barrier of N-force laid down by some government to mark a forbidden zone, but in this human-less region such a notion would have been absurd.

Finally pulling myself together, I decided to investigate in a cautious way. Holding my knife as far as possible ahead of me, so that it might be first to feel the strange force, I started once more for the shining crystal – preparing to advance step by step with the greatest deliberation. At the third step I was brought up short by the impact of the knife-point on an apparently solid surface – a solid surface where my eyes saw nothing.

After a moment's recoil I gained boldness. Extending my gloved left hand, I verified the presence of invisible solid matter – or a tactile illusion of solid matter – ahead of me. Upon moving my hand I found that the barrier was of substantial extent, and of an almost glassy smoothness, with no evidence of the joining of separate blocks. Nerving myself for further experiments, I removed a glove and tested the thing with my bare hand. It was indeed hard and glassy, and of a curious coldness as contrasted with the air around. I strained my eyesight to the utmost in an effort to glimpse some trace of the obstructing substance, but could discern nothing whatsoever. There was not even any evidence of refractive power as judged by the aspect of the landscape ahead. Absence of reflective power was proved by the lack of a glowing image of the sun at any point.

Burning curiosity began to displace all other feelings, and I enlarged my investigations as best I could. Exploring with my hands, I found that the barrier extended from the ground to some level higher than I could reach, and that it stretched off indefinitely on both sides. It was, then, a *wall* of some kind – though all guesses as to its materials and its purpose were beyond me. Again I thought of the mirage-plant and the dreams it induced, but a moment's reasoning put this out of my head.

Knocking sharply on the barrier with the hilt of my knife,

and kicking at it with my heavy boots, I tried to interpret the sounds thus made. There was something suggestive of cement or concrete in these reverberations, though my hands had found the surface more glassy or metallic in feel. Certainly, I was confronting something strange beyond all previous experience.

The next logical move was to get some idea of the wall's dimensions. The height problem would be hard, if not insoluble, but the length and shape problem could perhaps be sooner dealt with. Stretching out my arms and pressing close to the barrier, I began to edge gradually to the left – keeping very careful track of the way I faced. After several steps I concluded that the wall was not straight, but that I was following part of some vast circle or ellipse. And then my attention was distracted by something wholly different – something connected with the still-distant crystal which had formed the object of my quest.

I have said that even from a greater distance the shining object's position seemed indefinably queer – on a slight mound rising from the slime. Now – at about a hundred yards – I could see plainly despite the engulfing mist just what that mound was. It was the body of a man in one of the Crystal Company's leather suits, lying on his back, and with his oxygen mask half buried in the mud a few inches away. In his right hand, crushed convulsively against his chest, was the crystal which had led me here – a spheroid of incredible size, so large that the dead fingers could scarce close over it. Even at the given distance I could see that the body was a recent one. There was little visible decay, and I reflected that in this climate such a thing meant death not more than a day before. Soon the hateful farnoth-flies would begin to cluster about the corpse. I wondered who the man was. Surely no one I had seen on this trip. It must have been one of the old-timers absent on a long roving commission, who had come to this especial region independently of Anderson's survey. There he lay, past all trouble, and with the rays of the great crystal streaming out from between his stiffened fingers.

For fully five minutes I stood there staring in bewilderment and apprehension. A curious dread assailed me, and I

had an unreasonable impulse to run away. It could not
have been done by those slinking man-lizards, for he still
held the crystal he had found. Was there any connexion
with the invisible wall? Where had he found the crystal?
Anderson's instrument had indicated one in this quarter
well before this man could have perished. I now began to
regard the unseen barrier as something sinister, and re-
coiled from it with a shudder. Yet I knew I must probe the
mystery all the more quickly and thoroughly because of
this recent tragedy.

Suddenly – wrenching my mind back to the problem I
faced – I thought of a possible means of testing the wall's
height, or at least of finding whether or not it extended
indefinitely upward. Seizing a handful of mud, I let it drain
until it gained some coherence and then flung it high in
the air toward the utterly transparent barrier. At a height of
perhaps fourteen feet it struck the invisible surface with a
resounding splash, disintegrating at once and oozing downward in disappearing streams with surprising rapidity.
Plainly, the wall was a lofty one. A second handful, hurled
at an even sharper angle, hit the surface about eighteen feet
from the ground and disappeared as quickly as the first.

I now summoned up all my strength and prepared to
throw a third handful as high as I possibly could. Letting
the mud drain, and squeezing it to maximum dryness, I
flung it up so steeply that I feared it might not reach the
obstructing surface at all. It did, however, and this time it
crossed the barrier and fell in the mud beyond with a violent spattering. At last I had a rough idea of the height of
the wall, for the crossing had evidently occurred some
twenty or twenty-one feet aloft.

With a nineteen- or twenty-foot vertical wall of glassy
flatness, ascent was clearly impossible. I must, then, continue to circle the barrier in the hope of finding a gate, an
ending, or some sort of interruption. Did the obstacle form
a complete round or other closed figure, or was it merely
an arc or semi-circle? Acting on my decision, I resumed
my slow leftward circling, moving my hands up and down
over the unseen surface on the chance of finding some window or other small aperture. Before starting, I tried to mark

my position by kicking a hole in the mud, but found the slime too thin to hold any impression. I did, though, gauge the place approximately by noting a tall cycad in the distant forest which seemed just on a line with the gleaming crystal a hundred yards away. If no gate or break existed I could now tell when I had completely circumnavigated the wall.

I had not progressed far before I decided that the curvature indicated a circular enclosure of about a hundred yards' diameter – providing the outline was regular. This would mean that the dead man lay near the wall at a point almost opposite the region where I had started. Was he just inside or just outside the enclosure? This I would soon ascertain.

As I slowly rounded the barrier without finding any gate, window, or other break, I decided that the body was lying within. On closer view the features of the dead man seemed vaguely disturbing. I found something alarming in his expression, and in the way the glassy eyes stared. By the time I was very near I believed I recognized him as Dwight, a veteran whom I had never known, but who was pointed out to me at the post last year. The crystal he clutched was certainly a prize – the largest single specimen I had ever seen.

I was so near the body that I could – but for the barrier – have touched it, when my exploring left hand encountered a corner in the unseen surface. In a second I had learned that there was an opening about three feet wide, extending from the ground to a height greater than I could reach. There was no door, nor any evidence of hingemarks bespeaking a former door. Without a moment's hesitation I stepped through and advanced two paces to the prostrate body – which lay at right angles to the hallway I had entered, in what seemed to be an intersecting, doorless corridor. It gave me a fresh curiosity to find that the interior of this vast enclosure was divided by partitions.

Bending to examine the corpse, I discovered that it bore no wounds. This scarcely surprised me, since the continued presence of the crystal argued against the pseudo-reptilian natives. Looking about for some possible cause of death, my eyes lit upon the oxygen mask lying close to the body's feet. Here, indeed, was something significant. Without this device no human being could breathe the air of Venus for more than thirty seconds, and Dwight – if it were he – had obviously lost his. Probably it had been carelessly buckled, so that the weight of the tubes worked the straps loose – a thing which could not happen with a Dubois sponge-reservoir mask. The half-minute of grace had been too short to allow the man to stoop and recover his protection – or else the cyanogen content of the atmosphere was abnormally high at the time. Probably he had been busy admiring the crystal – wherever he may have found it. He had, apparently, just taken it from the pouch in his suit, for the flap was unbuttoned.

I now proceeded to extricate the huge crystal from the dead prospector's fingers – a task which the body's stiffness made very difficult. The spheroid was larger than a man's fist, and glowed as if alive in the reddish rays of the western-ing sun. As I touched the gleaming surface I shuddered involuntarily – as if by taking this precious object I had transferred to myself the doom which had overtaken its earlier bearer. However, my qualms soon passed, and I carefully buttoned the crystal into the pouch of my leather suit. Superstition has never been one of my failings.

Placing the man's helmet over his dead, staring face, I straightened up and stepped back through the unseen doorway to the entrance hall of the great enclosure. All my curiosity about the strange edifice now returned, and I racked my brain with speculations regarding its material, origin, and purpose. That the hands of men had reared it I could not for a moment believe. Our ships first reached Venus only seventy-two years ago, and the only human beings on the planet have been those at Terra Nova. Nor does human knowledge include any perfectly transparent, non-refractive solid such as the substance of this building. Prehistoric human invasions of Venus can be pretty well ruled out, so that one must turn to the idea of native construction. Did a forgotten race of highly-evolved beings precede the man-lizards as masters of Venus? Despite their elaborately-built cities, it seemed hard to credit the pseudo-reptiles with anything of this kind. There must have been another race aeons ago, of which this is perhaps the last

relique. Or will other ruins of kindred origin be found by
future expeditions? The *purpose* of such a structure passes
all conjecture – but its strange and seemingly non-practical
material suggests a religious use.

Realising my inability to solve these problems, I decided
that all I could do was to explore the invisible structure
itself. That various rooms and corridors extended over the
seemingly unbroken plain of mud I felt convinced ; and I
believed that a knowledge of their plan might lead to something significant. So, feeling my way back through the doorway and edging past the body, I began to advance along
the corridor toward those interior regions whence the dead
man had presumably come. Later on I would investigate
the hallway I had left.

Groping like a blind man despite the misty sunlight, I
moved slowly onward. Soon the corridor turned sharply
and began to spiral in toward the centre in ever-diminishing
curves. Now and then my touch would reveal a doorless
intersecting passage, and I several times encountered junc-
tions with two, three, and four diverging avenues. In these
latter cases I always followed the inmost route, which
seemed to form a continuation of the one I had been traversing. There would be plenty of time to examine the branches
after I had reached and returned from the main regions. I
can scarcely describe the strangeness of the experience –
threading the unseen ways of an invisible structure reared
by forgotten hands on an alien planet!

At last, still stumbling and groping, I felt the corridor end
in a sizeable open space. Fumbling about, I found I was in a
circular chamber about ten feet across ; and from the position of the dead man against certain distant forest landmarks I judged that this chamber lay at or near the centre
of the edifice. Out of it opened five corridors besides the
one through which I had entered, but I kept the latter in
mind by sighting very carefully past the body to a particular
tree on the horizon as I stood just within the entrance.

There was nothing in this room to distinguish it – merely
the floor of thin mud which was everywhere present. Wondering whether this part of the building had any roof, I
repeated my experiment with an upward-flung handful of

mud, and found at once that no covering existed. If there had ever been one, it must have fallen long ago, for not a trace of debris or scattered blocks ever halted my feet. As I reflected, it struck me as distinctly odd that this apparently primordial structure should be so devoid of tumbling masonry, gaps in the walls, and other common attributes of dilapidation.

What was it? What had it ever been? Of what was it made? Why was there no evidence of separate blocks in the glassy, bafflingly homogeneous walls? Why were there no traces of doors, either interior or exterior? I knew only that I was in a round, roofless, doorless edifice of some hard, smooth, perfectly transparent, non-refractive and non-reflective material, a hundred yards in diameter, with many corridors, and with a small circular room at the centre. More than this I could never learn from a direct investigation.

I now observed that the sun was sinking very low in the west – a golden-ruddy disc floating in a pool of scarlet and orange above the mist-clouded trees of the horizon. Plainly, I would have to hurry if I expected to choose a sleeping-spot on dry ground before dark. I had long before decided to camp for the night on the firm, mossy rim of the plateau near the crest whence I had first spied the shining crystal, trusting to my usual luck to save me from an attack by the man-lizards. It has always been my contention that we ought to travel in parties of two or more, so that someone can be on guard during sleeping hours, but the really small number of night attacks makes the Company careless about such things. Those scaly wretches seem to have difficulty in seeing at night, even with curious glow torches.

Having picked out again the hallway through which I had come, I started to return to the structure's entrance. Additional exploration could wait for another day. Groping a course as best I could through the spiral corridor – with only general sense, memory, and a vague recognition of some of the ill-defined weed patches on the plain as guides – I soon found myself once more in close proximity to the corpse. There were now one or two farnoth flies swooping over the helmet-covered face, and I knew that decay was

setting in. With a futile instinctive loathing I raised my hand
to brush away his vanguard of the scavengers – when a
strange and astonishing thing became manifest. An invisible
wall, checking the sweep of my arm, told me that – notwithstanding my careful retracing of the way – I had not
indeed returned to the corridor in which the body lay.
Instead, I was in a parallel hallway, having no doubt taken
some wrong turn or fork among the intricate passages behind.

Hoping to find a doorway to the exit hall ahead, I continued my advance, but presently came to a blank wall. I
would, then, have to return to the central chamber and
steer my course anew. Exactly where I had made my mistake
I could not tell. I glanced at the ground to see if by any
miracle guiding footprints had remained, but at once realised that the thin mud held impressions only for a very
few moments. There was little difficulty in finding my way
to the centre again, and once there I carefully reflected on
the proper outward course. I had kept too far to the right
before. This time I must take a more leftward fork somewhere – just where, I could decide as I went.

As I groped ahead a second time I felt quite confident
of my correctness, and diverged to the left at the junction I
was sure I remembered. The spiralling continued, and I
was careful not to stray into any intersecting passages.
Soon, however, I saw to my disgust that I was passing the
body at a considerable distance; this passage evidently
reached the outer wall at a point much beyond it. In the
hope that another exit might exist in the half of the wall I
had not yet explored, I pressed forward for several paces,
but eventually came once more to a solid barrier. Clearly,
the plan of the building was even more complicated than I
had thought.

I now debated whether to return to the centre again or
whether to try some of the lateral corridors extending toward the body. If I chose this second alternative, I would
run the risk of breaking my mental pattern of where I was;
hence I had better not attempt it unless I could think of
some way of leaving a visible trail behind me. Just how to
leave a trail would be quite a problem, and I ransacked my

mind for a solution. There seemed to be nothing about my person which could leave a mark on anything, nor any material which I could scatter – or minutely subdivide and scatter.

My pen had no effect on the invisible wall, and I could not lay a trail of my precious food tablets. Even had I been willing to spare the latter, there would not have been even nearly enough – besides which the small pellets would have instantly sunk from sight in the thin mud. I searched my pockets for an old-fashioned note-book – often used unofficially on Venus despite the quick rotting-rate of paper in the planet's atmosphere – whose pages I could tear up and scatter, but could find none. It was obviously impossible to tear the tough, thin metal of this revolving decay-proof record scroll, nor did my clothing offer any possibilities. In Venus's peculiar atmosphere I could not safely spare my stout leather suit, and underwear had been eliminated because of the climate.

I tried to smear mud on the smooth, invisible walls after squeezing it as dry as possible, but found that it slipped from sight as quickly as did the height-testing handfuls I had previously thrown. Finally I drew out my knife and attempted to scratch a line on the glassy, phantom surface – something I could recognize with my hand, even though I would not have the advantage of seeing it from afar. It was useless, however, for the blade made not the slightest impression on the baffling, unknown material.

Frustrated in all attempts to blaze a trail, I again sought the round central chamber through memory. It seemed easier to get back to this room than to steer a definite, predetermined course away from it, and I had little difficulty in finding it anew. This time I listed on my record scroll every turn I made – drawing a crude hypothetical diagram of my route, and marking all diverging corridors. It was, of course, maddeningly slow work when everything had to be determined by touch, and the possibilities of error were infinite ; but I believed it would pay in the long run.

The long twilight of Venus was thick when I reached the central room, but I still had hopes of gaining the outside before dark. Comparing my fresh diagram with previous recollections, I believed I had located my original mistake, so once more set out confidently along the invisible hallways. I veered further to the left than during my previous attempts, and tried to keep track of my turnings on the record scroll in case I was still mistaken. In the gathering dusk I could see the dim line of the corpse, now the centre of a loathsome cloud of farnoth-flies. Before long, no doubt, the mud-dwelling sificlighs would be oozing in from the plain to complete the ghastly work. Approaching the body with some reluctance I was preparing to step past it when a sudden collision with a wall told me I was again astray.

I now realized plainly that I was lost. The complications of this building were too much for offhand solution, and I would probably have to do some careful checking before I could hope to emerge. Still, I was eager to get to dry ground before total darkness set in ; hence I returned once more to the centre and began a rather aimless series of trials and errors – making notes by the light of my electric lamp. When I used this device I noticed with interest that it produced no reflection – not even the faintest glistening – in the transparent walls around me. I was, however, prepared for this ; since the sun had at no time formed a gleaming image in the strange material.

I was still groping about when the dusk became total. A heavy mist obscured most of the stars and planets, but the earth was plainly visible as a glowing, bluish-green point in the southeast. It was just past opposition, and would have been a glorious sight in a telescope. I could even make out the moon beside it whenever the vapours momentarily thinned. It was now impossible to see the corpse – my only landmark – so I blundered back to the central chamber after a few false turns. After all, I would have to give up hope of sleeping on dry ground. Nothing could be done till daylight, and I might as well make the best of it here. Lying down in the mud would not be pleasant, but in my leather suit it could be done. On former expeditions I had slept under even worse conditions, and now sheer exhaustion would help to conquer repugnance.

So here I am, squatting in the slime of the central room and making these notes on my record scroll by the light of the electric lamp. There is something almost humorous in my strange, unprecedented plight. Lost in a building without doors – a building which I cannot see! I shall doubtless get out early in the morning, and ought to be back at Terra Nova with the crystal by late afternoon. It certainly is a beauty – with surprising lustre even in the feeble light of this lamp. I have just had it out examining it. Despite my fatigue, sleep is slow in coming, so I find myself writing at great length. I must stop now. Not much danger of being bothered by those cursed natives in this place. The thing I like least is the corpse – but fortunately my oxygen mask saves me from the worst effects. I am using the chlorate cubes very sparingly. Will take a couple of food tablets now and turn in. More later.

Later – Afternoon, VI, 13

There has been more trouble than I expected. I am still in the building, and will have to work quickly and wisely if I expect to rest on dry ground tonight. It took me a long time to get to sleep, and I did not wake till almost noon today. As it was, I would have slept longer but for the glare of the sun through the haze. The corpse was a rather bad sight – wriggling with sificlighs, and with a cloud of farnoth-flies around it. Something had pushed the helmet away from the face, and it was better not to look at it. I was doubly glad of my oxygen mask when I thought of the situation.

At length I shook and brushed myself dry, took a couple of food tablets, and put a new potassium chlorate cube in the electrolyser of the mask. I am using these cubes slowly, but wish I had a larger supply. I felt much better after my sleep, and expected to get out of the building very shortly.

Consulting the notes and sketches I had jotted down, I was impressed by the complexity of the hallways, and by the possibility that I had made a fundamental error. Of the six openings leading out of the central space, I had chosen a certain one as that by which I had entered – using a sighting-arrangement as a guide. When I stood just within the opening, the corpse fifty yards away was exactly in

line with a particular lepidodendron in the far-off forest.
Now it occurred to be that this sighting might not have
been of sufficient accuracy – the distance of the corpse
making its difference of direction in relation to the horizon
compartively slight when viewed from the openings next to
that of my first ingress. Moreover, the tree did not differ as
distinctly as it might from other lepidodendra on the horizon.

Putting the matter to a test, I found to my chagrin that I
could not be sure which of three openings was the right
one. Had I traversed a different set of windings at each
attempted exit? This time I would be sure. It struck me
that despite the impossibility of trail-blazing there was one
marker I could leave. Though I could not spare my suit, I
could – because of my thick head of hair – spare my helmet ; and this was large and light enough to remain visible
above the thin mud. Accordingly I removed the roughly
hemispherical device and laid it at the entrance of one
of the corridors – the right-hand one of the three I must try.

I would follow this corridor on the assumption that it
was correct ; repeating what I seemed to recall as the proper
turns, and constantly consulting and making notes. If I did
not get out, I would systematically exhaust all possible
variations ; and if these failed, I would proceed to cover
the avenues extending from the next opening in the same
way – continuing to the third opening if necessary. Sooner
or later I could not avoid hitting the right path to the exit,
but I must use patience. Even at worst, I could scarcely fail
to reach the open plain in time for a dry night's sleep.

Immediate results were rather discouraging, though they
helped me eliminate the right-hand opening in little more
than an hour. Only a succession of blind alleys, each ending
at a great distance from the corpse, seemed to branch from
this hallway ; and I saw very soon that it had not figured at
all in the previous afternoon's wanderings. As before, however, I always found it relatively easy to grope back to the
central chamber.

About 1 P.M. I shifted my helmet marker to the next opening and began to explore the hallways beyond it. At first I
thought I recognized the turnings, but soon found myself

in a wholly unfamiliar set of corridors. I could not get near
the corpse, and this time seemed cut off from the central
chamber as well, even though I thought I had recorded
every move I made. There seemed to be tricky twists and
crossings too subtle for me to capture in my crude diagrams, and I began to develop a kind of mixed anger and
discouragement. While patience would of course win in
the end, I saw that my searching would have to be minute,
tireless, and long-continued.

Two o'clock found me still wandering vainly through
strange corridors – constantly feeling my way, looking alternately at my helmet and at the corpse, and jotting data
on my scroll with decreasing confidence. I cursed the stupid-
ity and idle curiosity which had drawn me into this tangle
of unseen walls – reflecting that if I had let the thing alone
and headed back as soon as I had taken the crystal from
the body, I would even now be safe at Terra Nova.

Suddenly it occurred to me that I might be able to tunnel under the invisible walls with my kinfe, and thus effect
a short cut to the outside – or to some outward-leading
corridor. I had no means of knowing how deep the building's foundations were, but the omnipresent mud argued
the absence of any floor save the earth. Facing the distant
and increasingly horrible corpse, I began a course of fever-
ish digging with the broad, sharp blade.

There was about six inches of semi-liquid mud, below
which the density of the soil increased sharply. This lower
soil seemed to be of a different colour – a greyish clay
rather like the formation near Venus's north pole. As I
continued downward close to the unseen barrier I saw that
the ground was getting harder and harder. Watery mud
rushed into the excavation as fast as I removed the clay,
but I reached through it and kept on working. If I could
bore any kind of a passage beneath the wall, the mud would
not stop my wriggling out.

About three feet down, however, the hardness of the soil
halted my digging seriously. Its tenacity was beyond anything I had encountered before, even on this planet, and
was linked with an anomalous heaviness. My knife had to
split and chip the tightly packed clay, and the fragments I

brought up were like solid stones or bits of metal. Finally even this splitting and chipping became impossible, and I had to cease my work with no lower edge of wall in reach.

The hour-long attempt was a wasteful as well as futile one, for it used up great stores of my energy and forced me both to take an extra food tablet, and to put an additional chlorate cube in the oxygen mask. It had also brought a pause in the day's gropings, for I am still much too exhausted to walk. After cleaning my hands and arms of the worst of the mud I sat down to write these notes – leaning against an invisible wall and facing away from the corpse.

That body is simply a writhing mass of vermin now – the odour has begun to draw some of the slimy akmans from the far-off jungle. I notice that many of the efjeh-weeds on the plain are reaching out necrophagous feelers toward the thing ; but I doubt if any are long enough to reach it. I wish some really carnivorous organisms like the skorahs would appear, for then they might scent me and wriggle a course through the building toward me. Things like that have an odd sense of direction. I could watch them as they came, and jot down their approximate route if they failed to form a continuous line. Even that would be a great help. When I met any the pistol would make short work of them.

But I can hardly hope for as much as that. Now that these notes are made I shall rest a while longer, and later will do some more groping. As soon as I get back to the central chamber – which ought to be fairly easy – I shall try the extreme left-hand opening. Perhaps I can get outside by dusk after all.

Night – VI, 13

New trouble. My escape will be tremendously difficult, for there are elements I had not suspected. Another night here in the mud, and a fight on my hands tomorrow. I cut my rest short and was up and groping again by four o'clock. After about fifteen minutes I reached the central chamber and moved my helmet to mark the last of the three possible doorways. Starting through this opening, I seemed to find the going more familiar, but was brought up short in less than five minutes by a sight that jolted me more than I can describe.

It was a group of four or five of those detestable man-lizards emerging from the forest far off across the plain. I could not see them distinctly at that distance, but thought they paused and turned toward the trees to gesticulae, after which they were joined by fully a dozen more. The augmented party now began to advance directly toward the invisible building, and as they approached I studied them carefully. I had never before had a close view of the things outside the streamy shadows of the jungle.

The resemblance to reptiles was perceptible, though I knew it was only an apparent one, since these beings have no point of contact with terrestrial life. When they drew nearer they seemed less truly reptilian – only the flat head and the green, slimy, frog-like skin carrying out the idea. They walked erect on their odd, thick stumps, and their suction-discs made curious noises in the mud. These were average specimens, about seven feet in height, and with four long, ropy pectoral tentacles. The motions of those tentacles – if the theories of Fogg, Ekberg, and Janat are right, which I formerly doubted but am now more ready to believe – indicated that the things were in animated conversation.

I drew my flame pistol and was ready for a hard fight. The odds were bad. but the weapon gave me a certain advantage. If the things knew this building they would come through it after me, and in this way would form a key to getting out ; just as carnivorous skorahs might have done. That they would attack me seemed certain ; for even though they could not see the crystal in my pouch, they could divine its presence through that special sense of theirs.

Yet, surprisingly enough, they did not attack me. Instead they scattered and formed a vast circle around me – at a distance which indicated that they were pressing close to the unseen wall. Standing there in a ring, the beings stared silently and inquisitively at me, waving their tentacles and sometimes nodding their heads and gesturing with their upper limbs. After a while I saw others issue from the forest, and these advanced and joined the curious crowd. Those near the corpse looked briefly at it but made no move to disturb it. It was a horrible sight, yet the man-lizards seemed quite unconcerned. Now and then one of them would brush away the farnoth-flies with its limbs or tentacles, or crush a wriggling sificligh or akman, or an outreaching efjeh-weed, with the suction discs on its stumps.

Staring back at these grotesque and unexpected intruders, and wondering uneasily why they did not attack me at once, I lost for the time being the will-power and nervous energy to continue my search for a way out. Instead I leaned limply against the invisible wall of the passage where I stood, letting my wonder merge gradually into a chain of the wildest speculations. A hundred mysteries which had previously baffled me seemed all at once to take on a new and sinister significance, and I trembled with an acute fear unlike anything I had experienced before.

I believed I knew why these repulsive beings were hovering expectantly around me. I believed, too, that I had the secret of the transparent structure at last. The alluring crystal which I had seized, the body of the man who had seized it before me – all these things began to acquire a dark and threatening meaning.

It was no common series of mischances which had made me lose my way in this roofless, unseen tangle of corridors. Far from it. Beyond doubt, the place was a genuine maze – a labyrinth deliberately built by these hellish beings whose craft and mentality I had so badly underestimated. Might I not have suspected this before, knowing of their uncanny architectural skill? The purpose was all too plain. It was a trap – a trap set to catch human beings, and with the crystal spheroid as bait. These reptilian things, in their war on the takers of crystals, had turned to strategy and were using our own cupidity against us.

Dwight – if this rotting corpse were indeed he – was a victim. He must have been trapped some time ago, and had failed to find his way out. Lack of water had doubtless maddened him, and perhaps he had run out of chlorate cubes as well. Probably his mask had not slipped accidentally after all. Suicide was a likelier thing. Rather than face a lingering death he had solved the issue by removing the mask deliberately and letting the lethal atmosphere do its work at once. The horrible irony of his fate lay in his position – only a few feet from the saving exit he had failed to find. One minute more of searching and he would have been safe.

And now I was trapped as he had been. Trapped, and with this circling herd of curious starers to mock at my predicament. The thought was maddening, and as it sank in I was seized with a sudden flash of panic which set me running aimlessly through the unseen hallways. For several moments I was essentially a maniac – stumbling, tripping, bruising myself on the invisible walls, and finally collapsing in the mud as a panting, lacerated heap of mindless, bleeding flesh.

The fall sobered me a bit, so that when I slowly struggled to my feet I could notice things and exercise my reason. The circling watchers were swaying their tentacles in an odd, irregular way suggestive of sly, alien laughter, and I shook my fist savagely at them as I rose. My gesture seemed to increase their hideous mirth – a few of them clumsily imitating it with their greenish upper limbs. Shamed into sense, I tried to collect my faculties and take stock of the situation.

After all, I was not as badly off as Dwight has been. Unlike him, I knew what the situation was – and forewarned is forearmed. I had proof that the exit was attainable in the end, and would not repeat his tragic art of impatient despair. The body – or skeleton, as it would soon be – was constantly before me as a guide to the sought-for aperture, and dogged patience would certainly take me to it if I worked long and intelligently enough.

I had, however, the disadvantage of being surrounded by these reptilian devils. Now that I realised the nature of the trap – whose invisible material argued a science and technology beyond anything on earth – I could no longer discount the mentality and resources of my enemies. Even with my flame-pistol I would have a bad time getting away – though boldness and quickness would doubtless see me through in the long run.

But first I must reach the exterior – unless I could lure or provoke some of the creatures to advance toward me.

As I prepared my pistol for action and counted over my generous supply of ammunition it occurred to me to try the effect of its blasts on the visible walls. Had I overlooked a feasible means of escape? There was no clue to the chemical composition of the transparent barrier, and conceivably it might be something which a tongue of fire could cut like cheese. Choosing a section facing the corpse, I carefully discharged the pistol at close range and felt with my knife where the blast had been aimed. Nothing was changed. I had seen the flame spread when it struck the surface, and now I realised that my hope had been vain. Only a long, tedious search for the exit would ever bring me to the outside.

So, swallowing another food tablet and putting another cube in the electrolyser of my mask, I recommenced the long quest; retracing my steps to the central chamber and starting out anew. I constantly consulted my notes and sketches, and made fresh ones – taking one false turn after another, but staggering on in desperation till the afternoon light grew very dim. As I persisted in my quest I looked from time to time at the silent circle of mocking stares, and noticed a gradual replacement in their ranks. Every now and then a few would return to the forest, while others would arrive to take their places. The more I thought of their tactics the less I liked them, for they gave me a hint of the creatures' possible motives. At any time these devils could have advanced and fought me, but they seemed to prefer watching my struggles to escape. I could not but infer that they enjoyed the spectacle – and this made me shrink with double force from the prospect of falling into their hands.

With the dark I ceased my searching, and sat down in the mud to rest. Now I am writing in the light of my lamp, and will soon try to get some sleep. I hope tomorrow will see me out; for my canteen is low, and lacol tablets are a poor substitute for water. I would hardly dare to try the moisture in this slime, for none of the water in the mud-regions is potable except when distilled. That is why we run such long pipe lines to the yellow clay regions – or depend on rain-water when those devils find and cut our pipes. I have none too many chlorate cubes either, and must try to cut down my oxygen consumption as much as I can. My tunnelling attempt of the early afternoon, and my later panic flight, burned up a perilous amount of air. Tomorrow I will reduce physical exertion to the barest minimum until I meet the reptiles and have to deal with them. I must have a good cube supply for the journey back to Terra Nova. My enemies are still on hand; I can see a circle of their feeble glow-torches around me. There is a horror about those lights which will keep me awake.

Night – VI, 14

Another full day of searching and still no way out! I am beginning to be worried about the water problem, for my canteen went dry at noon. In the afternoon there was a burst of rain, and I went back to the central chamber for the helmet which I had left as a marker – using this as a bowl and getting about two cupfuls of water. I drank most of it, but have put the slight remainder in my canteen. Lacol tablets make little headway against real thirst, and I hope there will be more rain in the night. I am leaving my helmet bottom up to catch any that falls. Food tablets are none too plentiful, but not dangerously low. I shall halve my rations from now on. The chlorate cubes are my real worry, for even without violent exercise the day's endless tramping burned a dangerous number. I feel weak from my forced economies in oxygen, and from my constantly mounting thirst. When I reduce my food I suppose I shall feel still weaker.

There is something damnable – something uncanny – about this labyrinth. I could swear that I had eliminated certain turns through charting, and yet each new trial belies some assumption I had thought established. Never before did I realise how lost we are without visual landmarks. A blind man might do better – but for most of us *sight* is the king of the senses. The effect of all these fruitless wanderings is one of profound discouragement. I can understand how poor Dwight must have felt. His corpse is now just a skeleton, and the sificlighs and akmans and farnoth-flies are gone. The efjen-weeds are nipping the leather clothing to pieces, for they were longer and faster-growing than I had expected. And all the while those relays of tentacled starers stand gloatingly around the barrier laughing at me and enjoying my misery. Another day and I shall go mad if I do not drop dead from exhaustion.

However, there is nothing to do but persevere. Dwight would have got out if he had kept on a minute longer. It is just possible that somebody from Terra Nova will come looking for me before long, although this is only my third day out. My muscles ache horribly, and I can't seem to rest at all lying down on this loathsome mud. Last night, despite my terrific fatigue, I slept only fitfully, and tonight I fear will be no better. I live in an endless nightmare – poised between waking and sleeping, yet neither truly awake nor truly asleep. My hand shakes, I can write no more for the time being. That circle of feeble glow-torches is hideous.

Late Afternoon – VI, 15

Substantial progress! Looks good. Very weak, and did not sleep much till daylight. Then I dozed till noon, though without being at all rested. No rain, and thirst leaves me very weak. Ate an extra food tablet to keep me going, but without water it didn't help much. I dared to try a little of the slime water just once, but it made me violently sick and left me even thirstier than before. Must save chlorate cubes, so am nearly suffocating for lack of oxygen. Can't walk much of the time, but manage to crawl in the mud. About 2 P.M. I thought I recognised some passages, and got substantially nearer the corpse – or skeleton – than I had been since the first day's trials. I was sidetracked once in a blind alley, but recovered the main trail with the aid of my chart and notes. The trouble with these jottings is that there are so many of them. They must cover three feet of the record scroll, and I have to stop for long periods to untangle them. My head is weak from thirst, suffocation, and exhaustion, and I cannot understand all I have set down. Those damnable green things keep staring and laughing with their tentacles, and sometimes they gesticulate in a way that makes

me think they share some terrible joke just beyond my
perception.

It was three o'clock when I really struck my stride. There
was a doorway which, according to my notes, I had not
traversed before; and when I tried it I found I could crawl
circuitously toward the weed-twined skeleton. The route
was a sort of spiral, much like that by which I had first
reached the central chamber. Whenever I came to a lateral
doorway or junction I would keep to the course which
seemed best to repeat that original journey. As I circled
nearer and nearer to my gruesome landmark, the watchers
outside intensified their cryptic gesticulations and sardonic
silent laughter. Evidently they saw something grimly amusing in my progress – perceiving no doubt how helpless I
would be in any encounter with them. I was content to leave
them to their mirth; for although I realised my extreme
weakness, I counted on the flame pistol and its numerous
extra magazines to get me through the vile reptilian phalanx.

Hope now soared high, but I did not attempt to rise to
my feet. Better crawl now, and save my strength for the
coming encounter with the man-lizards. My advance was
very slow, and the danger of straying into some blind alley
very great, but none the less I seemed to curve steadily
toward my osseous goal. The prospect gave me new
strength, and for the nonce I ceased to worry about my
pain, my thirst, and my scant supply of cubes. The creatures
were now all massing around the entrance – gesturing, leaping, and laughing with their tentacles. Soon, I reflected, I
would have to face the entire horde – and perhaps such
reinforcements as they would receive from the forest.

I am now only a few yards from the skeleton, and am
pausing to make this entry before emerging and breaking
through the noxious band of entities. I feel confident that
with my last ounce of strength I can put them to flight
despite their numbers, for the range of this pistol is tremendous. Then a camp on the dry moss at the plateau's
edge, and in the morning a weary trip through the jungle to
Terra Nova. I shall be glad to see living men and the buildings of human beings again. The teeth of that skull gleam
and grin horribly.

Toward Night – VI, 15

Horror and despair. Baffled again! After making the previous entry I approached still closer to the skeleton, but
suddenly encountered an intervening wall. I had been de-
ceived once more, and was apparently back where I had
been three days before, on my first futile attempt to leave
the labyrinth. Whether I screamed I do not know – perhaps
I was too weak to utter a sound. I merely lay dazed in the
mud for a long period, while the greenish things outside
leaped and laughed and gestured.

After a time I became more fully conscious. My thirst
and weakness and suffocation were fast gaining on me, and
with my last bit of strength I put a new cube in the electrolyser – recklessly, and without regard for the needs of my
journey to Terra Nova. The fresh oxygen revived me
slightly, and enabled me to look about more alertly.

It seemed as if I were slightly more distant from poor
Dwight than I had been at the first disappointment, and
I dully wondered if I could be in some other corridor a
trifle more remote. With this faint shadow of hope I labor-
iously dragged myself forward – but after a few feet encountered a dead end as I had on the former occasion.

This, then, was the end. Three days had taken me nowhere, and my strength was gone. I would soon go mad
from thirst, and I could no longer count on cubes enough to
get me back. I feebly wondered why the nightmare things
had gathered so thickly around the entrance as they mocked
me. Probably this was part of the mockery – to make me
think I was approaching an egress which they knew did
not exist.

I shall not last long, though I am resolved not to hasten
matters as Dwight did. His grinning skull has just turned
toward me, shifted by the groping of one of the efjeh-weeds
that are devouring his leather suit. The ghoulish stare of
those empty eye-sockets is worse than the staring of those
lizard horrors. It lends a hideous meaning to that dead,
white-toothed grin.

I shall lie very still in the mud and save all the strength I
can. This record – which I hope may reach and warn those
who come after me – will soon be done. After I stop writ-

ing I shall rest a long while. Then, when it is too dark for those frightful creatures to see, I shall muster up my last reserves of strength and try to toss the record scroll over the wall and the intervening corridor to the plain outside. I shall take care to send it toward the left, where it will not hit the leaping band of mocking beleaguers. Perhaps it will be lost forever in the thin mud – but perhaps it will land in some widespread clump of weeds and ultimately reach the hands of men.

If it does survive to be read, I hope it may do more than merely warn men of this trap. I hope it may teach our race to let those shining crystals stay where they are. They belong to Venus alone. Our planet does not truly need them, and I believe we have violated some obscure and mysterious law – some law buried deep in the arcana of the cosmos – in our attempts to take them. Who can tell what dark, potent, and widespread forces spur on these reptilian things who guard their treasure so strangely? Dwight and I have paid, as others have paid and will pay. But it may be that these scattered deaths are only the prelude of greater horrors to come. Let us leave to Venus that which belongs only to Venus.

*

I am very near death now, and fear I may not be able to throw the scroll when dusk comes. If I cannot, I suppose the man-lizards will seize it, for they will probably realise what it is. They will not wish anyone to be warned of the labyrinth – and they will not know that my message holds a plea in their own behalf. As the end approaches I feel more kindly toward the things. In the scale of cosmic entity who can say which species stands higher, or more nearly approaches a space-wide organic norm – theirs or mine?

*

I have just taken the great crystal out of my pouch to look at in my last moments. It shines fiercely and menacingly in the red rays of the dying day. The leaping horde have noticed it, and their gestures have changed in a way I cannot understand. I wonder why they keep clustered around the entrance instead of concentrating at a still closer point in the transparent wall.

❋

I am growing numb and cannot write much more. Things whirl around me, yet I do not lose consciousness. Can I throw this over the wall? That crystal glows so, yet the twilight is deepening.

❋

Dark. Very weak. They are still laughing and leaping around the doorway, and have started those hellish glow-torches.

❋

Are they going away? I dreamed I heard a sound ... light in the sky....

REPORT OF WESLEY P. MILLER, SUPT, GROUP A, VENUS CRYSTAL CO.

(TERRA NOVA ON VENUS – VI, 16)

Our Operative A-49, Kenton J. Stanfield of 5317 Marshall Street, Richmond, Va., left Terra Nova early on VI, 12, for a short-term trip indicated by detector. Due back 13th or 14th. Did not appear by evening of 15th, so Scouting Plane FR-58 with five men under my command set out at 8 P.M. to follow route with detector. Needle showed no change from earlier readings.

Followed needle to Erycinian Highland, played strong searchlights all the way. Triple-range flame-guns and D-radiation-cylinders could have dispersed any ordinary hostile force of natives, or any dangerous aggregation of carnivorous skorahs.

When over the open plain on Eryx we saw a group of moving lights which we knew were native glow-torches. As we approached, they scattered into the forest. Probably seventy-five to a hundred in all. Detector indicated crystal on spot where they had been. Sailing low over this spot, our lights picked out objects on the ground. Skeleton tangled in efjeh-weeds, and complete body ten feet from it. Brought plane down near bodies, and corner of wing crashed on unseen obstruction.

Approaching bodies on foot, we came up short against a smooth, invisible barrier which puzzled us enormously. feeling along it near the skeleton, we struck an opening, beyond which was a space with another opening leading to the skeleton. The latter, though robbed of clothing by weeds, had one of the company's numbered metal helmets beside it. It was Operative B-9, Frederick N. Dwight of Keonig's division, who had been out of Terra Nova for two months on a long commission.

Between this skeleton and the complete body there seemed to be another wall, but we could easily identify the second man as Stanfield. He had a record scroll in his left hand and a pen in his right, and seemed to have been writing when he died. No crystal was visible, but the detector indicated a huge specimen near Stanfield's body.

We had great difficulty in getting at Stanfield, but finally succeeded. The body was still warm, and a great crystal lay beside it, covered by the shallow mud. We at once studied the record scroll in the left hand, and prepared to take certain steps based on its data. The contents of the scroll forms the long narrative prefixed to this report; a narrative whose main descriptions we have verified, and which we append as an explanation of what was found. The later parts of this account show mental decay, but there is no reason to doubt the bulk of it. Stanfield obviously died of a combination of thirst, suffocation, cardiac strain, and psychological depression. His mask was in place, and freely generating oxygen despite an alarmingly low cube supply.

Our plane being damaged, we sent a wireless and called out Anderson with Repair Plane FG.7, a crew of wreckers, and a set of blasting materials. By morning FH-58 was fixed, and went back under Anderson carrying the two bodies and the crystal. We shall bury Dwight and Stanfield in the company graveyard, and ship the crystal to Chicago

on the next earth-bound liner. Later, we shall adopt Stanfield's suggestion – the sound one in the saner, earlier part
of his report – and bring across enough troops to wipe out
the natives altogether. With a clear field, there can be scarcely any limit to the amount of crystal we can secure.

In the afternoon we studied the invisible building or trap
with great care, exploring it with the aid of long guiding
cords, and preparing a complete chart for our archives. We
were much impressed by the design, and shall keep specimens of the substance for chemical analysis. All such knowledge will be useful when we take over the various cities of
the natives. Our type C diamond drills were able to bite
into the unseen material, and wreckers are now planting
dynamite preparatory to a thorough blasting. Nothing will
be left when we are done. The edifice forms a distinct menace to aerial and other possible traffic.

In considering the plan of the labyrinth one is impressed
not only with the irony of Dwight's fate, but with that of
Stanfield's as well. When trying to reach the second body
from the skeleton, we could find no access on the right, but
Markheim found a doorway from the first inner space some
fifteen feet past Dwight and four or five past Stanfield. Beyond this was a long hall which we did not explore till
later, but on the right-hand side of that hall was another
doorway leading directly to the body. Stanfield could have
reached the outside entrance by walking twenty-two or
twenty-three feet if he had found the opening which lay
directly *behind* him – an opening which he overlooked in
his exhaustion and despair.

The Evil Clergyman

I was shown into the attic chamber by a grave, intelligent-looking man with quiet clothes and an iron-gray beard, who spoke to me in this fashion:

'Yes, *he* lived here – but I don't advise your doing anything. Your curiosity makes you irresponsible. *We* never come here at night, and it's only because of *his* will that we keep it this way. You know what *he* did. That abominable society took charge at last, and we don't know where *he* is buried. There was no way the law or anything else could reach the society.

'I hope you won't stay till after dark. And I beg of you to let that thing on the table – the thing that looks like a match-box – alone. We don't know what it is, but we suspect it has something to do with what *he* did. We even avoid looking at it very steadily.'

After a time the man left me alone in the attic room. It was very dingy and dusty, and only primitively furnished, but it had a neatness which showed it was not a slum-denizen's quarters. There were shelves full of theological and classical books, and another bookcase containing treatises on magic – Paracelsus, Albertus Magnus, Trithemius, Hermes Trismegistus, Borellus, and others in strange alphabet whose titles I could not decipher. The furniture was very plain. There was a door, but it led only into a closet. The only egress was the aperture in the floor up to which the crude, steep staircase led. The windows were of bull's-eye pattern, and the black oak beams bespoke unbelievable antiquity. Plainly, this house was of the Old World. I seemed to know where I was, but cannot recall what I then knew. Certainly the town was *not* London. My impression is of a small seaport.

The small object on the table fascinated me intensely. I seemed to know what to do with it, for I drew a pocket electric light – or what looked like one – out of my pocket and nervously tested its flashes. The light was not white but violet, and seemed less like true light than like some radioactive bombardment. I recall that I did not regard it as a common flashlight – indeed, I *had* a common flashlight in another pocket.

It was getting dark, and the ancient roofs and chimney-pots outside looked very queer through the bull's-eye window-panes. Finally I summoned up courage and propped the small object up on the table against a book – then turned the rays of the peculiar violet light upon it. The light seemed now to be more like a rain of hail or small violet particles than like a continuous beam. As the particles struck the glassy surface at the center of the strange device, they seemed to produce a crackling noise like the sputtering of a vacuum tube through which sparks are passed. The dark glassy surface displayed a pinkish glow, and a vague white shape seemed to be taking form at its center. Then I noticed that I was not alone in the room – and put the ray-projector back in my pocket.

But the newcomer did not speak – nor did I hear any sound whatever during all the immediately following moments. Everything was shadowy pantomime, as if seen at a vast distance through some intervening haze – although on the other hand the newcomer and all subsequent comers loomed large and close, as if both near and distant, according to some abnormal geometry.

The newcomer was a thin, dark man of medium height attired in the clerical garb of the Anglican church. He was apparently about thirty years old, with a sallow, olive complexion and fairly good features, but an abnormally high forehead. His black hair was well cut and neatly brushed, and he was clean-shaven though blue-chinned with a heavy growth of beard. He wore rimless spectacles with steel bows. His build and lower facial features were like other clergymen I had seen, but he had a vastly higher forehead, and was darker and more intelligent-looking – also more subtly and concealedly *evil*-looking. At the present moment – having just lighted a faint oil lamp – he looked nervous, and before I knew it he was casting all his magical books into a fireplace on the window side of the room (where the wall slanted sharply) which I had not noticed before. The flames devoured the volumes greedily – leaping up in

strange colors and emitting indescribably hideous odors as
the strangely hieroglyphed leaves and wormy bindings succumbed to the devastating element. All at once I saw there
were others in the room – grave-looking men in clerical
costume, one of whom wore the bands and knee-breeches
of a bishop. Though I could hear nothing, I could see that
they were bringing a decision of vast import to the first-
comer. They seemed to hate and fear him at the same time,
and he seemed to return these sentiments. His face set itself into a grim expression, but I could see his right hand
shaking as he tried to grip the back of a chair. The bishop
pointed to the empty case and to the fireplace (where the
flames had died down amidst a charred, non-committal
mass), and seemed filled with a peculiar loathing. The first-
comer then gave a wry smile and reached out with his left
hand toward the small object on the table. Everyone then
seemed frightened. The procession of clerics began filing
down the steep stairs through the trap-door in the floor,
turning and making menacing gestures as they left. The
bishop was last to go.

The first-comer now went to a cupboard on the inner side
of the room and extracted a coil of rope. Mounting a chair,
he attached one end of the rope to a hook in the great exposed central beam of black oak, and began making a noose
with the other end. Realizing he was about to hang himself,
I started forward to dissuade or save him. He saw me and
ceased his preparations, looking at me with a kind of
triumph which puzzled and disturbed me. He slowly stepped
down from the chair and began gliding toward me with a
positively wolfish grin on his dark, thin-lipped face.

I felt somehow in deadly peril, and drew out the peculiar
ray-projector as a weapon of defense. Why I thought it
could help me, I do not know. I turned it on – full in his
face, and saw the sallow features glow first with violet and
then with pinkish light. His expression of wolfish exultation
began to be crowded aside by a look of profound fear –
which did not, however, wholly displace the exultation. He
stopped in his tracks – then, flailing his arms wildly in the
air, began to stagger backwards. I saw he was edging toward
the open stair-well in the floor, and tried to shout a warning,

but he did not hear me. In another instant he had lurched
backward through the opening and was lost to view.

I found difficulty in moving toward the stair-well, but
when I did get there I found no crushed body on the floor
below. Instead there was a clatter of people coming up
with lanterns, for the spell of phantasmal silence had
broken, and I once more heard sounds and saw figures as
normally tri-dimensional. Something had evidently drawn a
crowd to this place. Had there been a noise I had not heard?

Presently the two people (simple villagers, apparently)
farthest in the lead saw me – and stood paralyzed. One of
them shrieked loudly and reverberantly:

'Ahrrh! ... It be'ee, zur? Again?'

Then they all turned and fled frantically. All, that is, but
one. When the crowd was gone I saw the grave-bearded
man who had brought me to this place – standing alone
with a lantern. He was gazing at me gaspingly and fascin-
atedly, but did not seem afraid. Then he began to ascend
the stairs, and joined me in the attic. He spoke:

So you *didn't* let it alone! I'm sorry. I know what has
happened. It happened once before, but the man got frightened and shot himself. You ought not to have made *him*
come back. You know what *he* wants. But you mustn't get
frightened like the other man he got. Something very
strange and terrible has happened to you, but it didn't get
far enough to hurt your mind and personality. If you'll
keep cool, and accept the need for making certain radical
readjustments in your life, you can keep right on enjoying
the world, and the fruits of your scholarship. But you can't
live here – and I don't think you'll wish to go back to London. I'd advise America.

'You mustn't try anything more with that – thing. Nothing can be put back now. It would only make matters worse
to do – or summon – anything. You are not as badly off a
you might be – but you must get out of here at once and
stay away. You'd better thank Heaven it didn't go
further....'

'I'm going to prepare you as bluntly as I can. There's
been a certain change – in your personal appearance. *He*
always causes that. But in a new country you can get used

to it. There's a mirror up at the other end of the room, and I'm going to take you to it. You'll get a shock – though you will see nothing repulsive.'

I was now shaking with a deadly fear, and the bearded man almost had to hold me up as he walked me across the room to the mirror, the faint lamp (i.e., that formerly on the table, not the still fainter lantern he had brought) in his free hand. This is what I saw in the glass:

A thin, dark man of medium stature attired in the clerical garb of the Anglican church, apparently about thirty, and with rimless, steel-bowed glasses glistening beneath a sallow, olive forehead of abnormal height.

It was the silent first-comer who had burned his books.

For all the rest of my life, in outward form, I was to be that man!

Early Tales

*Apart from some inconsequential juvenilia written begin-
ning when he was six years old, H. P. Lovecraft preserved
only a few of what he called his early tales – that is, stories
written in his teens and twenties, having destroyed most of
them. These tales are manifestly early stories, uncertain
and imperfect, written after a period during which he had
put down little fiction.*

*The earliest of these narratives dates back to Lovecraft's
fifteenth year, and presumably all but The Transition of
Juan Romero were written when he was between fifteen and
twenty. The Transition of Juan Romero was written when
Lovecraft's interest in fiction, some years dormant, was
once more revived, and only a few years before he began to
write the main body of his fiction.*

*Since these early tales, particularly The Beast in the Cave
and The Alchemist show great promise, it is only to be
speculated about whether that early promise would have
been fulfilled sooner had Lovecraft's fiction then earned
the encouragement it merited. He lost here at least a decade
of his creative life, when, discouraged in his late teens, he
abandoned the writing of fiction almost until the advent of
Weird Tales.*

The Beast in the Cave

The horrible conclusion which had been gradually obtrud-
ing itself upon my confused and reluctant mind was now an
awful certainty. I was lost, completely, hopelessly lost in
the vast and labyrinthine recess of the Mammoth Cave.

Turn as I might, in no direction could my straining vision seize on any object capable of serving as a guidepost to set me on the outward path. That nevermore should I behold the blessed light of day, or scan the pleasant hills and dales of the beautiful world outside, my reason could no longer entertain the slightest unbelief. Hope had departed. Yet, indoctrinated as I was by a life of philosophical study, I derived no small measure of satisfaction from my unimpassioned demeanour ; for although I had frequently read of the wild frenzies into which were thrown the victims of similar situation, I experienced none of these, but stood quiet as soon as I clearly realised the loss of my bearings.

Nor did the thought that I had probably wandered beyond the utmost limits of an ordinary search cause me to abandon my composure even for a moment. If I must die, I reflected, then was this terrible yet majestic cavern as welcome a sepulchre as that which any churchyard might afford, a conception which carried with it more of tranquillity than of despair.

Starving would prove my ultimate fate ; of this I was certain. Some, I knew, had gone mad under circumstances such as these, but I felt that this end would not be mine. My disaster was the result of no fault save my own, since unknown to the guide I had separated myself from the regular party of sightseers ; and, wandering for over an hour in forbidden avenues of the cave, had found myself unable to retrace the devious windings which I had pursued since forsaking my companions.

Already my torch had begun to expire ; soon I would be enveloped by the total and almost palpable blackness of the bowels of the earth. As I stood in the waning, unsteady light, I idly wondered over the exact circumstances of my coming end. I remembered the accounts which I had heard of the colony of consumptives, who, taking their residence in this gigantic grotto to find health from the apparently salubrious air of the underground world, with its steady, uniform temperature, pure air, and peaceful quiet, had found, instead, death in strange and ghastly form. I had seen the sad remains of their ill-made cottages as I passed them by with the party, and had wondered what unnatural influence a long sojourn in this immense and silent cavern would exert upon one as healthy and vigorous as I. Now, I grimly told myself, my opportunity for settling this point had arrived, provided that want of food should not bring me too speedy a departure from this life.

As the last fitful rays of my torch faded into obscurity, I resolved to leave no stone unturned, no possible means of escape neglected ; so, summoning all the powers possessed by my lungs, I set up a series of loud shoutings, in the vain hope of attracting the attention of the guide by my clamour. Yet, as I called, I believed in my heart that my cries were to no purpose, and that my voice, magnified and reflected by the numberless ramparts of the black maze about me, fell upon no ears save my own.

All at once, however, my attention was fixed with a start as I fancied that I heard the sound of soft approaching steps on the rocky floor of the cavern.

Was my deliverance about to be accomplished so soon? Had, then, all my horrible apprehensions been for naught, and was the guide, having marked my unwarranted absence from the party, following my course and seeking me out in this limestone labyrinth? Whilst these joyful queries arose in my brain, I was on the point of renewing my cries, in order that my discovery might come the sooner, when in an instant my delight was turned to horror as I listened ; for my ever acute ear, now sharpened in even greater degree by the complete silence of the cave, bore to my benumbed understanding the unexpected and dreadful knowledge that these footfalls were *not like those of any mortal man*. In the unearthly stillness of this subterranean region, the tread of the booted guide would have sounded like a series of sharp and incisive blows. These impacts were soft, and stealthy, as of the paws of some feline. Besides, when I listened carefully, I seemed to trace the falls of *four* instead of *two* feet.

I was now convinced that I had by my own cries aroused and attracted some wild beast, perhaps a mountain lion which had accidentally strayed within the cave. Perhaps, I considered, the Almighty had chosen for me a swifter and more merciful death than that of hunger ; yet the instinct

of self-preservation, never wholly dormant, was stirred in
my breast, and though escape from the on-coming peril
might but spare me for a sterner and more lingering end, I
determined nevertheless to part with my life at as high a
price as I could command. Strange as it may seem, my mind
conceived of no intent on the part of the visitor save that of
hostility. Accordingly, I became very quiet, in the hope
that the unknown beast would, in the absence of a guiding
sound, lose its direction as had I, and thus pass me by. But
this hope was not destined for realisation, for the strange
footfalls steadily advanced, the animal evidently having obtained my scent, which in an atmosphere so absolutely free
from all distracting influences as is that of the cave, could
doubtless be followed at great distance.

Seeing therefore that I must be armed for defense against
an uncanny and unseen attack in the dark, I groped about
me the largest of the fragments of rock which were strewn
upon all parts of the floor of the cavern in the vicinity, and
grasping one in each hand for immediate use, awaited with
resignation the inevitable result. Meanwhile the hideous
pattering of the paws drew near. Certainly, the conduct of
the creature was exceedingly strange. Most of the time, the
tread seemed to be that of a quadruped, walking with a
singular *lack of unison* betwixt hind and fore feet, yet at
brief and infrequent intervals I fancied that but two feet
were engaged in the process of locomotion. I wondered
what species of animal was to confront me; it must, I
thought, be some unfortunate beast who had paid for its
curiosity to investigate one of the entrances of the fearful
grotto with a life-long confinement in its interminable recesses. It doubtless obtained as food the eyeless fish, bats
and rats of the cave, as well as some of the ordinary fish
that are wafted in at every freshet of Green River, which
communicates in some occult manner with the waters of
the cave. I occupied my terrible vigil with grotesque conjectures of what alteration cave life might have wrought
in the physical structure of the beast, remembering the
awful appearances ascribed by local tradition to the consumptives who had died after long residence in the cave.
Then I remembered with a start that, even should I suc-

ceed in felling my antagonist, I should *never behold its form*, as my torch had long since been extinct, and I was entirely unprovided with matches. The tension on my brain now became frightful. My disordered fancy conjured up hideous and fearsome shapes from the sinister darkness that surrounded me, and that actually seemed to *press* upon my body. Nearer, nearer, the dreadful footfalls approached. It seemed that I must give vent to a piercing scream, yet had I been sufficiently irresolute to attempt such a thing, my voice could scarce have responded. I was petrified, rooted to the spot. I doubted if my right arm would allow me to hurl its missile at the oncoming thing when the crucial moment should arrive. Now the steady *pat, pat*, of the steps was close at hand; now *very* close. I could hear the laboured breathing of the animal, and terror-struck as I was, I realised that it must have come from a considerable distance, and was correspondingly fatigued. Suddenly the spell broke. My right hand, guided by my ever trustworthy sense of hearing, threw with full force the sharp-angled bit of limestone which it contained, toward that point in the darkness from which emanated the breathing and pattering, and, wonderful to relate, it nearly reached its goal, for I heard the thing jump landing at a distance away, where it seemed to pause.

Having readjusted my aim, I discharged my second missile, this time most effectively, for with a flood of joy I listened as the creature fell in what sounded like a complete collapse, and evidently remained prone and unmoving. Almost overpowered by the great relief which rushed over me, I reeled back against the wall. The breathing continued, in heavy, gasping inhalations and expirations, whence I realised that I had no more than wounded the creature. And now all desire to examine the *thing* ceased. At last something allied to groundless, superstitious fear had entered my brain, and I did not approach the body, nor did I continue to cast stones at it in order to complete the extinction of its life. Instead, I ran at full speed in what was, as nearly as I could estimate in my frenzied condition, the direction from which I had come. Suddenly I heard a sound, or rather, a regular succession of sounds. In another instant they had resolved themselves into a series of sharp, metallic clicks. This time there was no doubt. *It was the guide.* And then I shouted, yelled, screamed, even shrieked with joy as I beheld in the vaulted arches above the faint and glimmering effulgence which I knew to be the reflected light of an approaching torch. I ran to meet the flare, and before I could completely understand what had occurred, was lying upon the ground at the feet of the guide, embracing his boots and gibbering, despite my boasted reserve, in a most meaningless and idiotic manner, pouring out my terrible story, and at the same time overwhelming my auditor with protestations of gratitude. At length, I awoke to something like my normal consciousness. The guide had noted my absence upon the arrival of the party at the entrance of the cave, and had, from his own intuitive sense of direction, proceeded to make a thorough canvass of by-passages just ahead of where he had last spoken to me, locating my whereabouts after a quest of about four hours.

By the time he had related this to me, I, emboldened by his torch and his company, began to reflect upon the strange beast which I had wounded but a short distance back in the darkness, and suggested that we ascertain, by the flashlight's aid, what manner of creature was my victim. Accordingly I retraced my steps, this time with a courage born of companionship, to the scene of my terrible experience. Soon we descried a white object upon the floor, an object whiter even than the gleaming limestone itself. Cautiously advancing, we gave vent to a simultaneous ejaculation of wonderment, for of all the unnatural monsters either of us had in our lifetimes beheld, this was in surpassing degree the strangest. It appeared to be an anthropoid ape of large proportions, escaped, perhaps, from some itinerant menagerie. Its hair was snow-white, a thing due no doubt to the bleaching action of a long existence within the inky confines of the cave, but it was also surprisingly thin, being indeed largely absent save on the head, where it was of such length and abundance that it fell over the shoulders in considerable profusion. The face was turned away from us, as the creature lay almost directly upon it. The inclination of the limbs was very singular, ex-

plaining, however, the alternation in their use which I had
before noted, whereby the beast used sometimes all four,
and on other occasions but two for its progress. From the
tips of the fingers or toes, long rat-like claws extended. The
hands or feet were not prehensile, a fact that I ascribed to
that long residence in the cave which, as I before mentioned, seemed evident from the all-pervading and almost
unearthly whiteness so characteristic of the whole ana-
tomy. No tail seemed to be present.

The respiration had now grown very feeble, and the
guide had drawn his pistol with the evident intent of des-
patching the creature, when a sudden *sound* emitted by the
latter caused the weapon to fall unused. The sound was of a
nature difficult to describe. It was not like the normal note
of any known species of simian, and I wonder if this unnatural quality were not the result of a long continued and
complete silence, broken by the sensations produced by
the advent of the light, a thing which the beast could not
have seen since its first entrance into the cave. The sound,
which I might feebly attempt to classify as a kind of deep-
tone chattering, was faintly continued.

All at once a fleeting spasm of energy seemed to pass
through the frame of the beast. The paws went through a
convulsive motion, and the limbs contracted. With a jerk,
the white body rolled over so that its face was turned in
our direction. For a moment I was so struck with horror
at the eyes thus revealed that I noted nothing else. They
were black, those eyes, deep jetty black, in hideous contrast
to the snow-white hair and flesh. Like those of other cave
denizens, they were deeply sunken in their orbits, and were
entirely destitute of iris. As I looked more closely, I saw
that they were set in a face less prognathous than that of
the average ape, and infinitely less hairy. The nose was
quite distinct. As we gazed upon the uncanny sight presented to our vision, the thick lips opened, and several
sounds issued from them, after which the *thing* relaxed in
death.

The guide clutched my coatsleeve and trembled so
violently that the light shook fitfully, casting weird moving
shadows on the walls.

I made no motion, but stood rigidly still, my horrified eyes fixed upon the floor ahead.

The fear left, and wonder, awe, compassion, and reverence succeeded in its place, for the *sounds* uttered by the stricken figure that lay stretched out on the limestone had told us the awesome truth. The creature I had killed, the strange beast of the unfathomed cave, was, or had at one time been a MAN!!!

April 21, 1905

The Alchemist

High up, crowning the grassy summit of a swelling mount whose sides are wooded near the base with the gnarled trees of the primeval forest stands the old chateau of my ancestors. For centuries its lofty battlements have frowned down upon the wild and rugged countryside about, serving as a home and stronghold for the proud house whose honored line is older even than the moss-grown castle walls. These ancient turrets, stained by the storms of generations and crumbling under the slow yet mighty pressure of time, formed in the ages of feudalism one of the most dreaded and formidable fortresses in all France. From its machicolated parapets and mounted battlements Barons, Counts, and even Kings had been defied, yet never had its spacious halls resounded to the footsteps of the invader.

But since those glorious years, all is changed. A poverty but little above the level of dire want, together with a pride of name that forbids its alleviation by the pursuits of commercial life, have prevented the scions of our line from maintaining their estates in pristine splendour ; and the falling stones of the walls, the overgrown vegetation in the parks, the dry and dusty moat, the ill-paved courtyards,

and toppling towers without, as well as the sagging floors,
the worm-eaten wainscots, and the faded tapestries within,
all tell a gloomy tale of fallen grandeur. As the ages
passed, first one, then another of the four great turrets
were left to ruin, until at last but a single tower housed the
sadly reduced descendants of the once mighty lords of the
estate.

It was in one of the vast and gloomy chambers of this
remaining tower that I, Antoine, last of the unhappy and
accursed Counts de C—, first saw the light of day, ninety
long years ago. Within these walls and amongst the dark
and shadowy forests, the wild ravines and grottos of the
hillside below, were spent the first years of my troubled
life. My parents I never knew. My father had been killed
at the age of thirty-two, a month before I was born, by
the fall of a stone somehow dislodged from one of the deserted parapets of the castle. And my mother having died
at my birth, my care and education devolved solely upon
one remaining servitor, an old and trusted man of considerable intelligence, whose name I remember as Pierre. I
was an only child and the lack of companionship which
this fact entailed upon me was augmented by the strange
care exercised by my aged guardian, in excluding me from
the society of the peasant children whose abodes were scattered here and there upon the plains that surround the base
of the hill. At that time, Pierre said that this restriction was
imposed upon me because my noble birth placed me above
association with such plebeian company. Now I know that
its real object was to keep from my ears the idle tales of
the dread curse upon our line that were nightly told and
magnified by the simple tenantry as they conversed in
hushed accents in the glow of their cottage hearths.

Thus isolated, and thrown upon my own resources, I
spent the hours of my childhood in poring over the ancient
tomes that filled the shadow-haunted library of the chateau,
and in roaming without aim or purpose through the per-
petual dust of the spectral wood that clothes the side of
the hill near its foot. It was perhaps an effect of such surroundings that my mind early acquired a shade of melan-
choly. Those studies and pursuits which partake of the

dark and occult in nature most strongly claimed my attention.

Of my own race I was permitted to learn singularly little, yet what small knowledge of it I was able to gain seemed to depress me much. Perhaps it was at first only the manifest reluctance of my old preceptor to discuss with me my paternal ancestry that gave rise to the terror which I ever felt at the mention of my great house, yet as I grew out of childhood, I was able to piece together disconnected fragments of discourse, let slip from the unwilling tongue which had begun to falter in approaching senility, that had a sort of relation to a certain circumstance which I had always deemed strange, but which now became dimly terrible. The circumstance to which I allude is the early age at which all the Counts of my line had met their end. Whilst I had hitherto considered this but a natural attribute of a family of short-lived men, I afterward pondered long upon these premature deaths, and began to connect them with the wanderings of the old man, who often spoke of a curse which for centuries had prevented the lives of the holders of my title from much exceeding the span of thirty-two years. Upon my twenty-first birthday, the aged Pierre gave to me a family document which he said had for many generations been handed down from father to son, and continued by each possessor. Its contents were of the most startling nature, and its perusal confirmed the gravest of my apprehensions. At this time, my belief in the supernatural was firm and deep-seated, else I should have dismissed with scorn the incredible narrative unfolded before my eyes.

The paper carried me back to the days of the thirteenth century, when the old castle in which I sat had been a feared and impregnable fortress. It told of a certain ancient man who had once dwelled on our estates, a person of no small accomplishments, though little above the rank of peasant, by name, Michel, usually designated by the surname of Mauvais, the Evil, on account of his sinister reputation. He had studied beyond the custom of his kind, seeking such things as the Philosopher's Stone or the Elixir of Eternal Life, and was reputed wise in the terrible secrets of

Black Magic and Alchemy. Michel Mauvais had one son, named Charles, a youth as proficient as himself in the hidden arts, who had therefore been called Le Sorcier, or the Wizard. This pair, shunned by all honest folk, were suspected of the most hideous practices. Old Michel was said to have burnt his wife alive as a sacrifice to the Devil, and the unaccountable disappearance of many small peasant children was laid at the dreaded door of these two. Yet through the dark natures of the father and son ran one redeeming ray of humanity; the evil old man loved his offspring with fierce intensity, whilst the youth had for his parent a more than filial affection.

One night the castle on the hill was thrown into the wildest confusion by the vanishment of young Godfrey, son to Henri, the Count. A searching party, headed by the frantic father, invaded the cottage of the sorcerers and there came upon old Michel Mauvais, busy over a huge and violently boiling cauldron. Without certain cause, in the ungoverned madness of fury and despair, the Count laid hands on the aged wizard, and ere he released his murderous hold, his victim was no more. Meanwhile, joyful servants were proclaiming the finding of young Godfrey in a distant and unused chamber of the great edifice, telling too late that poor Michel had been killed in vain. As the Count and his associates turned away from the lowly abode of the alchemist, the form of Charles Le Sorcier appeared through the trees. The excited chatter of the menials standing about told him what had occurred, yet he seemed at first unmoved at his father's fate. Then, slowly advancing to meet the Count, he pronounced in dull yet terrible accents the curse that ever afterward haunted the house of C—.

'May ne'er a noble of they murd'rous line
Survive to reach a greater age than thine!'

spake he, when, suddenly leaping backwards into the black woods, he drew from his tunic a phial of colourless liquid which he threw into the face of his father's slayer as he disappeared behind the inky curtain of the night. The Count died without utterance, and was buried the next day, but little more than two and thirty years from the hour of his birth. No trace of the assassin could be found, though relentless bands of peasants scoured the neighboring woods and the meadowland around the hill.

Thus time and the want of a reminder dulled the memory of the curse in the minds of the late Count's family, so that when Godfrey, innocent cause of the whole tragedy and now bearing the title, was killed by an arrow whilst hunting at the age of thirty-two, there were no thoughts save those of grief at his demise. But when, years afterward, the next young Count, Robert by name, was found dead in a nearby field of no apparent cause, the peasants told in whispers that their seigneur had but lately passed his thirty-second birthday when surprised by early death. Louis, son to Robert, was found drowned in the moat at the same fateful age, and thus down through the centuries ran the ominous chronicle: Henris, Roberts, Antoines, and Armands snatched from happy and virtuous lives when little below the age of their unfortunate ancestor at his murder.

That I had left at most but eleven years of further existence was made certain to me by the words which I had read. My life, previously held at small value, now became dearer to me each day, as I delved deeper and deeper into the mysteries of the hidden world of black magic. Isolated as I was, modern science had produced no impression upon me, and I laboured as in the Middle Ages, as wrapt as had been old Michel and young Charles themselves in the acquisition of demonological and alchemical learning. Yet read as I might, in no manner could I account for the strange curse upon my line. In unusually rational moments I would even go so far as to seek a natural explanation, attributing the early deaths of my ancestors to the sinister Charles Le Sorcier and his heirs; yet, having found upon careful inquiry that there were no known descendants of the alchemist, I would fall back to occult studies, and once more endeavor to find a spell that would release my house from its terrible burden. Upon one thing I was absolutely resolved. I should never wed, for, since no other branch of my family was in existence, I might thus end the curse with myself.

As I drew near the age of thirty, old Pierre was called

to the land beyond. Alone I buried him beneath the stones
of the courtyard about which he had loved to wander in
life. Thus was I left to ponder on myself as the only human
creature within the great fortress, and in my utter solitude
my mind began to cease its vain protest against the impending doom, to become almost reconciled to the fate
which so many of my ancestors had met. Much of my time
was now occupied in the exploration of the ruined and
abandoned halls and towers of the old chateau, which in
youth fear had caused me to shun, and some of which old
Pierre had once told me had not been trodden by human
foot for over four centuries. Strange and awesome were
many of the objects I encountered. Furniture, covered by
the dust of ages and crumbling with the rot of long dampness, met my eyes. Cobwebs in a profusion never before
seen by me were spun everywhere, and huge bats flapped
their bony and uncanny wings on all sides of the otherwise
untenanted gloom.

Of my exact age, even down to days and hours, I kept a
most careful record, for each movement of the pendulum
of the massive clock in the library told off so much of
my doomed existence. At length I approached that time
which I had so long viewed with apprehension. Since most
of my ancestors had been seized some little while before
they reached the exact age of Count Henri at his end, I was
every moment on the watch for the coming of the unknown
death. In what strange form the curse should overtake me,
I knew not; but I was resolved at least that it should not
find me a cowardly or a passive victim. With new vigour I
applied myself to my examination of the old chateau and
its contents.

It was upon one of the longest of all my excursions of
discovery in the deserted portion of the castle, less than a
week before that fatal hour which I felt must mark the utmost limit of my stay on earth, beyond which I could have
not even the slightest hope of continuing to draw breath,
that I came upon the culminating event of my whole life. I
had spent the better part of the morning in climbing up
and down half ruined staircases in one of the most dilapidated of the ancient turrets. As the afternoon progressed, I

sought the lower levels, descending into what appeared
to be either a mediaeval place of confinement, or a more
recently excavated storehouse for gunpowder. As I slowly
traversed the nitre-encrusted passageway at the foot of
the last staircase, the paving became very damp, and soon
I saw by the light of my flickering torch that a blank, water-
stained wall impeded my journey. Turning to retrace my
steps, my eye fell upon a small trapdoor with a ring, which
lay directly beneath my foot. Pausing, I succeeded with
difficulty in raising it, whereupon there was revealed a black
aperture, exhaling noxious fumes which caused my torch
to sputter, and disclosing in the unsteady glare the top of
a flight of stone steps.

As soon as the torch which I lowered into the repellent
depths burned freely and steadily, I commenced my descent. The steps were many, and led to a narrow stone-
flagged passage which I knew must be far underground.
This passage proved of great length, and terminated in a
massive oaken door, dripping with the moisture of the
place, and stoutly resisting all my attempts to open it. Ceasing after a time my efforts in this direction, I had proceeded
back some distance toward the steps when there suddenly
fell to my experience one of the most profound and maddening shocks capable of reception by the human mind.
Without warning, I heard the heavy door behind me creak
slowly open upon its rusted hinges. My immediate sensations were incapable of analysis. To be confronted in a
place as thoroughly deserted as I had deemed the old castle
with evidence of the presence of man or spirit produced
in my brain a horror of the most acute description. When
at last I turned and faced the seat of the sound, my eyes
must have started from their orbits at the sight that they
beheld.

There in the ancient Gothic doorway stood a human
figure. It was that of a man clad in a skull-cap and long
mediaeval tunic of dark colour. His long hair and flowing
beard were of a terrible and intense black hue, and of incredible profusion. His forehead, high beyond the usual
dimensions ; his cheeks, deep-sunken and heavily lined with
wrinkles ; and his hands, long, claw-like, and gnarled, were

of such a deadly marble-like whiteness as I have never elsewhere seen in man. His figure, lean to the proportions of a skeleton, was strangely bent and almost lost within the voluminous folds of his peculiar garment. But strangest of all were his eyes, twin caves of abysmal blackness, profound in expression of understanding, yet inhuman in degree of wickedness. These were now fixed upon me, piercing my soul with their hatred, and rooting me to the spot whereon I stood.

At last the figure spoke in a rumbling voice that chilled me through with its dull hollowness and latent malevolence. The language in which the discourse was clothed was that debased form of Latin in use amongst the more learned men of the Middle Ages, and made familiar to me by my prolonged researches into the works of the old alchemists and demonologists. The apparition spoke of the curse which had hovered over my house, told me of my coming end, dwelt on the wrong perpetrated by my ancestor against old Michel Mauvais, and gloated over the revenge of Charles Le Sorcier. He told how young Charles has escaped into the night, returning in after years to kill Godfrey the heir with an arrow just as he approached the age which had been his father's at his assassination ; how he had secretly returned to the estate and established himself, unknown, in the even then deserted subterranean chamber whose doorway now framed the hideous narrator, how he had seized Robert, son of Godfrey, in a field, forced poison down his throat, and left him to die at the age of thirty-two, thus maintaing the foul provisions of his vengeful curse. At this point I was left to imagine the solution of the greatest mystery of all, how the curse had been fulfilled since that time when Charles Le Sorcier must in the course of nature have died, for the man digressed into an account of the deep alchemical studies of the two wizards, father and son, speaking most particularly of the researches of Charles Le Sorcier concerning the elixir which should grant to him who partook of it eternal life and youth.

His enthusiasm had seemed for the moment to remove from his terrible eyes the black malevolence that had first

so haunted me, but suddenly the fiendish glare returned
and, with a shocking sound like the hissing of a serpent,
the stranger raised a glass phial with the evident intent of
ending my life as had Charles Le Sorcier, six hundred years
before, ended that of my ancestor. Prompted by some pre-
serving instinct of self-defense, I broke through the spell
that had hitherto held me immovable, and flung my now
dying torch at the creature who menaced my existence. I
heard the phial break harmlessly against the stones of the
passage as the tunic of the strange man caught fire and lit
the horrid scene with a ghastly radiance. The shriek of
fright and impotent malice emitted by the would-be assassin proved too much for my already shaken nerves, and
I fell prone upon the slimy floor in a total faint.

When at last my senses returned, all was frightfully dark,
and my mind, remembering what had occurred, shrank
from the idea of beholding any more ; yet curiosity over-
mastered all. Who, I asked myself, was this man of evil,
and how came he within the castle walls? Why should he
seek to avenge the death of Michel Mauvais, and how had
the curse been carried on through all the long centuries
since the time of Charles Le Sorcier? The dread of years
was lifted from my shoulder, for I knew that he whom I
had felled was the source of all my danger from the curse ;
and now that I was free, I burned with the desire to learn
more of the sinister thing which had haunted my line for
centuries, and made of my own youth one long-continued
nightmare. Determined upon further exploration, I felt in
my pockets for flint and steel, and lit the unused torch
which I had with me.

First of all, new light revealed the distorted and blackened form of the mysterious stranger. The hideous eyes
were now closed. Disliking the sight, I turned away and
entered the chamber beyond the Gothic door. Here I found
what seemed much like an alchemist's laboratory. In one
corner was an immense pile of shining yellow metal that
sparkled gorgeously in the light of the torch. It may have
been gold, but I did not pause to examine it, for I was
strangely affected by that which I had undergone. At the
farther end of the apartment was an opening leading out

into one of the many wild ravines of the dark hillside forest. Filled with wonder, yet now realizing how the man had obtained access to the chauteau, I proceeded to return. I had intended to pass by the remains of the stranger with averted face but, as I approached the body, I seemed to hear emanating from it a faint sound, as though life were not yet wholly extinct. Aghast, I turned to examine the charred and shrivelled figure on the floor.

Then all at once the horrible eyes, blacker even than the seared face in which they were set, opened wide with an expression which I was unable to interpret. The cracked lips tried to frame words which I could not well understand. Once I caught the name of Charles Le Sorcier, and again I fancied that the words 'years' and 'curse' issued from the twisted mouth. Still I was at a loss to gather the purport of his disconnnected speech. At my evident ignorance of his meaning, the pitchy eyes once more flashed malevolently at me, until, helpless as I saw my opponent to be, I trembled as I watched him.

Suddenly the wretch, animated with his last burst of strength, raised his piteous head from the damp and sunken pavement. Then, as I remained, paralyzed with fear, he found his voice and in his dying breath screamed forth those words which have ever afterward haunted my days and nights. 'Fool!' he shrieked, 'Can you not guess my secret? Have you no brain whereby you may recognize the will which has through six long centuries fulfilled the dreadful curse upon the house? Have I not told you of the great elixir of eternal life? Know you not how the secret of Alchemy was solved? I tell you, it is I! I! I! that have lived for six hundred years to maintain my revenge, for I am Charles Le Sorcier!'

Poetry and the Gods

A damp gloomy evening in April it was, just after the close of the Great War, when Marcia found herself alone with strange thoughts and wishes, unheard-of yearnings which floated out of the spacious twentieth-century drawing room, up the deeps of the air, and eastward to olive groves in distant Arcady which she had seen only in her dreams. She had entered the room in abstraction, turned off the glaring chandeliers, and now reclined on a soft divan by a solitary lamp which shed over the reading table a green glow as soothing as moonlight when it issued through the foliage about an antique shrine.

Attired simply, in a low-cut black evening dress, she appeared outwardly a typical product of modern civilization; but tonight she felt the immeasurable gulf that separated her soul from all her prosiac surroundings. Was it because of the strange home in which she lived, that abode of coldness where relations were always strained and the inmates scarcely more than strangers? Was it that, or was it some greater and less explicable misplacement in time and space, whereby she had been born too late, too early, or too far away from the haunts of her spirit ever to harmonize with the unbeautiful things of contemporary reality? To dispel the mood which was engulfing her more and more deeply each moment, she took a magazine from the table and searched for some healing bit of poetry. Poetry had always relieved her troubled mind better than anything else, though many things in the poetry she had seen detracted from the influence. Over parts of even the sublimest verses hung a chill vapor of sterile ugliness and restraint, like dust on a window-pane through which one views a magnificent sunset.

Listlessly turning the magazine's pages, as if searching for an elusive treasure, she suddenly came upon something which dispelled her languor. An observer could have read her thoughts and told that she had discovered some image or dream which brought her nearer to her unattained goal

than any image or dream she had seen before. It was only a
bit of *vers libre*, that pitiful compromise of the poet who
overleaps prose yet falls short of the divine melody of numbers ; but it had in it all the unstudied music of a bard who
lives and feels, who gropes ecstatically for unveiled beauty.
Devoid of regularity, it yet had the harmony of winged,
spontaneous words, a harmony missing from the formal,
convention-bound verse she had known. As she read on,
her surroundings gradually faded, and soon there lay about
her only the mists of dream, the purple, star-strewn mists
beyond time, where only Gods and dreamers walk.

Moon over Japan,
White butterfly moon !
Where the heavy-lidded Buddhas dream
To the sound of the cuckoo's call . . .
The white wings of moon butterflies
Flicker down the the streets of the city,
Blushing into silence the useless wicks of sound-lanterns
    in the hands of girls

Moon over the tropics,
A white-curved bud
Opening its petals slowly in the warmth of heaven . . .

The air is full of odours
And languorous warm sounds . . .
A flute drones its insect music to the night
Below the curving moon-petal of the heavens.

Moon over China,
Weary moon on the river of the sky,
The stir of light in the willows is like the flashing
    of a thousand silver minnows
Through dark shoals ;
The tiles on graves and rotting temples flash like ripples,
The sky is flecked with clouds like the scales of a dragon.

Amid the mists of dream the reader cried to the rhythmical stars, of her delight at the coming of a new age of
song, a rebirth of Pan. Half closing her eyes, she repeated
words whose melody lay hidden like crystals at the bot-

tom of a stream before dawn, hidden but to gleam effulgently at the birth of day.

> Moon over Japan,
> White butterfly moon!

> Moon over the tropics,
> A white curved bud
> Opening its petals slowly in the warmth of heaven.
> The air is full of odours
> And languorous warm sounds . . .

> Moon over China,
> Weary moon on the river of the sky . . .

Out of the mists gleamed godlike the form of a youth, in winged helmet and sandals, caduceus-bearing, and of a beauty like to nothing on earth. Before the face of the sleeper he thrice waved the rod which Apollo had given him in trade for the nine-corded shell of melody, and upon her brow he placed a wreath of myrtle and roses. Then, adoring, Hermes spoke:

'O Nymph more fair than the golden-haired sisters of Cyene or the sky-inhabiting Atlantides, beloved of Aphrodite and blessed of Pallas, thou hast indeed discovered the secret of the Gods, which lieth in beauty and song. O Prophetess more lovely than the Sybil of Cumae when Apollo first knew her, thou has truly spoken of the new age, for even now on Maenalus, Pan sighs and stretches in his sleep, wishful to wake and behold about him the little rose-crowned fauns and the antique Satyrs. In thy yearning hast thou divined what no mortal, saving only a few whom the world rejects, remembereth: *that the Gods were never dead,* but only sleeping the sleep and dreaming the dreams of Gods in lotos-filled Hesperian gardens beyond the golden sunset. And now draweth nigh the time of their awakening, when coldness and ugliness shall perish, and Zeus sit once more on Olympus. Already the sea about Paphos trembleth into a foam which only ancient skies have looked on before, and at night on Helicon the shepherds hear strange murmurings and half-remembered notes. Woods and fields are tremulous at twilight with the shimmering of white saltant forms, and immemorial Ocean yields up curious sights beneath thin moons. The Gods are patient, and have slept long, but neither man nor giant shall defy the Gods forever. In Tartarus the Titans writhe and beneath the fiery Aetna groan the children of Uranus and Gaea. The day now dawns when man must answer for centuries of denial, but in sleeping the Gods have grown kind and will not hurl him to the gulf made for deniers of Gods. Instead will their vengeance smite the darkness, fallacy and ugliness which have turned the mind of man ; and under the sway of bearded Saturnus shall mortals, once more sacrificing unto him, dwell in beauty and delight. This night shalt thou know the favour of the Gods, and behold on Parnassus those dreams which the Gods have through ages sent to earth to show that they are not dead. For poets are the dreams of Gods, and in each and every age someone hath sung unknowingly the message and the promise from the lotos-gardens beyond the sunset.'

Then in his arms Hermes bore the dreaming maiden through the skies. Gentle breezes from the tower of Aiolas wafted them high above warm, scented seas, till suddenly they came upon Zeus, holding court upon double-headed Parnassus, his golden throne flanked by Apollo and the Muses on the right hand, and by ivy-wreathed Dionysus and pleasure-flushed Bacchae on the left hand. So much of splendour Marcia had never seen before, either awake or in dreams, but its radiance did her no injury, as would have the radiance of lofty Olympus ; for in this lesser court the Father of Gods had tempered his glories for the sight of mortals. Before the laurel-draped mouth of the Corycian cave sat in a row six noble forms with the aspect of mortals, but the countenances of Gods. These the dreamer recognized from images of them which she had beheld, and she knew that they were none else than the divine Maeonides, the avernian Dante, the more than mortal Shakespeare, the chaos-exploring Milton, the cosmic Goethe and the musalan Keats. These were those messengers whom the Gods had sent to tell men that Pan had passed not away, but only slept ; for it is in poetry that Gods speak to men. Then spake the Thunderer:

'O Daughter – for, being one of my endless line, thou
art indeed my daughter – behold upon ivory thrones of
honour the august messengers Gods have sent down that
in the words and writing of men there may be still some
traces of divine beauty. Other bards have men justly
crowned with enduring laurels, but these hath Apollo
crowned, and these have I set in places apart, as mortals
who have spoken the language of the Gods. Long have we
dreamed in lotos-gardens beyond the West, and spoken
only through our dreams; but the time approaches when
our voices shall not be silent. It is a time of awakening and
change. Once more hath Phaeton ridden low, searing the
fields and drying the streams. In Gaul lone nymphs with
disordered hair weep beside fountains that are no more,
and pine over rivers turned red with the blood of mortals.
Ares and his train have gone forth with the madness of
Gods and have returned Deimos and Phobos glutted
with unnatural delight. Tellus moons with grief, and the
faces of men are as the faces of Erinyes, even as when As-
traea fled to the skies, and the waves of our bidding en-
compassed all the land saving this high peak alone. Amidst
this chaos, prepared to herald his coming yet to conceal his
arrival, even now toileth our latest born messenger, in
whose dreams are all the images which other messengers
have dreamed before him. He it is that we have chosen to
blend into one glorious whole all the beauty that the world
hath known before, and to write words wherein shall echo
all the wisdom and the loveliness of the past. He it is who
shall proclaim our return and sing of the days to come
when Fauns and Dryads shall haunt their accustomed
groves in beauty. Guided was our choice by those who
now sit before the Corycian grotto on thrones of ivory,
and in whose songs thou shalt hear notes of sublimity by
which years hence thou shalt know the greater messenger
when he cometh. Attend their voices as one by one they
sing to thee here. Each note shall thou hear again in the
poetry which is to come, the poetry which shall bring peace
and pleasure to thy soul, though search for it through bleak
years thou must. Attend with diligence, for each chord that
vibrates away into hiding shall appear again to thee after

thou hast returned to earth, as Alpheus, sinking his waters into the soul of Hellas, appears as the crystal arethusa in remote Sicilia.'

Then arose Homeros, the ancient among bards, who took his lyre and chaunted his hymn to Aphrodite. No word of Greek did Marcia know, yet did the message not fall vainly upon her ears, for in the cryptic rhythm was that which spake to all mortals and Gods, and needed no interpreter.

So too the songs of Dante and Goethe, whose unknown words clave the ether with melodies easy to read and adore. But at last remembered accents resounded before the listener. It was the Swan of Avon, once a God among men, and still a God among Gods:

> Write, write, that from the bloody course of war,
> My dearest master, your dear son, may hie ;
> Bless him at home in peace, whilst I from far,
> His name with zealous fervour sanctify.

Accents still more familiar arose as Milton, blind no more, declaimed immortal harmony:

> Or let thy lamp at midnight hour
> Be seen in some high lonely tower,
> Where I might oft outwatch the Bear
> With thrice-great Hermes, or unsphere
> The spirit of Plato, to unfold
> What worlds or what vast regions hold
> The immortal mind, that hath forsook
> Her mansion in this fleshly nook.

* * * * *

> Sometime let gorgeous tragedy
> In sceptered pall come sweeping by,
> Presenting Thebes. or Pelop's line,
> Or the tale of Troy divine.

Last of all came the young voice of Keats, closest of all the messengers to the beauteous faun-folk:

Heard melodies are sweet, but those unheard
Are sweeter ; therefore, yet sweet pipes, play on . . .

* * * * *

When old age shall this generation waste,
Tho shalt remain, in midst of other woe
Than ours, a friend to man, to whom thou say'st
'Beauty is truth – truth beauty' – that is all
Ye know on earth, and all ye need to know.

As the singer ceased, there came a sound in the wind blowing from far Egypt, where at night Aurora mourns by the Nile for her slain Memnon. To the feet of the Thunderer flew the rosy-fingered Goddess and, kneeling, cried, 'Master, it is time I unlocked the Gates of the East.' And Phoebus, handing his lyre to Calliope, his bride among the Muses, prepared to depart for the jewelled and columnraised Palace of the Sun, where fretted the steeds already harnessed to the golden car of Day. So Zeus descended from his carven throne and placed his hand upon the head of Marcia, saying:

'Daughter, the dawn is nigh, and it is well that thou shouldst return before the awakening of mortals to thy home. Weep not at the bleakness of thy life, for the shadow of false faiths will soon be gone and the Gods shall once more walk among men. Search thou unceasingly for our messenger, for in him wilt thou find peace and comfort. By his word shall thy steps be guided to happiness, and in his dreams of beauty shall thy spirit find that which it craveth.' As Zeus ceased, the young Hermes gently seized the maiden and bore her up toward the fading stars, up and westward over unseen seas.

* * *

Many years have passed since Marcia dreamt of the Gods and of their Parnassus conclave. Tonight she sits in the same spacious drawing-room, but she is not alone. Gone is the old spirit of unrest, for beside her is one whose name is luminous with celebrity: the young poet of poets at whose feet sits all the world. He is reading from a manuscript words which none has ever heard before, but which when heard will bring to men the dreams and the fancies they lost so many centuries ago, when Pan lay down to doze in Arcady, and the great Gods withdrew to sleep in lotosgardens beyond the lands of the Hesperides. In the subtle cadences and hidden melodies of the bard the spirit of the maiden had found rest at last, for there echo the divinest notes of Thracian Orpheus, notes that moved the very rocks and trees by Hebrus' banks. The singer ceases, and with eagerness asks a verdict, yet what can Marcia say but that the strain is 'fit for the Gods'?

And as she speaks there comes again a vision of Parnassus and the far-off sound of a mighty voice saying, 'By his word shall thy steps be guided to happiness, and in his dreams of beauty shall thy spirit find all that it craveth.'

The Street

There be those who say that things and places have souls, and there be those who say they have not ; I dare not say, myself, but I will tell of the Street.

Men of strength and honour fashioned that Street: good valiant men of our blood who had come from the Blessed Isles across the sea. At first it was but a path trodden by bearers of water from the woodland spring to the cluster of houses by the beach. Then, as more men came to the growing cluster of houses and looked about for places to dwell, they built cabins along the north side, cabins of stout oaken logs with masonry on the side toward the forest, for many Indians lurked there with fire-arrows. And in a few years more, men built cabins on the south side of the Street.

Up and down the Street walked grave men in conical hats, who most of the time carried muskets or fowling pieces. And there were also their bonneted wives and sober children. In the evening these men with their wives and children would sit about gigantic hearths and read and speak. Very simple were the things of which they read and spoke, yet things which gave them courage and goodness and helped them by day to subdue the forest and till the fields. And the children would listen and learn of the laws and deeds of old, and of that dear England which they had never seen or could not remember.

There was war, and thereafter no more Indians troubled the Street. The men, busy with labour, waxed prosperous and as happy as they knew how to be. And the children grew up comfortable, and more families came from the Mother Land to dwell on the Street. And the children's children, and the newcomers' children, grew up. The town was now a city, and one by one the cabins gave place to houses – simple, beautiful houses of brick and wood, with stone steps and iron railings and fanlights over the doors. No flimsy creations were these houses, for they were made to serve many a generation. Within there were carven mantels and graceful stairs, and sensible, pleasing furniture, china, and silver, brought from the Mother Land.

So the Street drank in the dreams of a young people and rejoiced as its dwellers became more graceful and happy. Where once had been only strength and honour, taste and learning now abode as well. Books and paintings and music came to the houses, and the young men went to the university which rose above the plain to the north. In the place of conical hats and small-swords, of lace and snowy periwigs, there were cobblestones over which clattered many a blooded horse and rumbled many a gilded coach; and brick sidewalks with horse blocks and hitching-posts.

There were in that Street many trees: elm and oaks and maples of dignity; so that in the summer, the scene was all soft verdure and twittering bird-song. And behind the houses were walled rose-gardens with hedged paths and sundials, where at evening the moon and stars would shine bewitchingly while fragrant blossoms glistened with dew.

So the Street dreamed on, past wars, calamities, and change. Once most of the young men went away, and some never came back. That was when they furled the old flag and put up a new banner of stripes and stars. But though men talked of great changes, the Street felt them not, for its folk were still the same, speaking of the old familiar things in the old familiar accents. And the trees still sheltered singing birds, and at evening the moon and stars looked down upon dewy blossoms in the walled rose-gardens.

In time there were no more swords, three-cornered hats, or periwigs in the Street. How strange seemed the inhabitants with their walking-sticks, tall beavers, and cropped heads! New sounds came from the distance – first strange puffings and shrieks from the river a mile away, and then, many years later, strange puffings and shrieks and rumblings from other directions. The air was not quite so pure as before, but the spirit of the place had not changed. The blood and soul of their ancestors had fashioned the Street. Nor did the spirit change when they tore open the earth to lay down strange pipes, or when they set up tall posts bearing weird wires. There was so much ancient lore in that Street, that the past could not easily be forgotten.

Then came days of evil, when many who had known the Street of old knew it no more, and many knew it who had not known it before, and went away, for their accents were coarse and strident, and their mien and faces unpleasing. Their thoughts, too, fought with the wise just spirit of the Street, so that the Street pined silently as its houses fell into decay, and its trees died one by one, and its rose-gardens grew rank with weeds and waste. But it felt a stir of pride one day when again marched forth young men, some of whom never came back. These young men were clad in blue.

With the years, worse fortune came to the Street. Its trees were all gone now, and its rose-gardens were displaced by the backs of cheap, ugly new buildings on parallel streets. Yet the houses remained, despite the ravages of the years and the storms and worms, for they had been made to serve many a generation. New kinds of faces appeared in the Street, swarthy, sinister faces with furtive eyes and odd features, whose owners spoke unfamiliar words and placed signs in known and unknown characters upon most of the musty houses. Push-carts crowded the gutters. A sordid, undefinable stench settled over the place, and the ancient spirit slept.

Great excitement once came to the Street. War and revolution were raging across the seas; a dynasty had collapsed, and its degenerate subjects were flocking with dubious intent to the Western Land. Many of these took lodgings in the battered houses that had once known the songs of birds and the scent of roses. Then the Western Land itself awoke and joined the Mother Land in her titanic struggle for civilization. Over the cities once more floated the old flag, companioned by the new flag, and by a plainer, yet glorious tri-colour. But not many flags floated over the Street, for therein brooded only fear and hatred and ignorance. Again young men went forth, but not quite as did the young men of those other days. Something was lacking. And the sons of those young men of other days, who did indeed go forth in olive-drab with the true spirit of their ancestors, went from distant places and knew not the Street and its ancient spirit.

Over the seas there was a great victory, and in triumph most of the young men returned. Those who had lacked something lacked it no longer, yet did fear and hatred and ignorance still brood over the Street; for many had stayed behind, and many strangers had come from distant places to the ancient houses. And the young men who had returned dwelt there no longer. Swarthy and sinister were most of the strangers, yet among them one might find a few faces like those who fashioned the Street and moulded its spirit. Like and yet unlike, for there was in the eyes of all a weird, unhealthy glitter as of greed, ambition, vindictiveness, or misguided zeal. Unrest and treason were abroad amongst an evil few who plotted to strike the Western Land its death blow, that they might mount to power over its ruins, even as assassins had mounted in that unhappy, frozen land from whence most of them had come. And the heart of that plotting was in the Street, whose crumb-

ling houses teemed with alien makers of discord and echoed
with the plans and speeches of those who yearned for the
appointed day of blood, flame and crime.

Of the various odd assemblages in the Street, the law said
much but could prove little. With great diligence did men
of hidden badges linger and listen about such places as
Petrovitch's Bakery, the squalid Rifkin School of Modern
Economics, the Circle Social Club, and the Liberty Café.
There congregated sinister men in great numbers, yet always was their speech guarded or in a foreign tongue. And
still the old houses stood, with their forgotten lore of nobler,
departed centuries; of sturdy Colonial tenants and dewy
rose-gardens in the moonlight. Sometimes a lone poet or
traveler would come to view them, and would try to picture them in their vanished glory; yet of such travelers
and poets there were not many.

The rumour now spread widely that these houses contained the leaders of a vast band of terrorists, who on a
designated day were to launch an orgy of slaughter for the
extermination of America and of all the fine old traditions
which the Street had loved. Handbills and papers fluttered
about filthy gutters; handbills and papers printed in many
tongues and in many characters, yet all bearing messages of
crime and rebellion. In these writings the people were
urged to tear down the laws and virtues that our fathers
had exalted, to stamp out the soul of the old America –
the soul that was bequeathed through a thousand and a
half years of Anglo-Saxon freedom, justice, and modera-
tion. It was said that the swart men who dwelt in the Street
and congregated in its rotting edifices were the brains of a
hideous revolution, that at their word of command many
millions of brainless, besotted beasts would stretch forth
their noisome talons from the slums of a thousand cities,
burning, slaying, and destroying till the land of our fathers
should be no more. All this was said and repeated, and
many looked forward in dread to the fourth day of July,
about which the strange writings hinted much; yet could
nothing be found to place the guilt. None could tell just
whose arrest might cut off the damnable plotting at its
source. Many times came bands of blue-coated police to

search the shaky houses, though at last they ceased to come; for they too had grown tired of law and order, and had abandoned all the city to its fate. Then men in olive-drab came, bearing muskets, till it seemed as if in its sad sleep the Street must have some haunting dreams of those other days, when musket-bearing men in conical hats walked along it from the woodland spring to the cluster of houses by the beach. Yet could no act be performed to check the impending cataclysm, for the swart, sinister men were old in cunning.

So the Street slept uneasily on, till one night there gathered in Petrovitch's Bakery and the Rifkin School of Modern Economics, and the Circle Social Club, and Liberty Café, and in other places as well, vast hordes of men whose eyes were big with horrible triumph and expectation. Over hidden wires strange messages traveled, and much was said of still stranger messages yet to travel; but most of this was not guessed till afterward, when the Western Land was safe from the peril. The men in olive-drab could not tell what was happening, or what they ought to do; for the swart, sinister men were skilled in subtlety and concealment.

And yet the men in olive-drab will always remember that night, and will speak of the Street as they tell of it to their grandchildren; for many of them were sent there toward morning on a mission unlike that which they had expected. It was known that this nest of anarchy was old, and that the houses were tottering from the ravages of the years and the storms and worms; yet was the happening of that summer night a surprise because of its very queer uniformity. It was, indeed, an exceedingly singular happening, though after all, a simple one. For without warning, in one of the small hours beyond midnight, all the ravages of the years and the storms and the worms came to a tremendous climax; and after the crash there was nothing left standing in the Street save two ancient chimneys and part of a stout brick wall. Nor did anything that had been alive come alive from the ruins. A poet and a traveler, who came with the mighty crowd that sought the scene, tell odd stories. The poet says that all through the hours before dawn he beheld sordid ruins indistinctly in the glare of the arc-lights; that there loomed above the wreckage another picture wherein he could describe moonlight and fair houses and elms and oaks and maples of dignity. And the traveler declares that instead of the place's wonted stench there lingered a delicate fragrance as of roses in full bloom. But are not the dreams of poets and the tales of travelers notoriously false?

There be those who say that things and places have souls, and there be those who say they have not; I dare not say, myself, but I have told you of the Street.

The Transition of Juan Romero

Of the events which took place at the Norton Mine on October eighteenth and nineteenth, 1894, I have no desire to speak. A sense of duty to science is all that impels me to recall, in the last years of my life, scenes and happenings fraught with a terror doubly acute because I cannot wholly define it. But I believe that before I die I should tell what I know of the – shall I say *transition* – of Juan Romero.

My name and origin need not be related to posterity; in fact, I fancy it is better that they should not be, for when a man suddenly migrates to the States or the Colonies, he leaves his past behind him. Besides, what I once was is not in the least relevant to my narrative; save perhaps the fact that during my service in India I was more at home amongst white-bearded native teachers than amongst my brother-officers. I had delved not a little into odd Eastern lore when overtaken by the calamities which brought about my new life in America's vast West – a life wherein I found it well to accept a name – my present one – which is very common and carries no meaning.

In the summer and autumn of 1894 I dwelt in the drear

expanses of the Cactus Mountains, employed as a common
labourer at the celebrated Norton Mine, whose discovery
by an aged prospector some years before had turned the
surrounding region from a nearly unpeopled waste to a
seething cauldron of sordid life. A cavern of gold, lying
deep beneath a mountain lake, had enriched its venerable
finder beyond his wildest dreams, and now formed the
seat of extensive tunneling operations on the part of the
corporation to whiih it had finally been sold. Additional
grottoes had been found, and the yield of yellow metal
was exceedingly great ; so that a mighty and heterogeneous
army of miners toiled day and night in the numerous passages and rock hollows. The Superintendent, a Mr. Arthur,
often discussed the singularity of the local geological for-
mations ; speculating on the probable extent of the chain
of caves, and estimating the future of the titanic mining
enterprises. He considered the auriferous cavities the result of the action of water, and believed the last of them
would soon be opened.

It was not long after my arrival and employment that
Juan Romero came to the Norton Mine. One of a large
herd of unkempt Mexicans attracted thither from the
neighboring country, he at first attracted attention only
because of his features ; which though plainly of the Red
Indian type, were yet remarkable for their light colour
and refined conformation, being vastly unlike those of the
average 'greaser' or Piute of the locality. It is curious that
although he differed so widely from the mass of Hispani-
cised and tribal Indians, Romero gave not the least impression of Caucasian blood. It was not the Castilian conquis-
tador or the American pioneer, but the ancient and noble
Aztec, whom imagination called to view when the silent
peon would rise in the early morning and gaze in fascination at the sun as it crept above the eastern hills, meanwhile
stretching out his arms to the orb as if in the performance of some rite whose nature he did not himself com-
prehend. But save for his face, Romero was not in any
way suggestive of nobility. Ignorant and dirty, he was at
home amongst the other brown-skinned Mexicans ; having
come (so I was afterward told) from the very lowest sort

of surroundings. He had been found as a child in a crude mountain hut, the only survivor of an epidemic which had stalked lethally by. Near the hut, close to a rather unusual rock fissure, had lain two skeletons, newly picked by vultures, and presumably forming the sole remains of his parents. No one recalled their identity, and they were soon forgotten by the many. Indeed, the crumbling of the adobe hut and the closing of the rock-fissure by a subsequent avalanche had helped to efface even the scene from recollection. Reared by a Mexican cattle-thief who had given him his name, Juan differed little from his fellows.

The attachment which Romero manifested toward me was undoubtedly commenced through the quaint and ancient Hindoo ring which I wore when not engaged in active labour. Of its nature, and manner of coming into my possession, I cannot speak. It was my last link with a chapter of my life forever closed, and I valued it highly. Soon I observed that the odd-looking Mexican was likewise interested ; eyeing it with an expression that banished all suspicion of mere covetousness. Its hoary hieroglyphs seemed to stir some faint recollection in his untutored but active mind, though he could not possibly have beheld their like before. Within a few weeks after his advent, Romero was like a faithful servant to me ; this notwithstanding the fact that I was myself but an ordinary miner. Our conversation was necessarily limited. He knew but a few words of English, while I found my Oxonian Spanish was something quite different from the patois of the peon of New Spain.

The event which I am about to relate was unheralded by long premonitions. Though the man Romero had interested me, and though my ring had affected him peculiarly, I think that neither of us had any expectation of what was to follow when the great blast was set off. Geological considerations had dictated an extension of the mine directly downward from the deepest part of the subterranean area ; and the belief of the Superintendent that only solid rock would be encountered, had led to the placing of a prodigious charge of dynamite. With this work Romero and I were not connected, wherefore our first knowledge of ex-

traordinary conditions came from others. The charge,
heavier perhaps than had been estimated, had seemed to
shake the entire mountain. Windows in shanties on the
slope outside were shattered by the shock, whilst miners
throughout the nearer passages were knocked from their
feet. Jewel Lake, which lay above the scene of action,
heaved as in a tempest. Upon investigation it was seen that
a new abyss yawned indefinitely below the seat of the blast ;
an abyss so monstrous that no handy line might fathom it,
nor any lamp illuminate it. Baffled, the excavators sought a
conference with the Superintendent, who ordered great
lengths of rope to be taken to the pit, and spliced and
lowered without cessation till a bottom might be discovered.

Shortly afterward the pale-faced workmen apprised the
Superintendent of their failure. Firmly though respect-
fully, they signified their refusal to revisit the chasm or
indeed to work further in the mine until it might be sealed.
Something beyond their experience was evidently confronting them, for so far as they could ascertain, the void below was infinite. The Superintendent did not reproach
them. Instead, he pondered deeply, and made plans for
the following day. The night shift did not go on that evening.

At two in the morning a lone coyote on the mountain
began to howl dismally. From somewhere within the
works a dog barked an answer ; either to the coyote – or
to something else. A storm was gathering around the peaks
of the range, and weirdly shaped clouds scudded horribly
across the blurred patch of celestial light which marked a
gibbous moon's attempts to shine through many layers of
cirro-stratus vapours. It was Romero's voice, coming from
the bunk above, that awakened me, a voice excited and
tense with some vague expectation I could not understand:

'¡Madre de Dios! – El sonido – ese sonido – ¡orga Vd! –
¡lo oyte Vd? – Senor, THAT SOUND!'

I listened, wondering what sound he meant. The coyote,
the dog, the storm, all were audible ; the last named now

gaining ascendancy as the wind shrieked more and more frantically. Flashes of lightning were visible through the bunk-house window. I questioned the nervous Mexican, repeating the sounds I had heard:

'¿El coyote? – ¿el perro? – ¿el viento?'

But Romero did not reply. Then he commenced whispering as in awe:

'El ritmo, Senor – el ritmo de la tierra – THAT THROB DOWN IN THE GROUND!'

And now I also heard; heard and shivered and without knowing why. Deep, deep, below me was a sound – a rhythm, just as the peon had said – which, though exceedingly faint, yet dominated even the dog, the coyote, and the increasing tempest. To seek to describe it was useless – for it was such that no description is possible. Perhaps it was like the pulsing of the engines far down in a great liner, as sensed from the deck, yet it was not so mechanical; not so devoid of the element of life and consciousness. Of all its qualities, *remoteness* in the earth most impressed me. To my mind rushed fragments of a passage in Joseph Glanvil which Poe has quoted with tremendous effect* –

'– the vastness, profundity, and unsearchableness of His works, *which have a depth in them greater than the well of Democritus.*'

Suddenly Romero leaped from his bunk, pausing before me to gaze at the strange ring on my hand, which glistened queerly in every flash of lightning, and then staring intently in the direction of the mine shaft. I also rose, and both stood motionless for a time, straining our ears as the uncanny rhythm seemed more and more to take on a vital quality. Then without apparent volition we began to move toward the door, whose rattling in the gale held a comforting suggestion of earthly reality. The chanting in the depths – for such the sound now seemed to be – grew in volume and distinctness; and we felt irresistibly urged out into the storm and thence to the gaping blackness of the shaft.

*Motto of *A Descent into the Maelstrom.*

We encountered no living creature, for the men of the
night shift had been released from duty, and were doubtless
at the Dry Gulch settlement pouring sinister rumours into
the ear of some drowsy bartender. From the watchman's
cabin, however, gleamed a small square of yellow light like
a guardian eye. I dimly wondered how the rhythmic sound
had affected the watchman ; but Romero was moving more
swiftly now, and I followed without pausing.

As we descended the shaft, the sound beneath grew de-
finitely composite. It struck me as horribly like a sort of
Oriental ceremony, with beating of drums and chanting of
many voices. I have, as you are aware, been much in India.
Romero and I moved without material hesitancy through
drifts and down ladders ; ever toward the thing that allured
us, yet ever with a pitifully helpless fear and reluctance.
At one time I fancied I had gone mad – this was when, on
wondering how our way was lighted in the absence of lamp
or candle, I realized that the ancient ring on my finger was
glowing with eery radiance, diffusing a pallid lustre through
the damp, heavy air around.

It was without warning that Romero, after clambering
down one of the many wide ladders, broke into a run and
left me alone. Some new and wild note in the drumming
and chanting, perceptible but slightly to me, had acted on
him in a startling fashion ; and with a wild outcry he forged
ahead unguided in the cavern's gloom. I heard his repeated
shrieks before me, as he stumbled awkwardly along the
level places and scrambled madly down the rickety ladders.
And frightened as I was, I yet retained enough of my perception to note that his speech, when articulate, was not of
any sort known to me. Harsh but impressive polysyllables
had replaced the customary mixture of bad Spanish and
worse English, and of these, only the oft repeated cry
'*Huitzilopotchli*' seemed in the least familiar. Later I de-
finitely placed that word in the works of a great historian*
– and shuddered when the association came to me.

The climax of that awful night was composite but fairly
brief, beginning just as I reached the final cavern of the
journey. Out of the darkness immediately ahead burst a
*Prescott, Conquest of Mexico

final shriek from the Mexican, which was joined by such a chorus of uncouth sound as I could never hear again and survive. In that moment it seemed as if all the hidden terrors and monstrosities of earth had become articulate in an effort to overwhelm the human race. Simultaneously the light from my ring was extinguished, and I saw a new light glimmering from lower space but a few yards ahead of me. I had arrived at the abyss, which was now redly aglow, and which had evidently swallowed up the unfortunate Romero. Advancing, I peered over the edge of that chasm which no line could fathom, and which was now a pandemonium of flickering flame and hideous uproar. At first I beheld nothing but a seething blur of luminosity; but then shapes, all infinitely distant, began to detach themselves from the confusion, and I saw – was it Juan Romero? – *but God! I dare not tell you what I saw!* ... Some power from heaven, coming to my aid, obliterated both sights and sounds in such a crash as may be heard when two universes collide in space. Chaos supervened, and I knew the peace of oblivion.

I hardly know how to continue, since conditions so singular are involved; but I will do my best, not even trying to differentiate betwixt the real and the apparent. When I awakened. I was safe in my bunk and the red glow of dawn was visible at the window. Some distance away the lifeless body of Juan Romero lay upon a table, surrounded by a group of men, including the camp doctor. The men were discussing the strange death of the Mexican as he lay asleep; a death seemingly connected in some way with the terrible bolt of lightning which had struck and shaken the mountain. No direct cause was evident, and an autopsy failed to show any reason why Romero should not be living. Snatches of conversation indicated beyond a doubt that neither Romero nor I had left the bunk-house during the night; that neither had been awake during the frightful storm which had passed over the Cactus range. That storm, said men who had ventured down the mine-shaft, had caused extensive caving-in, and had completely closed the deep abyss which had created so much apprehension the day before. When I asked the watchman what sounds he had heard prior to the mighty thunder-bolt; he mentioned a coyote, a dog, and the snarling mountain wind – nothing more. Nor do I doubt his word.

Upon the resumption of work, Superintendent Arthur called upon some especially dependable men to make a few investigations around the spot where the gulf had appeared. Though hardly eager, they obeyed, and a deep boring was made. Results were very curious. The roof of the void, as seen when it was open, was not by any means thick; yet now the drills of the investigators met what appeared to be a limitless extent of solid rock. Finding nothing else, not even gold, the Superintendent abandoned his attempts; but a perplexed look occasionally steals over his countenance as he sits thinking at his desk.

One other thing is curious. Shortly after waking on that morning after the storm, I noticed the unaccountable absence of my Hindoo ring from my finger. I had prized it greatly, yet nevertheless felt a sensation of relief at its disappearance. If one of my fellow-miners appropriated it, he must have been quite clever in disposing of his booty, for despite advertisements and a police search the ring was never seen again. Somehow I doubt if it was stolen by mortal hands, for many strange things were taught me in India.

My opinion of my whole experience varies from time to time. In broad daylight, and at most seasons I am apt to think the greater part of it a mere dream; but sometimes in the autumn, about two in the morning when the winds and animals howl dismally, there comes from inconceivable depths below a damnable suggestion of rhythmical throbbing . . . and I feel that the transition of Juan Romero was a terrible one indeed.

September 16, 1919.

Four Fragments

These fragments found among Lovecraft's papers are presumably his attempts to set down in rudimentary form, preparatory to expansion into longer stories, some of his dreams. None was ever expanded. Keys to the dream sources of some of these fragments can be found in Lovecraft's letters.

Azathoth

When age fell upon the world, and wonder went out of the minds of men ; when grey cities reared to smoky skies tall towers grim and ugly, in whose shadow none might dream of the sun or of Spring's flowering meads ; when learning stripped Earth of her mantle of beauty, and poets sang no more save of twisted phantoms seen with bleared and inward-looking eyes ; when these things had come to pass, and childish hopes had gone away for ever, there was a man who traveled out of life on a quest into the spaces whither the world's dreams had fled.

Of the name and abode of this man but little is written, for they were of the waking world only ; yet it is said that both were obscure. It is enough to know that he dwelt in a city of high walls where sterile twilight reigned, and that he toiled all day among shadow and turmoil, coming home at evening to a room whose one window opened not on the fields and groves but on a dim court where other windows stared in dull despair. From that casement one might see only walls and windows, except sometimes when one leaned far out and peered aloft at the small stars that passed. And because mere walls and windows must soon drive to madness a man who dreams and reads much, the dweller in that room used night after night to lean out and peer aloft to glimpse some fragment of things beyond the waking world and the greyness of tall cities. After years he began to call the slow-sailing stars by name, and to follow them in fancy when they glided regretfully out of sight; till at length his vision opened to many secret vistas whose existence no common eye suspects. And one night a mighty gulf was bridged, and the dream-haunted skies swelled down to the lonely watcher's window to merge with the close air of his room and make him a part of their fabulous wonder.

There came to that room wild streams of violet midnight glittering with dust of gold ; vortices of dust and fire, swirling out of the ultimate spaces and heavy with perfumes from beyond the worlds. Opiate oceans poured there, litten by suns that the eye may never behold and having in their whirlpools strange dolphins and sea-nymphs of unrememberable deeps. Noiseless infinity eddied around the dreamer and wafted him away without even touching the body that leaned stiffly from the lonely window ; and for days not counted in men's calendars the tides of far spheres bore him gently to join the dreams for which he longed ; the dreams that men have lost. And in the course of many cycles they tenderly left him sleeping on a green sunrise shore ; a green shore fragrant with lotus-blossoms and starred by red camalates. . . .

(circa 1922)

The Descendant

Writing on what the doctor tells me is my deathbed, my most hideous fear is that the man is wrong. I suppose I shall seem to buried next week, but. . . .

In London there is a man who screams when the church
bells ring. He lives all alone with his streaked cat in Gray's
Inn, and people call him harmlessly mad. His room is filled
with books of the tamest and most puerile kind, and hour
after hour he tries to lose himself in their feeble pages. All
he seeks from life is not to think. For some reason thought
is very horrible to him, and anything which stirs the imagination he flees as a plague. He is very thin and grey and
wrinkled, but there are those who declare he is not nearly
so old as he looks. Fear has its grisly claws upon him, and
a sound will make him start with staring eyes and sweat-
beaded forehead.. Friends and companions he shuns, for
he wishes to answer no questions. Those who once knew
him as scholar and aesthete say it is very pitiful to see him
now. He dropped them all years ago, and no one feels sure
whether he left the country or merely sank from sight in
some hidden byway. It is a decade now since he moved
into Gray's Inn, and of where he had been he would say
nothing till the night young Williams bought the *Necronomicon*.

Williams was a dreamer, and only twenty-three, and when
he moved into the ancient house he felt a strangeness and
a breath of cosmic wind about the grey wizened man in
the next room. He forced his friendship where old friends
dared not force theirs, and marvelled at the fright that sat
upon this gaunt, haggard watcher and listener. For that
the man always watched and listened no one could doubt.
He watched and listened with his mind more than with his
eyes and ears, and strove every moment to drown something in his ceaseless poring over gay, insipid novels. And
when the church bells rang he would stop his ears and
scream, and the grey cat that dwelt with him would howl in
unison till the last peal died reverberantly away.

But try as Williams would, he could not make his neigh-
bour speak of anything profound or hidden. The old man
would not live up to his aspect and manner, but would feign
a smile and a light tone and prattle feverishly and frantically of cheerful trifles ; his voice every moment rising and
thickening till at last it would split in a piping and inco-
herent falsetto. That his learning was deep and thorough,

his most trivial remarks made abundantly clear; and Williams was not surprised to hear that he had been to Harrow and Oxford. Later it developed that he was none other than Lord Northam, of whose ancient hereditary castle on the Yorkshire coast so many odd things were told; but when Williams tried to talk of the castle, and of its reputed Roman origin, he refused to admit that there was anything unusual about it. He even tittered shrilly when the subject of the supposed under-crypts, hewn out of the solid crag that frowns on the North Sea, was brought up.

So matters went till that night when Williams brought home the infamous *Necronomicon* of the mad Arab Abdul Alhazred. He had known of the dreaded volume since his sixteenth year, when his dawning love of the bizarre had led him to ask queer questions of a bent old bookseller in Chandos Street; and he had always wondered why men paled when they spoke of it. The old bookseller had told him that only five copies were known to have survived the shocked edicts of the priests and lawgivers against it and that all of them were locked up with frightened care by custodians who had ventured to begin a reading of the hateful black-letter. But now, at last, he had not only found an accessible copy but had made it his own at a ridiculously low figure. It was at a Jew's shop in the squalid precincts of Clare Market, where he had often bought strange things before, and he almost fancied the gnarled old Levite smiled amidst tangles of beard as the great discovery was made. The bulky leather cover with the brass clasp had been so prominently visible, and the price was so absurdly slight.

The one glimpse he had had of the title was enough to send him into transports, and some of the diagrams set in the vague Latin text excited the tensest and most disquieting recollections in his brain. He felt it was highly necessary to get the ponderous thing home and begin deciphering it, and bore it out of the shop with such precipitate haste that the old Jew chuckled disturbingly behind him. But when at last it was safe in his room he found the combination of black-letter and debased idiom too much for his powers as a linguist, and reluctantly called on his

strange frightened friend for help with the twisted, mediaeval Latin. Lord Northam was simpering inanities to his
streaked cat, and started violently when the young man
entered. Then he saw the volume and shuddered wildly,
and fainted altogether when Williams uttered the title. It
was when he regained his senses that he told his story; told
his fantastic figment of madness in frantic whispers lest
his friend be not quick to burn the accured book and give
wide scattering to its ashes.

There must, Lord Northam whispered, have been something wrong at the start; but it would never have come to a
head if he had not explored too far. He was the nineteenth
Baron of a line whose beginnings went uncomfortably far
back into the past – unbelievably far, if vague tradition
could be heeded, for there were family tales of a descent
from pre-Saxon times, when a certain Luneus Gabinius
Capito, military tribune in the Third Augustan Legion then
station at Lindum in Roman Britain, had been summarily
expelled from his command for participation in certain
rites unconnected with any known religion. Gabinius had,
the rumour ran, come upon the cliffside cavern where
strange folk met together and made the Elder Sign in the
dark; strange folk whom the Britons knew not save in fear,
and who were the last to survive from a great land in the
west that had sunken, leaving only the islands with the
roths and circles and shrines of which Stonehenge was the
greatest. There was no certainty, of course, in the legend
that Gabinius had built an impregnable fortress over the
forbidden cave and founded a line which Pict and Saxon,
Dane and Norman were powerless to obliterate; or in the
tacit assumption that from this line sprang the bold companion and lieutenant of the Black Prince whom Edward
Third created Baron of Northam. These things were not
certain, yet they were often told; and in truth the stone-
work of Northam Keep did look alarmingly like the
masonry of Hadrian's Wall. As a child Lord Northam had
had peculiar dreams when sleeping in the older parts of
the castle, and had acquired a constant habit of looking
back through his memory for half-amorphous scenes and
patterns and impressions which formed no part of his wak-

ing experience. He became a dreamer who found life tame
and unsatisfying; a searcher for strange realms and rela-
tionships once familiar, yet lying nowhere in the visible
regions of the Earth.

Filled with a feeling that our tangible world is only an
atom in a fabric vast and ominous, and that unknown de-
mesnes press on and permeate the sphere of the known
at every point, Northam in youth and young manhood
drained in turn the founts of formal religion and occult
mystery. Nowhere, however, could he find ease and content; and as he grew older the staleness and limitations of
life became more and more maddening to him. During
the 'nineties he dabbled in Satanism, and at all times he
devoured avidly any doctrine or theory which seemed to
promise escape from the close vistas of science and the
dully unvarying laws of Nature. Books like Ignatius Don-
nelly's chimerical account of Atlantis he absorbed with
zest, and a dozen obscure precursors of Charles Fort enthralled him with their vagaries. He would travel leagues to
follow up a furtive village tale of abnormal wonder, and
once went into the desert of Araby to seek a Nameless
City of faint report, which no man has ever beheld. There
rose within him the tantalising faith that somewhere an
easy gate existed, which if one found would admit him
freely to those outer deeps whose echoes rattled so dimly
at the back of his memory. It might be in the visible world,
yet it might be only in his mind and soul. Perhaps he held
within his own half-explored brain that cryptic link which
would awaken him to Elder and future lives in forgotten
dimensions; which would bind him to the stars, and to the
infinities and eternities beyond them. . . .
(circa 1926)

The Book

My memories are very confused. There is even much doubt as to where they begin ; for at times I feel appalling vistas of years stretching behind me, while at other times it seems as if the present moment were an isolated point in a grey, formless infinity. I am not even certain how I am communicating this message. While I know I am speaking, I have a vague impression that some strange and perhaps terrible mediation will be needed to bear what I say to the points where I wish to be heard. My identity, too, is bewilderingly cloudy. I seem to have suffered a great shock – perhaps from some utterly monstrous outgrowth of my cycles of unique, incredible experience.

These cycles of experience, of course, all stem from that worm-riddled book. I remember when I found it – in a dimly lighted place near the black, oily river where the mists always swirl. That place was very old, and the ceiling-high shelves full of rotting volumes reached back endlessly through windowless inner rooms and alcoves. There were, besides, great formless heaps of books on the floor and in crude bins ; and it was in one of these heaps that I found the thing. I never learned its title, for the early pages were missing ; but it fell open toward the end and gave me a glimpse of something which sent my senses reeling.

There was a formula – a sort of list of things to say and do – which I recognised as something black and forbidden ; something which I had read of before in furtive paragraphs of mixed abhorrence and fascination penned by those strange ancient delvers into the universe's guarded secrets whose decaying texts I loved to absorb. It was a key – a guide – to certain gateways and transitions of which mystics have dreamed and whispered since the race was young, and which lead to freedoms and discoveries beyond the three dimensions and realms of life and matter that we know. Not for centuries had any man recalled its vital substance or known where to find it, but this book was very old indeed. No printing-press, but the hand of some half-crazed monk, had traced these ominous Latin phrases in uncials of awesome antiquity.

I remember how the old man leered and tittered, and made a curious sign with his hand when I bore it away. He had refused to take pay for it, and only long afterward did I guess why. As I hurried home through those narrow, winding, mist-cloaked waterfront streets I had a frightful impression of being stealthily followed by softly padding feet. The centuried, tottering houses on both sides seemed alive with a fresh and morbid malignity – as if some hitherto closed channel of evil understanding had abruptly been opened. I felt that those walls and overhanging gables of mildewed brick and fungoid plaster and timber – with eye-like, diamond-paned windows that leered – could hardly desist from advancing and crushing me ... yet I had read only the least fragment of that blasphemous rune before closing the book and bringing it away.

I remember how I read the book at last – white-faced, and locked in the attic room that I had long devoted to strange searchings. The great house was very still, for I had not gone up till after midnight. I think I had a family then – though the details are very uncertain – and I know there were many servants. Just what the year was, I cannot say; for since then I have known many ages and dimensions, and have had all my notions of time dissolved and refashioned. It was by the light of candles that I read – I recall the relentless dripping of the wax – and there were chimes that came every now and then from distant belfries. I seemed to keep track of those chimes with a peculiar intentness, as if I feared to hear some very remote, intruding note among them.

Then came the first scratching and fumbling at the dormer window that looked out high above the other roofs of the city. It came as I droned aloud the ninth verse of that primal lay, and I knew amidst my shudders what it meant. For he who passes the gateways always wins a shadow, and never again can he be alone. I had evoked – and the book was indeed all I had suspected. That night I passed the gateway to a vortex of twisted time and vision, and when morning found me in the attic room I saw in the walls and shelves and fittings that which I had never seen before.

Nor could I ever after see the world as I had known it. Mixed with the present scene was always a little of the past and a little of the future, and every once-familiar object loomed alien in the new perspective brought by my widened sight. From then on I walked in a fantastic dream of unknown and half-known shapes; and with each new gateway crossed, the less plainly could I recognise the things of the narrow sphere to which I had so long been bound. What I saw about me, none else saw; and I grew doubly silent and aloof lest I be thought mad. Dogs had a fear of me, for they felt the outside shadow which never left my side. But still I read more – in hidden, forgotten books and scrolls to which my new vision led me – and pushed through fresh gateways of space and being and life-patterns toward the core of the unknown cosmos.

I remember the night I made the five concentric circles of fire on the floor, and stood in the innermost one chanting that monstrous litany the messenger from Tartary had brought. The walls melted away, and I was swept by a black wind through gulfs of fathomless grey with the needle-like pinnacles of unknown mountains miles below me. After a while there was utter blackness, and then the light of myriad stars forming strange, alien constellations. Finally I saw a green-litten plain far below me, and discerned on it the twisted towers of a city built in no fashion I had ever known or read of or dreamed of. As I floated closer to that city I saw a great square building of stone in an open space, and felt a hideous fear clutching at me. I screamed and struggled, and after a blankness was again in my attic room sprawled flat over the five phosphorescent circles on the floor. In that night's wandering there was no more of strangeness than in many a former night's wandering; but there was more of terror because I knew I was closer to those outside gulfs and worlds than I had ever been before. Thereafter I was more cautious with my incantations, for I had no wish to be cut off from my body and from the earth in unknown abysses whence I could never return. . .

(circa 1934)

The Thing in the Moonlight

Morgan is not a literary man ; in fact he cannot speak English with any degree of coherency. That is what makes me wonder about the words he wrote, though others have laughed.

He was alone the evening it happened. Suddenly an unconquerable urge to write came over him, and taking pen in hand he wrote the following:

My name is Howard Phillips. I live at 66 College Street, in Providence, Rhode Island. On November 24, 1927 – for I know not even what the year may be now –, I fell asleep and dreamed, since when I have been unable to awaken.

My dream began in a dank, reed-choked marsh that lay under a gray autumn sky, with a rugged cliff of lichen-crusted stone rising to the north. Impelled by some obscure quest, I ascended a rift or cleft in this beetling precipice, noting as I did so the black mouths of many fearsome burrows extending from both walls into the depths of the stony plateau.

At several points the passage was roofed over by the choking of the upper parts of the narrow fissure ; these places being exceeding dark, and forbidding the perception of such burrows as may have existed there. In one such dark space I felt conscious of a singular accession of fright, as if some subtle and bodiless emanation from the abyss were engulfing my spirit ; but the blackness was too great for me to perceive the source of my alarm.

At length I emerged upon a tableland of moss-grown rock and scanty soil, lit by a faint moonlight which had replaced the expiring orb of day. Casting my eyes about, I beheld no living object ; but was sensible of a very peculiar stirring far below me, amongst the whispering rushes of the pestilential swamp I had lately quitted.

After walking for some distance, I encountered the rusty tracks of a street railway, and the worm-eaten poles which still held the limp and sagging trolley wire. Following this line, I soon came upon a yellow, vestibuled car numbered

1852 – of a plain, double-trucked type common from 1900
to 1910. It was untenanted, but evidently ready to start;
the trolley being on the wire and the air-brake now and
then throbbing beneath the floor. I boarded it and looked
vainly about for the light switch – noting as I did so the
absence of the controller handle, which thus implied the
brief absence of the motorman. Then I sat down in one of
the cross seats of the vehicle. Presently I heard a swishing
in the sparse grass toward the left, and saw the dark forms
of two men looming up in the moonlight. They had the
regulation caps of a railway company, and I could not
doubt but that they were conductor and motorman. Then
one of them *sniffed* with singular sharpness, and raised his
face to howl to the moon. The other dropped on all fours
to run toward the car.

I leaped up at once and raced madly out of that car
and across endless leagues of plateau till exhaustion forced
me to stop – doing this not because the conductor had
dropped on all fours, but because the face of the motorman was a mere white cone tapering to one blood-red-ten-
tacle. . . .

I was aware that I only dreamed, but the very aware-
ness was not pleasant.

Since that fearful night, I have prayed only for awakening – it has not come!

Instead I have found myself an *inhabitant* of this terrible dream-world! That first night gave way to dawn, and
I wandered aimlessly over the lonely swamp-lands. When
night came, I still wandered, hoping for awakening. But
suddenly I parted the weeds and saw before me the ancient railway car – and to one side a cone-faced thing lifted
its head and in the streaming moonlight howled strangely!

It has been the same each day. Night takes me always to
that place of horror. I have tried not moving, with the coming of nightfall, but I must walk in my slumber, for always
I awaken with the thing of dread howling before me in the
pale moonlight, and I turn and flee madly.

God! when will I awaken?

That is what Morgan wrote. I would go to 66 College
Street in Providence, but I fear for what I might find there.
(1934)

The following complete chronology of H. P. Lovecraft' work was set down by the author himself.

Dagon, 1917
The Tomb, 1917
Polaris, 1918
Beyond the Wall of Sleep, 1919
The Doom That Came to Sarnath, 1919
The Statement of Randolph Carter, 1919
The White Ship, 1919
Arthur Jermyn (The White Ape), 1920
The Cats of Ulthar, 1920
Celephais, 1920
From Beyond, 1920
The Picture in the House, 1920
The Temple, 1920
The Terrible Old Man, 1920
The Tree, 1920
The Moon-Bog, 1921
The Music of Erich Zann, 1921
The Nameless City, 1921
The Other Gods, 1921
The Outsider, 1921
The Quest of Iranon, 1921
Herbert West: Reanimator, 1921–1922
The Hound, 1922
Hypnos, 1922
The Lurking Fear, 1922
The Festival, 1923
The Rats in the Walls, 1923
The Unnamable, 1923
Imprisoned with the Pharaohs, 1924
The Shunned House, 1924
He, 1925
The Horror at Red Hook, 1925
In the Vault, 1925
The Call of Cthulhu, 1926
Cool Air, 1926
Pickman's Model, 1926
The Silver Key, 1926
The Strange High House in the Mist, 1926
The Colour out of Space, 1927
The Case of Charles Dexter Ward, 1927–1928
The Dunwich Horror, 1928

The Whisperer in Darkness, 1930
The Shadow over Innsmouth, 1931
At the Mountains of Madness, 1931
The Dreams in the Witch-House, 1932
Through the Gates of the Silver Key, 1932
The Thing on the Doorstep, 1933
The Shadow out of Time, 1934
In the Walls of Eryx, 1935
The Haunter of the Dark, 1935
The Evi Clergyman, 1937